SILENT
MURDERS

ALSO BY MARY MILEY

The Impersonator

SILENT MURDERS

MARY MILEY

MINOTAUR BOOKS

NEW YORK

SILENT MURDERS. Copyright © 2014 by Mary Miley Theobald.
All rights reserved. Printed in the United States of America. For information,
address St. Martin's Press, 175 Fifth Avenue, New York, N.Y. 10010.

www.minotaurbooks.com

Designed by Anna Gorovoy

Library of Congress Cataloging-in-Publication Data

Miley, Mary.
    Silent murders / Mary Miley.—First edition.
        pages   cm
    ISBN 978-1-250-05137-0 (hardcover)
    ISBN 978-1-4668-6518-1 (e-book)
    1. Actresses—Fiction.   2. Impersonation—Fiction.   [1. Hollywood
(Los Angeles, Calif.)—History—20th century—Fiction.]   I. Title.
    PS3613.I532244S55 2014
    813'.6—dc23

                                                         2014016746

Minotaur books may be purchased for educational, business,
or promotional use. For information on bulk purchases, please contact
Macmillan Corporate and Premium Sales Department at 1-800-221-7945,
extension 5442, or write specialmarkets@macmillan.com.

First Edition: September 2014

10 9 8 7 6 5 4 3 2 1

SILENT
MURDERS

Turns out vaudeville doesn't prepare you for Hollywood.

I'm a quick study and good at figuring things out, but it was a week before I could navigate the eighteen acres of stages, sets, and storage rooms at Pickford-Fairbanks Studios. It was another week before I got straight in my head the pecking order of all the directors, general managers, collaborators, producers, and other big shots and learned to tell the actors from the extras and the gaffers from the grips. To be safe, I called everyone mister or miss until they said otherwise.

Everyone called me Jessie. And everyone called me a lot. Officially I was assistant script girl to director Frank Richardson on the *Don Q, Son of Zorro* set, but anyone in the studio could waylay me at any time. I felt like a lowly worker bee, flitting in and out of the beehive on foraging expeditions.

"Jessie, run to Wardrobe and get Paul Burns—the Queen has ripped her ball gown."

"There you are, Jessie. We need wind. Find two electric fans, pronto."

"Oh, Jessie? More ice water for Mr. Fairbanks before he films that stunt again."

"Quick, Jessie, the shovel! Somebody oughta quit feeding those damned horses."

But I was lucky to have the job, and I loved being part of the excitement of creating moving pictures. Pickford-Fairbanks Studios made even Big Time vaudeville seem Small Time.

The film industry had started moving to the Los Angeles area a dozen years ago, drawn by sunshine, scenery, and cheap labor. I was part of that last feature. Locals called us moving picture people "movies" and avoided us when they could, but the number of "movies" grew with every passing day while locals seemed to evaporate into the warm, dry air. By my count, there were seventeen studios in town and Pickford-Fairbanks was not among the largest. But it was the only one started by actors: Mary Pickford and her husband, Douglas Fairbanks, the queen and king of Hollywood.

I'd been on the job two weeks when America's most famous leading man first took notice of me. We were in the early days of filming *Don Q, Son of Zorro*, shooting one of the final scenes (who knew the scenes weren't shot in sequence?), the one where Don Q has fled to his hideout in the ruins of the DeVega ancestral castle, when a hinge on the secret trapdoor came loose.

"Jessie! Find a grip right away."

I came across Zeke in the shade of a low-hanging eucalyptus at the edge of the back lot and pulled him from his lunch pail to the castle hideout. Crouching beside him, handing him his tools like a nurse in an operating room, I felt a prickly sensation on my neck. I've always been able to sense when I'm being watched—it comes from years of being on the stage where the ability to draw attention is essential to success.

"Who's that?" I heard a deep voice whisper.

"The new girl Friday, Jessie Beckett."

I stood up and turned to face the great Douglas Fairbanks, Son of Zorro, not three steps away.

He looked every inch the Spanish don of the last century, costumed in tight pants and a white blousy shirt with a flowing silk tie and bolero jacket. He had played the hero in the 1920 feature *Mark of Zorro*—a completely new style of picture full of action and adventure—and now, five years later, he was back for the sequel as Zorro's son, Don Q, wrongly accused of murdering the archduke and desperate to woo the fair Dolores. I'd seen him on the set, of course, but this was the first time we had actually been introduced.

From a distance, Douglas Fairbanks was a tanned, muscular young man, but up close, the receding hairline and the wrinkles around his mouth and eyes betrayed him. I felt a stab of sympathy. I, too, had specialized in younger roles, playing a fourteen-year-old in vaudeville with the Little Darlings well into my twenty-fifth year, and I understood all too well the terrifying prospect of aging out of one's livelihood. It had recently happened to me.

"How do you do, Mr. Fairbanks?" I said, looking steadily into his eyes, according him the respect he had earned without any of the toadying I knew he would loathe.

He gave me the once-over, stepped closer, locked those piercing gray-blue eyes on mine, and put both hands firmly on my shoulders. Without a word, he walked me backward until I bumped into a papier-mâché castle wall that looked more like the real thing than the real thing. Two dozen people on the set froze. With my shoulders pinned to the wall, I probably looked as thunderstruck as I felt.

"Chin up," he commanded in a voice that was clear and strong and accustomed to obedience. "Hold still, now." And yes, I did think, for one appalling moment, that he was going to kiss me, right there in front of the entire cast and crew.

Snatching a clipboard from the hand of an assistant, he set it on my head and made a pencil mark on the fake stone wall.

"How tall is she?" he demanded of no one in particular. An alert gaffer whipped out a tape measure and held one end at my heel.

"Five one," the man announced. "With shoes."

"I thought so. Exactly the same as my Mary. But not as slim, I'll wager. How much do you weigh?"

"Um . . . about a hundred pounds."

"Mary weighs ninety-five. And she struggles mightily to hold on to that number, I can tell you. Never touches sweets. Well, well, maybe we can use you as a stand-in sometime, eh, Jessie Beckett? A blond wig to cover up that auburn bob and you'd be all set."

A stand-in for the incomparable Mary Pickford, my idol and the most recognized face in the world? I swallowed hard but no words came out.

"All finished here." At that moment, the grip climbed through the trapdoor, oblivious to the odd scene that had just played out above him. The cast and crew scurried to resume their places and pretend nothing out of the ordinary had occurred.

It was a week or so after that incident, at a break during the brutal swordfight scene between our hero, Don Q, and the dastardly Don Sebastian, that Mr. Fairbanks sent for me to come to his dressing room. The makeup artist was leaving just as I arrived.

"Ah, there you are," said Mr. Fairbanks. "Come in, come in. Step lively, there isn't much time."

He must have sensed my nervousness because he lost no time in putting me at ease by telling me that Frank Richardson, the director, and Pauline Cox, the script girl who was training me, were pleased with the job I was doing. Then he asked how I liked working at Pickford-Fairbanks.

"I like it very much," I replied uneasily, fearing this was to be my last day.

"Frank says you were in vaudeville. What brought you to Hollywood?"

"I spent my life in vaudeville, but I was ready for a change. Twenty-five years was enough."

"Jesus, I thought you were about eighteen. How old are you?"

"Twenty-five. My mother was onstage while she was carrying me, so I tell people I started performing before I was born. Last fall, I took some civilian work and ended up with a broken leg and living with my grandmother in San Francisco while it mended. A vaudeville friend, Jack Benny, knew I'd had enough of the vagabond life and made inquiries for me. Zeppo Marx told Benny that Frank Richardson's script girl was planning to get married, and I applied for the position before Frank even knew she was leaving."

"If Zeppo vouched for you, I'm sure Frank counted himself lucky to get you." He offered me a Camel, which I declined, and he lit one of his own. "So you came to Hollywood to become a star, eh?"

"Doesn't everyone want to become a star?" I asked, relaxing a little now that I realized I wasn't going to be fired. "But I expect my years on the stage left me a little more realistic than most. I figure to learn all I can about the moving picture business— it's a lot different than vaudeville—and then I'll find out where I best fit in."

"Well, Jessie Beckett, I'll tell you where you best fit in. If you agree, that is. My personal assistant was called home to Texas yesterday to comfort her dying father. I need someone to fill her shoes for a while, and Frank offered you up. Pauline says it's okay; she's got six weeks before she leaves and that's plenty of time to get you trained. It's a temporary assignment, you understand," he warned. "When my assistant comes back, she picks up where she left off, and you're back with Frank. Are you interested?"

"Oh, yes, sir. Very much." In the distance, a harsh bell sounded, signaling the end of the break. Douglas Fairbanks extinguished his cigarette, picked up a stack of papers, and continued talking as we walked out of his dressing room toward the sunlit stage.

"Good girl. Job starts now. Here, take these folders to director Beaudine on the *Little Annie Rooney* set, call for the studio mail at the post office—something you'll do twice a day—take it to the office and my secretary will show you how to sort it and what to answer. Stop by Kress's and pick up a hat and some other things they'll have waiting for you. Bring them here before three. Do you have all that straight?"

Other than the fact that I had no idea where those places were, sure. "Yes, sir."

"'Sir' is for the stage, Jessie. 'Douglas' will do off it."

By now we had reached the castle-ruins set. The great actor threw back his shoulders, straightened his doublet, narrowed his eyes to a steely glare, lifted his chin, and transformed Douglas Fairbanks into the fearless Don Q, son of Zorro. "Robledo!" he barked imperiously, one hand held out, palm up. "My sword!" Both cameras rolled.

Douglas Fairbanks was as good as his word. When his assistant returned after a few weeks, I went back to working as the film's assistant script girl. But during those weeks, I learned my way around Hollywood, met a slew of big shots and stars, and got invited to the party where the first of the "Hollywood murders" took place.

2

"Are you very, very certain the invitation included me?" Myrna asked as we stepped off the electric streetcar— called Red Cars or Yellow Cars around here—on Saturday night and headed toward the home of one of Paramount's leading directors.

"Of course it did," I replied in a confident tone designed to conceal my own misgivings. In truth, it had been rather an odd invitation, extended on impulse only yesterday when I delivered some papers to the office of the famous director, Bruno Heilmann. I had no written invitation to get us past a butler. What if no one expected us? Being turned away like gate-crashers in front of other guests would be humiliating.

"I was at Bruno Heilmann's office on business three times this week, and yesterday I explained to him that it was my last day and that he could expect Mr. Fairbanks's regular assistant to pick the papers up on Monday. He looked at me like he was trying to figure out a puzzle, and then he said"—and here I mimicked him with my best German accent—" 'I'm hafing a party at my house tomorrow night. Everyone vill be there. Vill you come?'" So I said, 'Sure, what time do you want me?' and he said that most people would be arriving after nine. Then I asked, 'What do you want me to do?' He gave me the strangest look and said, 'Vat do you usually do at parties?' That was when I realized my mistake. 'You mean, you want me to come as a guest?' I said. 'Of course,' he said. 'Vat did you think I meant?' And I had to admit: 'I thought you were asking me to help out taking coats or passing caviar.' He laughed so hard he had to wipe his eyes."

Myrna was laughing, too. "You didn't!"

"I'm afraid I did. But the minute I understood it was an invitation and not a job, I thought how much I'd rather come with a friend. I figured since he was laughing, the odds were in my favor, so I asked. He said, 'A girlfriend or a boyfriend?' I said, 'A girlfriend who shares a house with me.' 'Is she pretty as you?' he asked. 'Prettier,' I said."

"Aw, come on!" she said, nudging me with her elbow.

Myrna was not a classic beauty like Gloria Swanson or Greta Garbo. Cataloged individually, her features were nothing unique—a cute upturned nose, wide-set blue eyes, and high cheekbones—but the package sure turned heads. At nineteen, her carrot hair was maturing to a more sophisticated hue, her freckles were fading, and her soft, sexy voice was deepening . . . not that that would help her until someone figured out how to make pictures with sound. I had been in vaudeville dance acts for years and was a pretty good hoofer myself, but Myrna was a gifted, classically trained dancer who made reaching for the salt look like something out of *Swan Lake*. She had recently left her dancing job for a shot at the silver screen. With the predictable outcome . . . that is, none. We met two months ago when I took a room in the house on Fernwood Avenue where she lived with Melva, Helen, and Lillian—all nice girls, but I liked Myrna best.

The noisy commercialism of Hollywood Boulevard faded behind us, replaced with the sound of crickets and the exotic fragrance of eucalyptus trees as we wound our way through the narrow roads of Whitley Heights. Although there were no street lamps, a nearly full moon lit our stage like a distant floodlight. "The stars are out tonight," I said.

"I hope I meet some. What if no one will talk to us?"

"Then we'll talk to each other. But don't worry. Douglas Fairbanks, at least, will talk to us. He told me he'd be there tonight for a short while, and he's always so kind to his people. And we're bound to know some of the others," I said with more hope than certainty. "Surely someone from *Son of Zorro* will be there. And maybe from *Ben-Hur*."

"Even so, they won't know me. I'm just an extra." Myrna was still glum over her recent failures. She had tested for the Virgin Mary with *Ben-Hur* but came away with only a $7.50-a-day job as a Roman senator's mistress at the chariot races. Earlier she'd tested for a role with the great Rudolph Valentino in *Cobra* but missed that one, as well. Too young for the part, Valentino had ruled.

We stepped through a gate and into a semicircular courtyard with five Spanish-style haciendas arranged in an arc around a dolphin fountain spouting streams of water. There was no mistaking the house—flaming torches lit the path to Bruno Heilmann's front door.

"Good thing Mr. Heilmann put torches out or we'd never have guessed which place was his," Myrna deadpanned.

I smiled. The Heilmann home could have doubled as an advertisement for the electric company, with light spilling out of every open door and window, raucous laughter surging and ebbing like waves at the seashore, and lively band music pulsating from behind the house, competing with the people indoors who were lustily singing to piano accompaniment. I'd been to parties in Hollywood, but nothing classy like this.

"It looks like he invited all the neighbors," I said, indicating the other four houses that were dark.

"That or they left town before the ruckus started!"

We approached the wide-open front door. Inside it was wall-to-wall actors, actresses, directors, and studio big shots, all dressed to the nines in dinner jackets and glamorous flapper dresses that bared more arms, shoulders, calves, and backs than you could see at a burlesque show. A thick haze of cigarette smoke clogged the air. Myrna and I exchanged nervous glances, put on our most confident smiles, and stepped into the foyer. When no one sprang from behind a corner to challenge us, my fears receded.

Bruno Heilmann didn't live in one of those flashy mansions you see photographed in *Motion Picture*, *Photoplay*, or any of the fan magazines. We could see most of the first floor from the foyer, all of it decorated in the modern German style, cold, spare, and angular, with subtle colors, no bric-a-brac, and lots of abstract paintings. Intimidating, like its owner, but not overly large. I guessed he didn't need a huge place, being a bachelor.

A butler descended the stairs to take our wraps. Several couples wobbled past him on their way to the second floor, planting each footstep with care and steadying themselves with the handrail.

I wore a custom-made, sleeveless tea-length frock, green to bring out the color in my eyes, with bugle beads sewn onto every square inch. It was expensive, left over from my last role, where I had played the part of a long-lost heiress in a swindle to bilk her relatives out of her fortune. No one cared to have the clothes back, so I kept them. Myrna was dressed in her finest, a blue silk backless with a handkerchief hem; not costly, but Myrna could wear rags and look like a million bucks. Still, she came across as very young and inexperienced. I made a mental note to keep an eye on her.

"Shall I use your new name?" I asked, thinking ahead to the introductions.

She nodded uncertainly, then sighed. "I suppose so. I've just started using it on the back of my photographs and to sign my checks."

"Good girl. It's a great name." The artistic, avant-garde crowd she hung around with had been urging her for some time to come up with a more distinctive-sounding moniker, and she had finally settled on one.

"Every one of my friends thought Williams was too ordinary for an actress. I still consider it a very, very good name, but . . . well, I guess they were right. Anyway, everyone had ideas for my new last name—someone suggested Myrna Lisa, can you believe that?" She giggled. "It's catchy all right, but I'd be too embarrassed to use something so silly."

There must have been a hundred people at the party already, with more arriving behind us. We surveyed the living room from our vantage point at the top of the steps and jostled our way through the crush toward an enormous slate patio ringed with more torches. Colorful Japanese lanterns dangled overhead. In the space of sixty seconds I'd spotted several familiar faces from the *Son of Zorro* and a few people I'd met on my Fairbanks errands. I began to breathe easier. I could fit in here.

A waiter came near us with a tray of canapés, and I managed to snatch one. Another was taking orders for the bar. Myrna and I were about to request gin rickeys when I caught sight of a waitress circulating the room with a tray of champagne. My all-time favorite.

"Wait, Myrna! Have you ever had champagne?"

She shook her head.

"Try this," I said, lifting two glasses off the tray and thanking the waitress with a smile.

She took a sip, but before I could hear her opinion, her eyes opened wide. "Gosh, there's Raoul Walsh," she said, pointing to the well-known director. I spun around. "He hired my dance troupe at Grauman's Egyptian to do the orgy scene in *The Wanderer*. I was drinking and hanging over a couch with a wine goblet, trying to do what they told me to do. It was really fun."

"Can you introduce me?"

Her mouth turned down. "He doesn't know me. I'm just a dancer."

The champagne was delicious and cold as ice. It had not taken me long to realize that in Hollywood, as elsewhere, Prohibition laws were treated with the scorn they deserved. Liquor was served at every party, brazenly, defiantly, without fear of raids, arrests, or fines, not merely because the police were bribed as they were in most cities, but because the studio bosses ran the show here. The police did what they were told.

Every man in the room was handsome and every woman beautiful, so why I should find myself staring at one particularly compelling, dark-haired gentleman, I do not know. He had just entered the house and was standing in the foyer unaccompanied, surveying the crowded room. His eyes worked from right to left quickly, then back again more methodically, until he had taken stock of every face. It reminded me of another man I used to know—a bootlegger—who did the same thing before entering a room. All at once a shout came from behind me, and an actor I recognized from the screen as Jack Pickford called, "Johnnie! Over here!" Only then did Johnnie descend the two steps into the living room and plunge into the party.

Someone tapped my shoulder and there was Douglas Fairbanks in his smart midnight-blue dinner jacket, looking like he'd just stepped out of a high-society picture. "Good evening, Jessie," he said, sipping a frosted glass of orange juice. "You're looking lovely tonight."

"Thank you. I'm here with a friend, and I'd like you to meet her. This is Myrna Loy." And for form's sake, I added the entirely unnecessary second half of the introduction, "Myrna, this is Douglas Fairbanks."

Douglas made a short bow. "Charmed, I'm sure, Miss Loy."

Myrna stood rooted to the rug, hopelessly tongue-tied. "Gee, Mr. Fairbanks. This is such an honor. I, um—I've seen all your pictures."

"Until recently, Myrna was a dancer at Grauman's Egyptian Theater," I said helpfully, nudging her with my elbow.

"Um, that's right, I used to dance the prologue to *Thief of Bagdad*." She was referring to the lavish live spectacle presented on the stage before every showing of Douglas's most recent film, a fairy tale with astonishing special effects that had been released last year and was still playing in many theaters.

"So you and I have shared the same stage, so to speak? Allow me to express my gratitude for your part in making my picture such a success. Ah, here she is . . . Mary, darling, I've told you about my temporary assistant. This is Jessie Beckett and her friend Myrna Loy."

As one of the few adults whose height matched that of "Little Mary" Pickford, I could look her straight in the eye. "I'm honored to meet you," I began, trying not to appear overawed by her presence and hoping she couldn't see my heart hammering beneath my frock. I'd seen her at the studio a few times, but being introduced socially almost took away my powers of speech. "I've learned so much from you over the years, I feel I owe whatever success I had in vaudeville to you."

"How very kind." Mary Pickford looked even prettier than she did in her pictures, with wide hazel eyes and delicate lips darkened red. Her voice was higher than I had imagined and soft as a cat's fur. For the party, she had swept her famous blond ringlets in a mass behind her head and donned a pale gold flapper dress embroidered with pearls. Hard to believe I was talking to the woman who had virtually invented film acting, the woman who had not only starred in hundreds of pictures, but who had started her own studio; the woman who could play a feisty eleven-year-old boy as convincingly as she did an old woman. I'd've rather met "Little Mary" than the queen of England.

"Douglas said you played children's roles in vaudeville?" she asked politely, sipping her orange juice and no doubt wondering why a lowly assistant script girl had been invited to this chic affair.

I nodded. "I grew up on stage, too. Just like you. My mother was a headliner, and she managed to keep both of us working most of the time." The truth was, things were pretty darn good while Mother was alive. It was later, after she died, that my life fell apart.

"No father?"

"Died."

Sympathy wrinkled her smooth brow. "Oh, Jessie, so did mine. And my mother took us kids—Lottie and Jack and me—on the stage and managed our careers. She still does. I don't know what I'd do without her. I'll bet you never went to school, either."

"You can't go to school when you move to a different city every week. My mother taught me my letters and numbers, and I read every book I could lay my hands on."

"I learned to read from the billboards along the train tracks," Miss Pickford said, shaking her head with the wonder of it. I was about to ask her what early roles she had played, when she said, "What sort of roles did you play?"

"My first was Moses in the bulrushes, the second was Baby Jesus. After that I specialized in kidnapped-baby roles, caterwauling like the devil during chase scenes. When I got old enough to memorize lines, I played the brat in *Ransom of Red Chief* and scenes from *Romeo and Juliet,* that sort of thing."

She gave a knowing nod and smiled at the recollection. "I played Juliet myself. I milked that death scene for all it was worth!"

"Juliet was my first death scene . . . they became something of a specialty for me: Juliet, Ophelia, Desdemona, Cleopatra—"

Miss Pickford's perfectly arched brows moved together in a slight frown. "Ophelia doesn't have a death scene."

I waved my hand dismissively. "Yes, I know. Shakespeare missed a real opportunity there, so we added one. Audiences love death scenes and mine were pretty darn convincing. As I got older, I continued with the kiddie roles. It was what I knew best and my size let me get away with it. I learned the tricks of the trade from watching your pictures."

Miss Pickford smiled, putting her hand lightly on my arm, almost as if we were real friends. "And what tricks were those?"

"Well, for one, to keep thin and flat-chested. And to make short, quick movements. Also, to add a skip to my step whenever possible. To accentuate my freckles and keep my fingernails short and unpolished. And of course, to keep my hair in long ringlets."

"But you've bobbed yours." She sounded envious.

"Just a couple months ago. I hated those curls!"

"I loathe mine. So babyish! Now don't you dare tell a soul I said that! Not a day goes by that I don't wish I could cut my hair, but my public would think it a betrayal as bad as Benedict Arnold's and would probably quit watching my pictures. I don't dare risk it."

I was more than a little surprised at this confession. Like most people, I had supposed that "The Most Popular Girl in America" did whatever she wanted. Suddenly I saw how naïve that was. In some respects, Mary Pickford was a prisoner of her image.

For a few minutes, we swapped recollections of night trains, dollar hotels, and boardinghouse food, until a waitress carrying a tray of champagne approached. I set my empty glass on the tray and picked up a full one. Miss Pickford glanced over her shoulder, then did the same, replacing her glass of orange juice with one of champagne.

"Don't tell Douglas," she said with an exaggerated wink. "He disapproves of alcohol. Usually I try to accommodate him, but, well, sometimes I get tired of pleasing everyone else."

At that moment, her attention was drawn to someone behind me. I turned to see her younger sister, Lottie Pickford, making her way unsteadily toward us. Lottie wore a wild look as she clutched at Mary's arm.

"Lottie, what on earth—"

"Can you—have you—" Her eyes darted around the room, frantically searching right and left.

"Lottie, darling, I'd like you to meet . . ." But Lottie must have spotted the person she was looking for, because she stumbled toward the stairs without uttering another syllable. A few steps away, Douglas took in the entire scene. His well-disciplined actor's features failed him for a moment and his eyes narrowed to dark slits. His lips tightened. With a jolt of surprise, I read disgust on his face. Clearly, Douglas despised his sister-in-law.

"I'm sorry . . ." Miss Pickford began, but I waved off her apology.

"I already know Lottie from *Son of Zorro*." Lottie had a small but significant role in the picture as Lola, the pretty servant girl who serves as a spy in Don Fabrique's employ and uncovers the blackmail plot. Lottie was usually late to work and often petulant, but no one dared reprimand the sister-in-law of Douglas Fairbanks. Only now did I realize his courteous treatment of her on the set masked his true feelings. And as I watched Lottie's behavior, I understood the reason for his contempt. Douglas Fairbanks despised liquor, and Lottie was a drunkard.

"Oh, of course you do. I forgot, you work for Frank Richardson now. Well, excuse Lottie's bad manners tonight, I'm afraid she's dealing with some—"

Whatever she was going to say was interrupted by a shrill scream and the sound of pottery breaking into a hundred pieces, followed by furious accusations from the other end of the room. Too short to see and too curious for my own good, I stepped up on one of the chairs that had been pushed against the wall.

Two women in sparkling gowns were hurling insults until one of them, the older one, lost all sense of decency and pulled back her bejeweled hand. With a lightning movement, she smacked the younger woman across the face, pushed through the throng toward the door, and stormed into the night. The victim staggered but did not fall, thanks to the quick reaction of a couple of men nearby who held her close. The stunned silence quickly filled with a babble of conversation as the guests analyzed the spat.

"Seems like a disagreement," I said lamely, stepping down off the chair. "I wonder who that was."

Miss Pickford sipped her champagne calmly. "That was Faye Gordon who just left." I looked surprised, as little Mary Pickford could not have seen over the heads to the other side of the room. She read the question in my eyes and gave a rueful smile. "I recognized her voice, and throwing breakables has become something of a trademark with Faye. Poor dear, she has had some bad luck lately, but she should learn to keep her temper in check, at least in public. And this," she said grandly as an attractive couple approached us, "this handsome man is my darling brother Jack and his wife, Marilyn Miller."

Compared to their famous sister, Jack and Lottie Pickford were amateurs, but they were good-looking and competent enough on-screen. Marilyn Miller and I were almost the same age, and I knew her from vaudeville. When she didn't seem to recognize me, I tried to spark her memory by saying, "It's so good to see you again, Marilyn. You may not remember, but we knew one another some years ago in vaudeville when we were children. You were touring with your family as the Five Columbians and my mother and I had a mother-daughter act."

She didn't respond. A little embarrassed, I tried again, "Remember how we were always dodging the sticklers who were trying to enforce the child labor laws?"

Then I looked at her more closely and noticed the empty eyes—her pupils were deep black pools so large I couldn't tell what color her irises were—and I guessed why so many party guests were going upstairs. Bruno Heilmann might flaunt the Prohibition laws downstairs, but even he couldn't be so cavalier about narcotics. I looked back at Jack Pickford. His pupils were enormous, as well. Cocaine or hashish, probably, although I'd seen enough heroin and morphine since I'd come to Hollywood to know those were popular party fare, too.

Marilyn and Jack did not incline toward conversation, at least not with me. Jack made a curt remark to his sister, then pulled his wife to the front hall where he erupted into a tirade, berating the stone-faced butler who had brought down the wrong wraps.

Miss Pickford didn't appear to notice. She reached toward Douglas, who was still chatting with Myrna and two other fawning women. "Duber, let's go or we'll be late to the Gishes." She turned back to me. "Douglas was right when he said I would enjoy meeting you, Jessie. I'm sure we'll see you around town in the near future, and we can talk again about vaudeville. Excuse us, please, we have another stop tonight before we can go home and relax."

The crowd did a Red Sea parting as the Hollywood royalty made for the exit. The champagne waitress passed again, this time giving me a long, measured look that I found disconcerting. Myrna lifted two glasses off her tray. "Here, let's toast! To the most exciting night of my life!" She bubbled more than the champagne. "Imagine, little Myrna Williams—I mean, Loy—talking to Douglas Fairbanks for ten whole minutes! No one would believe it back home in Montana. And did you get to meet Jack Pickford? Isn't he a dream?"

"Actually, we were introduced, but he wasn't in a sociable mood."

"Do you know the scandal about his first wife's death? You must remember! It was all over the newspapers about five years ago. Olive Thomas was her name. She was a real vamp, very, very gorgeous and a big star."

Who hadn't heard the tale? Actually knowing some of the people involved brought the story closer to home. I remembered Olive Thomas from her pictures and from her mysterious death in Paris.

Myrna continued. "I was only fourteen at the time, but I read all about it in the magazines. I never believed Jack's claim for a minute. You tell me, please, how anyone could accidentally drink an entire quart of nasty-tasting toilet-cleaning solution at three A.M. without noticing something tasted funny. Did you think it was suicide or murder?"

"I never could decide. The reports I read said it wasn't toilet cleaner, that Jack had lied so the press wouldn't learn the truth and ruin his career."

"What was it?"

"Bichloride of mercury. You know what that's for, don't you?" I had understood the sexual implications at the time, but Myrna was younger and probably never caught on. "Syphilis," I told her. "I kind of thought that maybe her death really *was* accidental, that both of them were so high on cocaine and booze that they didn't know what they were doing."

"I overheard my mother and her friends talking about it. One of the neighbors insisted that it was suicide, that Olive was depressed over their awful marriage. Another thought Jack murdered her. My mother still thinks that she was planning to poison Jack, but drank it herself instead by mistake, but that sounds impossible. I guess no one will ever know the truth."

"The French police certainly didn't bother to find out. They couldn't send the body home fast enough. The sad thing was that all those tales of wild living spilled over to Mary Pickford, dragging her name through the mud along with Jack's, even though she wasn't within a thousand miles of Paris and had nothing to do with any of it."

"Gosh," said Myrna, "that's not fair. Anyway, I'm surprised to see Jack and Marilyn together tonight. This month's *Photoplay* says they are getting a divorce, but they looked happy enough tonight."

"Myrna, those magazines are full of lies. You can't believe a word they print. All these big actors have press agents who'll say anything to get publicity. They make up ninety percent of it. Here, I'll prove it. You know how everyone says Douglas Fairbanks does all his own stunts? Well, he does most of them, true, but I've seen a stuntman do a few."

"Really?"

"Excuse me, don't I know you?" A woman wearing a short, chic gown came up to Myrna and me. "Weren't you at Pickfair last Christmas?"

Before I could respond, two young men cruised over. "Haven't we met before?" asked the one with the dimples. "Of course we have," said his friend, answering for me, "at the Montmartre that night Rudy was doing the tango, wasn't it?"

The cynic in me knew exactly what had prompted the sudden spike in our popularity—people had seen Douglas Fairbanks and the Pickfords talking to us and assumed we were "somebody." Somebody they couldn't quite place . . . Thus elevated to the ranks of the Hollywood elite for a few short hours, Myrna and I basked in our new status like two Cinderellas before the final stroke of midnight returned us to reality.

I t wasn't until after eleven that I finally saw our host. Bruno Heilmann approached our little circle and graciously nodded to me. It was as close as we had been all evening, and I was glad to have the opportunity to thank him for the invitation.

"Good evening, Mr. Heilmann," I began. "This is my friend Myrna Loy. Thank you so much for inviting us. We've been enjoying ourselves immensely tonight."

Bruno Heilmann had only to glance at Myrna's rapturous expression to know the truth of that statement. He was a big, attractive man in his early forties, I guessed, but as I examined his broad forehead, his large eyes behind round-rimmed glasses, his straight nose and strong jaw, it occurred to me that his appeal stemmed more from his authority than from his appearance. Power always looks handsome, and this was a powerful man, one who worked for Hollywood's most powerful studio, Paramount, for the most powerful studio boss, Adolph Zukor. He flattered Myrna for a moment with some pleasantries, then turned to me.

"So, you are no longer Douglas's little assistant, ja?" As he spoke, his eyes dropped from my face to my legs, then moved up slowly, pausing at my breasts before returning to my face. I felt naked.

"I'm afraid not," I said, pretending I hadn't noticed but blushing in spite of myself. "His regular girl will be back on the job on Monday."

"Then you are out of work, no? Perhaps I haf something for you. A pretty girl like you must haf many talents," he said, lightly brushing my cheek with his knuckles.

I didn't like the way he said it. I didn't like the way he looked me over. And it was all I could do not to flinch at his touch. Now I knew what motives had prompted his impulsive invitation. And just a couple of hours ago I had been thinking Myrna was naïve!

"Thank you very much, but I'll be returning to work as assistant script girl at *Son of Zorro*."

"Assistant script girl? Tsk-tsk. You look more capable than such a lowly job. I am certain we could find something more suited to your talents at Paramount."

"I am really quite happy where I am, thank you."

"And how is the new Zorro picture coming?"

How gullible did he think I was? I would not be dragged into a conversation that divulged anything about our films to a rival studio. "Right on schedule, Mr. Heilmann. Everything's smooth sailing so far."

"So you will still be . . . ah, *working* for the great Fairbanks?"

I knew what he was insinuating, the swine. Plenty of people had seen me going in and out of Douglas's dressing room over the past few weeks, and the gossip had obviously reached Heilmann. He probably had an informer on the Zorro set. It was not uncommon for studios to place their own people at competing

studios or bribe one of the production staff to report on develop-
ments. I felt my face grow warm. Douglas Fairbanks was America's
hero, even if he was in his forties. I'd read the shameless letters
that women all over the world wrote to him. I'd seen the beautiful leading ladies who surrounded him every day. But Douglas
Fairbanks's love for Mary Pickford was the stuff of legends, like
Tristan and Isolde, Romeo and Juliet, or Anthony and Cleopatra.
He hardly noticed the women he kissed on screen. He certainly
didn't notice me, not in that way.

Before I could respond, Lottie Pickford bumped hard into
Myrna from behind. "Oh!" gasped Myrna as her champagne
glass flew out of her hand and splintered on the floor, spattering
Heilmann and several guests. Lottie looked like a madwoman,
her pretty cheeks blotchy with rage. I couldn't tell if she had
stumbled into Myrna or pushed her on purpose. Tears had
smudged her kohl makeup, but she wasn't crying now.

With a string of profanity a sailor would envy, Lottie threw
garbled accusations at Heilmann that he did not wait to catch.
Sending an apologetic glance in my direction, he grabbed her
elbow to steer her away, but not before everyone in the room
heard her snarl, "The little tramp . . . treat me like that . . . I
could still . . . bastard . . . I could *kill* you . . ."

Myrna and I did our best to melt into the wall as Heilmann
dragged Lottie up the stairs.

"Parties certainly are lively around here," I said to Myrna.
"Let's get some more food and go out back to the music. It's so
smoky in here, I could use some fresh air."

We threaded through the hazy crush to the dining room
table where I filled my plate with mushrooms stuffed with crab
and cheese, asparagus tips, little oval slices of lamb and turkey,
olives, Waldorf salad, and other delicious bites I couldn't recognize. I continued on through the French doors. When I turned
around, Myrna had vanished. It took me a moment, then I spotted her huge grin. She was talking with a very tall young man,

handsome in a plain sort of way. Before I could wonder who he was, she pulled him toward me.

"Now I can introduce *you* to someone!" she crowed. "Jessie Beckett, this is Frank Cooper. Believe it or not, Frank grew up across the street from me on Fifth Avenue, but not Fifth Avenue in New York, Fifth Avenue in Helena, Montana. He's been in Hollywood a year now, and we run into each other now and then." She danced on her toes with excitement.

"Nice to meet you, Miss Beckett," he drawled, taking my small hand in his large one. "Myrna says you were a vaudeville star and work for Mr. Fairbanks now."

"She's being kind. I did a little of everything in vaudeville; now I'm just a script girl in training for the director of one of Mr. Fairbanks's pictures." He was a few years older than Myrna, a rugged sort, and I had no trouble imagining him as a logger or a cowboy or a sheriff from Montana. "Are you an actor?"

"Aimin' to be. Now I'm just an extra, like Myrna here. Been in two pictures so far, both westerns. Ten dollars a day. Who'd've thought little Myrna Williams and Judge Cooper's boy would be in the pictures?"

"I'm Myrna Loy now. Just made the change this week. What do you think?"

"Has a nice ring to it. I've changed my name, too. A lady casting director suggested Gary instead of Frank. She said it sounded rough and tough, like Gary, Indiana. Probably won't stick. Everyone calls me Coop anyway. Can I get you gals something more from the table?" He held out his own empty plate and headed toward the nearest spread of food. I'd never seen a man put away more than Gary Cooper did that night—he must have eaten ten times the amount Myrna and I ate together. I wondered how he stayed so slim.

We spent some time dancing to the lively music of the jazz band and did our best to drink all of Bruno Heilmann's champagne. Some of the younger set were throwing their arms and

legs in the air and toddling every step in the foxtrot, and everyone did the Charleston. A woman beside me shimmied until
some of the fringe on her dress flew off. I gave up trying to stick
close to Myrna—she was doing fine on her own, and I was having
a swell time.

Around midnight, someone tapped my shoulder. I turned to
see the champagne waitress.

"Excuse me, miss. Aren't you Chloë Randall's little girl from
vaudeville?"

Shocked silent at the unexpected thrust back in time, I
blinked before I found my voice. "Why—yes! How on earth—"

"I been looking at you all night, trying to think who you remind me of, and then it come to me. You're Chloë Randall's
little girl she called Baby."

"Yes! Oh, my goodness! Who are you?"

"You won't remember me; it was more than fifteen, maybe
twenty years ago, and you were just a kid. I'm Esther Frankel,
and I knew your ma when we was on stage. Not together, I don't
mean that. She sang, and I was with a German dance troupe.
But we were on the same circuit for a year and got to be friends.
I was awful sad when I heard she passed."

Suddenly, the party seemed frivolous. My eyes stung. I blinked
hard. "Esther. Yes, I remember her friend Esther. I remember
you."

She chuckled. "Well, you can't recognize me; I'm a lot fatter
than I was in those days. And you've changed a good bit, too, but
you haven't grown much. You are the spitting image of your
mother." She looked around furtively. "Look, I'd love to talk with
you a little, but I can't do that here. I'm working, you know, and
they wouldn't like me to mix with guests."

"Come on," I said, "let's slip into the kitchen."

"What's that? I don't hear so good, especially with all this
noise."

"I said, let's go into the kitchen. It'll be quieter."

We ducked through the swinging doors and into the relative stillness of a small butler's pantry. The kitchen counters were stacked high with food trays and pots and pans, and two men who could have been Mexican, wearing aprons lettered with CISNEROS BROTHERS CATERING, darted about in a frenzy coordinating the food and staff for this huge affair. I wanted to hear about my mother, and Esther wanted to hear about me, but the two chief cooks were throwing unhappy looks in my direction. I was distracting one of their workers.

Esther frowned. "Look, this won't do, either. Why don't you come by my place tomorrow? I have some playbills of your ma, maybe ones you haven't seen. We can have some coffee and a nice long talk about the old days, and you can tell me what you're doing here in Hollywood, and I can tell you what I remember 'bout your ma."

"Oh, Esther," I said, as she cupped one hand behind her ear, "you have no idea how much I'd love that! I was only twelve when she died, and I don't know anyone who knew her in her younger days."

"We won't be done here until late . . . two or three o'clock maybe. Still, I don't sleep late these days, no matter what. Come around ten or eleven. Here's my address." She scribbled on a notepad by the telephone on the wall. "The Red Car'll get you most of the way there, and then you can walk just three blocks."

She squeezed my hand, and on impulse I threw my arms around her in a big hug. "See you tomorrow, Esther."

When I returned to the patio, Myrna and Gary Cooper were still dancing. I waited until the music paused to pull her aside. "Myrna, the last Red Car runs at half after midnight, remember." She pouted prettily, but didn't protest. Neither of us could afford a taxi. We said good night to Coop, retrieved our wraps from the butler, and headed out the front door.

A couple dozen guests were gathered around the fountain where a lovely young actress was sitting in the water. It looked like the same girl who had been slapped earlier—if so, she'd recovered nicely. Several men were pouring martinis over her head, causing her to laugh prettily down the notes of a scale. Her wet clothing was plastered to her curves, revealing the fact that she had forgotten to wear undergarments. Someone picked up another young woman who gave a charming shriek as she was plopped in the water, too. Myrna and I crept along the edge of the courtyard in the shadows.

"Call me a scaredy-cat, but I'd rather not ruin my frock." Myrna giggled. "What a divine party! I'm so very, very glad you asked Bruno Heilmann to include me." She was a little tipsy. Well, so was I.

Walking none too steadily through the gate, we retraced our steps downhill toward Hollywood Boulevard. I felt as light as the breeze that teased our hair. It had been a perfect evening . . . a night to remember forever. Ten minutes later, we hopped the crowded streetcar heading east.

"Who was that old woman serving drinks?" asked Myrna, grabbing a hand strap since there was no place to sit. "I saw you talking to her like you knew her."

"Believe it or not, that was a friend of my mother's from vaudeville. I barely remember her from when I was a little girl. We couldn't talk at the party while she was working, but she invited me to her house for coffee tomorrow, and she's going to tell me some stories about my mother."

"Gosh, you must be excited!"

More than excited, I was thrilled. "She has a collection of playbills that includes some of my mother's. Seeing those . . ." I swallowed hard before I could continue. "You see, I don't have any photographs of my mother, and, well, seeing those playbills will . . ." I couldn't go on. I didn't need to. Myrna squeezed my hand.

Although it was after midnight, Hollywood Boulevard was ablaze with lights and alive with throngs of people milling in and out of restaurants, clubs, and speakeasies, hopping on and off the Red Cars at every intersection, some returning, like us, from a party, others heading out for further mischief. Shop doors stood open to the evening air. Flower stalls with pails full of colorful blossoms and white booths selling fresh orange juice did brisk business. Sleep came late to Hollywood.

"I sure liked your friend Gary Cooper. Is there any romance between you two?"

"Oh, no, not with Coop. He's just an old friend from home. We were never really close 'cause he's about four years older than me, and I barely knew him growing up. He's nice, but too quiet for my taste and kind of dull. And he's too tall for you!" she teased.

"Heck, everyone is too tall for me," I said cheerfully.

"How come you don't have a sweetheart, Jessie?"

The silence stretched between us as I considered how to respond. I had told Myrna and the girls I lived with that I was unattached, but was it true? Did I have a sweetheart? I had thought so, at one point. I had thought myself in love with a wonderful fellow who made my heart pound and my mouth go dry, but I guess I wasn't, not any longer.

Unfortunately, my pause made Myrna think she had offended me. "Never mind, it's none of my business," she said hastily.

I reassured her. "It's not that, Myrna. I'm afraid I really don't know how to answer. There was someone last fall when I was in Oregon. First I thought there was no chance for us; then for a short time, it seemed there might be. Turned out he wasn't the person I thought he was. He left right after I got hurt, and I don't know where he is now. And that's all for the best."

"Never mind, there are loads of eligible men in Hollywood. Maybe you'd like Coop. I was just kidding about his being too tall for you."

"Oh, thanks! Give me the dull ones, will you?" I teased.

We walked down the street a couple blocks, laughing most of

the way, then snagged a shortcut through an empty lot that came out near the rear door of our house. One of the girls had left the back light on for us, but the bulb was weak. I was fumbling through my purse for the key when Myrna gasped.

I whirled around and saw her face, white in the dim light. She was staring at the ground in horror. I followed her gaze and saw it.

A dead bird.

I don't know much about birds—perhaps it was a sparrow or a wren. Something small and brown and ordinary. Its little neck met its body at a right angle, clearly broken. It hadn't been there when we left.

"Oh, what a shame!" I thought she would pick it up and throw it in the bushes while I searched for my key, but she stood like a statue. I looked at her again. Her face was frozen with panic. A moment ago she had been giggling.

Now, I don't relish picking up dead animals myself, but I've had to deal with countless rodents in my life, and a bird wasn't going to send me into a fainting spell, as it clearly was Myrna. Without a word, I bent down and gingerly picked up the little corpse with my thumb and forefinger.

"Poor thing. It must have flown into the window and broken its neck."

Myrna twitched. Really, her reaction astonished me. She wasn't a child, and it was only a wild bird, not a pet. I took a couple steps to the hedge that separated our house from the neighbors and tossed it into the bushes.

"Come on, let's go inside." But she didn't move. She couldn't. Her eyes met mine, and I saw genuine fear. "It's all right, Myrna," I said gently. "It's just a wild bird."

"You don't understand."

"Understand what?"

"What it means."

"What *what* means?"

"There's an old Swedish saying that when a bird hits a window, someone is going to die."

So that's what was bothering her.

"No one has died," I pointed out. It didn't faze her. "Look, Myrna, there are a lot of old sayings, but they are only superstitions."

"Not this one."

4

woke early the next morning, too keyed up over the prospect
of visiting Esther Frankel to go back to sleep.

What child pays attention to her mother's friends? Certainly not me, but I did have hazy recollections of Esther. *Stay in
the room, Baby,* I could hear my mother say. *Esther and I are going
out tonight.* We toured the same circuit for a while, a few months,
a couple of years; I don't remember. It was nothing unusual. In
vaudeville, agents tend to book to a particular circuit—like the
Orpheum Circuit or Pantages, or Palace, or Keith—and those
acts would stop at the theaters on that circuit, in a certain order,
for the life of the contract. The theater bill changed every week,
and with nine or ten acts in a show, it was natural for some to
travel between cities in a loosely organized group. At some point
in my young life, Esther's German dance troupe had shared the

same billing as my mother's act. We may even have roomed with her for a while. I'd soon know all the details.

Meanwhile, I gathered my laundry and headed for the basement. There was just enough time before I left for my weekly battle with the Gainaday.

A surprise attack seemed best. Sneaking up on the contraption, I managed to fill its cylinder with soap and hot water before it caught on to my intentions, but the beast retaliated by yanking out its hose and spewing sudsy water all over the basement floor. By the time I had reattached the hose and regrouped for a second assault, its motor was coughing and shuddering like a consumptive, and I feared even my best swear words would not prevent the whole thing from rattling off its legs. A couple of sharp kicks showed it who was boss, and it settled down to swirl, lift, dip, and squeeze my clothes until they were passably clean. I stood guard through two clear water rinses to defend against an unexpected offensive and then fed each sodden garment through the wringer, one by one, wondering each time it pinched my fingers why it was that I struggled with the nasty behemoth every weekend, then reminding myself exactly how much it cost to send out to the Chinese laundry. In the end, I had not gained a day, as the name promised, but I had survived the hostilities and would live to fight again.

When everything was pinned to the line, I brewed a pot of coffee and settled down in the shade of a lemon tree to varnish my toenails and contemplate my visit to Esther's.

The screen door banged. I looked up. "Morning, Myrna. I hope the racket in the basement didn't wake you too early."

"Nah. I smelled the coffee. Thanks for making such a big pot."

"Figured we'd need it after last night."

"I feel fine, considering the gallons of champagne I swallowed. What a marvelous drink, champagne! I wonder who invented it? And what a grand party!" She sat on the edge of my lounge chair and sipped her coffee. "I was about to wash my hair but Melva slipped into the bathroom first."

"You could always use the basement sink."

"What, go down there alone? Turn my back on that nasty machine? Oh, what a nice color polish. Can I use some?"

The rental we girls shared had been a farmhouse when it was built before the turn of the century, back when Hollywood was known for nothing more than orange and lemon groves. The rusted pump in the backyard and the remnants of an outhouse told the tale of farm life before 1910. That's when the town annexed itself to Los Angeles in exchange for water and sewer services, and indoor plumbing came along. And that's when the owners squeezed a flush toilet in the space below the stairs and a bathtub at one end of the upstairs hall. We girls each had our own bedroom: there were three upstairs and two downstairs that had once been the dining room and parlor. Happy as a nesting hen, I hung gingham curtains and bought a rag rug for the bare oak floor. It was the first place I'd ever called my own, and the unaccustomed pleasure of possession made me almost giddy. Every time I walked into my room, I found myself inventorying each item: my pillow, my sheets, my cup, my very own, mine, all mine.

"You know that director fella I told you I met last night?" she said.

"Johnnie Something-or-other?"

"Salazar. He's with a small studio in Culver City, and he said they were testing next week for a film. He said I could come by Monday or Tuesday and test for a part."

"Really? That's swell."

"No promises, but who knows?"

"I didn't get to meet him."

"You were outside. Johnnie was talking to Jack Pickford, and he introduced himself."

I remembered the man. Jack Pickford's friend. Dark hair,

good-looking. I'd thought he was an actor. Well, there was no law against handsome directors, was there? "So you're going to Culver City tomorrow?"

She nodded. "No point in waiting until the second day."

I almost said, "The early bird gets the worm," but stopped myself just in time. Myrna didn't need reminding about the dead bird, and pointing out that no one had died last night would sound like "I told you so." Instead I asked, "What's the name of the studio?"

"I don't remember. I've got an address but forgot to jot down the name. It's not exactly MGM, but those fellas haven't been knocking on my door lately."

"When you have the name, I'll ask around at Pickford-Fairbanks if anyone has heard of it. Just to make sure it's on the up-and-up."

"That would be great."

"What's the film about? Did he say?"

"Something mythological. Jupiter and gods and goddesses and so forth. When Johnnie Salazar learned I was a dancer, he mentioned the role. Said they were looking for actresses who could dance. I'll probably just be another seven-dollar-a-day extra, but it comes in the nick of time," she confessed. "The only thing in the piggy bank's tummy is change, and rent's coming due."

"Myrna, you know you can always—"

"No," she said firmly. "Thank you, Jessie, you're a dear, but no. I'm a big girl, and I've managed to find jobs pretty steadily since I turned sixteen. If worse comes to worst, I can always beg Sid Grauman for my dancing job back. But I have a very, very good feeling about this part. Maybe once they see me in this mythology picture, MGM or Paramount or someone will sign me."

"I'm sure you're on your way!"

5

ater that morning I hopped the Red Car, fidgeting with the
anticipation of seeing Esther and some of Mother's old playbills. Like most vaudeville players, Mother saved every play-
bill in the bottom of her trunk, not just the ones with her name
in bold letters or her face in color. After she died, these were my
only link to her or to my childhood. They were the most valu-
able things I owned—at least they were until last fall, when my
uncle destroyed them in an act of petty revenge that left a gap-
ing hole in my heart. If I were very lucky today, Esther might
offer me one of hers to keep.

Even better was the prospect of hearing Esther's recollections
from the Good Old Days. I could scarcely believe my luck in
meeting her again after all these years, although it was really
not so shocking because Hollywood was full of vaudeville re-
fugees. Undoubtedly there would be stories I had never heard,

glimpses of my mother I had never seen, and memories I could add to my precious store and hug close at night.

I sprang to the ground when the Red Car slowed and waved to the conductor as I scurried in front of him. Apart from a few Sunday drivers, there was no traffic. Without much trouble, I found Esther's street and set off at a brisk pace through a quiet residential neighborhood not unlike my own, full of bungalows and cottages. Bees hummed and birds sang. Wildflowers grew alongside the road in patches of dirt that looked unfit for weeds, and around every house were beds of fragrant roses. Even the most lackadaisical gardener could grow flowers in this Garden of Eden.

Esther Frankel's boxy stucco apartment building sat on a corner next to a ramshackle boardinghouse. Cracks in the stucco had recently been patched but the workmen had not troubled to match the shade of the stucco to the original, and their carelessness gave the place a dilapidated appearance it did not deserve. As I approached, a gray-haired woman peered out at me over a window box of geraniums, following my progress up the walk with suspicious eyes until I disappeared from her view. The lobby was bare except for one exhausted chair and a pine table shoved up against the wall with a tray on it for outgoing mail. Above the table were two dozen mail slots for the residents. Glancing over the names, I found the Frankel apartment: third floor, number five.

I took the stairs two at a time to the top floor and checked numbers until I found 305. The door was cracked. Esther was expecting me. I knocked loudly as I pushed the crack a little wider.

"Esther? I'm here. It's me, Baby." The old nickname made me feel like a child again.

The homey parlor brought a smile to my face. Every tabletop was covered with a crocheted cloth, and a crocheted antimacassar protected the arms and back of every chair. A clothesline was stretched in front of the window with a few undergarments pinned to it, and I was surprised that Esther would leave that up for company. To my left, a Pullman kitchen had been squeezed into a closet. To my right was the bedroom.

She was hard of hearing. I didn't want to startle her. I called again, louder. "Esther? It's Baby, come to visit."

I crossed the parlor to the half-opened bedroom door and pushed it clear. My smile hardened. Esther was sprawled on the floor beside the bed.

"Esther!"

Horrified, I rushed to her side, thinking that she had fallen or fainted. When I saw her head, I knew she was dead.

No accidental fall could have caused that wound. She had been bludgeoned to death with some heavy object. The back of her head was bloody, her skull smashed, her hair matted. On the floor beside her lay a bronze statue of a rearing horse that was fixed to a marble-block base. Someone had come up on her from behind, grabbed hold of the horse statue, and clubbed her to death.

Stumbling backward with my hand to my mouth, I fought off nausea. My initial instinct was to run for help, but I had to be sure. I steeled myself and put one hand on her arm, taking care not to look at the bloody mess that had been her head. Her skin was cold. The blood was partly dried. No doctor could help Esther now. I needed the police.

Like most vaudeville players, I'd spent my life avoiding cops, not looking for them. The idea of summoning those blue uniforms filled me with such a fright I started shaking. They would accuse me of killing Esther. I had no witness to say that I didn't. I'd go to prison forever. I'd hang. I sucked in deep breaths to calm my pounding heart.

The better plan was to slip out quietly. Someone else would find her soon enough. Someone else could call the police. Getting involved could ruin my life.

Then I remembered the nosy old biddy in 101. She'd seen me

enter the building a few moments ago; she would see me exit. When the body was discovered, she'd tell the police about me. They'd conclude that I'd killed Esther and fled the scene. Someone of my description would not be difficult to track down in a town of this size. I was a newcomer, a vaudeville vagabond, no better than a gypsy or a hobo. It was always easier to pin crimes on our kind than to go to the trouble of hunting down the real offender.

Panic shouted, *Run! Head straight to the train station. Hop the next train out, change your name again, go to a big city where the police will never find you.*

My mother's voice steadied me. *Wait a minute, Baby. You haven't done anything wrong. You've lived in Hollywood for three months, longer than you have ever lived anywhere in your life. It feels good to put down roots, doesn't it? You have a job here and a start at a good career. Don't throw it all away too hastily.*

Mother was right. I loved Hollywood. It felt like my hometown. For the first time in my life, I belonged somewhere, and I wasn't going to give that up without a fight. I took another deep breath to steady my nerves.

The only thing worse than calling the police was *not* calling the police. I'd look guilty either way, but less so if I took the initiative. After all, murderers don't hang around after killing someone, waiting for the police to arrive, do they?

I looked about for a telephone, and that's when I saw them. Esther's playbills. Before she'd been attacked last night, she had dug them out of the trunk and laid them on her bed to sort through them, getting ready to show them to me the next day. There on the top was a blue and yellow poster dominated by a picture of my mother, smiling as if she had a wonderful secret she was about to share. It pulled me like a bug to light.

Hands trembling, I flipped through them. Esther had collected her friends' playbills as well as her own, and there were four—*four!!*—of singer Chloë Randall. Esther didn't need them now. They would just get thrown out. I knew she would want me to have them. I was certain of it.

It wasn't stealing. But the cops wouldn't see it that way. They might search me, thinking that I'd killed her to take something. If I said the playbills were mine, would they believe me? I could say they were mine, that Chloë Randall was my mother, but they would probably not believe me. Our names were not the same. I couldn't take the risk.

I rushed back into the parlor and rifled the drawers of Esther's oak desk. The search turned up most of what I was looking for—an envelope and a pencil. I folded the four playbills, stuck them into the envelope, and licked the flap. I had no stamp, but I knew how to send letters without stamps.

With an unsteady hand, I addressed the envelope to myself at Pickford-Fairbanks Studios, then wrote "Myrna Loy" and our Fernwood Avenue address in the upper left corner. When the post office saw the unstamped letter, they would "return to sender." In the unlikely event that a benevolent postman allowed it to go through, I could intercept it at the studio office.

I clattered down the stairs, put my letter in the outgoing mail tray underneath several others, and pounded on 101. "Open up! Quick!" The walls in this building were paper thin—I could hear the old woman shuffling toward the door. Finally the door cracked. She had it chained. No fool, she. Her scowl was fierce.

"Do you have a telephone? I need to call the police, quick! Esther Frankel's dead."

Her eyes widened with alarm. Her door closed. I waited for her to unlatch the chain. I heard nothing but silence. Horrid old woman!

I crossed the hall and put my ear to the door of 102. A fussy baby howled. I knocked. This time the door opened and a lanky young man told me they didn't have a telephone but the Joneses in 104 did. Thankfully, the Joneses were in. I placed the call.

"You can wait in here if you like, young lady," said Mr. Jones.

"That's quite an upset you've had. My wife will get you a nice cup of tea." I thanked him but Mrs. Jones was frying liver for Sunday supper and the smell was making me nauseous. I wanted to be alone with my thoughts before the melodrama went into its second act.

I was shocked. I was sad. I was angry. Who could have killed a defenseless woman like that, in the middle of the night? And why? I felt the loss keenly, although I hadn't known her well. Now I never would. Esther was gone and her departure closed the window to my past.

Police come quick when it's a murder.

    Two blue uniforms, one tall and tan, the other shorter and older, met me outside the building and followed me upstairs to Esther's apartment. On either side of us, hall doors opened and heads stuck out. Word spread like a bad smell seeping under the door. I stopped at Esther's place and motioned them inside ahead of me. I didn't want to look at her again.

    "Don't go anywhere," snapped the older man.

    "Yes, sir."

    Third-floor residents peered at me from the safety of their doorways as I leaned my back against the wall and looked at the ceiling. Snatches of conversation reached me from inside Esther's as the police gave the place a quick once-over.

    "Nothing's messed up . . . Doesn't look like anything's missing . . . Check the kitchen . . . Hey, lookahere, no one was looking for money—here's a few bucks in the sugar bowl . . ." I heard the clink of a china lid and I suspected there were now fewer bucks in the sugar bowl. "She's been dead awhile . . . Whaddya think? . . . Looks like it . . ."

The younger of the two—the one with brown eyes and curly brown hair sticking out from under his hat—went across the hall asking to use a phone to call for the doctor. I heard him introduce himself to the man as Officer Delaney. Moments later, Delaney went downstairs.

After a while, the shorter man came out of the apartment and joined me in the hall, a pencil and notepad in hand. One fierce glare from him sent the people in their doorways skulking back inside. Then he began with the questions.

"Name and address."

"Mine?"

He looked right and left. "Do I look like I'm talking to somebody else here?"

I gave him the name I had adopted a couple months ago and the Fernwood address, hoping he wouldn't be checking the mail tray downstairs.

"Lived there long?"

"Three months."

"Another country girl come to be a star, eh? When will you dames learn?"

That needed no response.

"Her name?" He jerked his head toward the body.

"Esther Frankel." I spelled it for him.

"You a relative?"

"No. Esther was a friend of my mother's when they were in vaudeville, fifteen or twenty years ago. She recognized me last night and invited me here to talk over old times. I really didn't know her personally."

"You know if she lives here alone? If she's married? If she has next of kin?"

"I'm afraid not, although she didn't mention a roommate or husband last night. I think you could tell by looking through her belongings if another person lives here. Or the neighbors might know."

His snort told me I could keep my suggestions to myself. I reminded myself of the cardinal rule for dealing with a policeman— say as little as possible. At this point, the curly-haired Officer Delaney rejoined us.

"You have a key?" he asked. I shook my head. "So if she was dead when you got here, who let you in?"

"The door was cracked open when I came up. I thought she had left it that way on purpose. She was expecting me." On reflection, I figured the killer must have left it open accidentally in his haste to flee, but I didn't volunteer my opinion again.

Officer Delaney examined the lock. "Look here, Brickles." He spoke to his partner. "What do you think about this?" They took turns kneeling beside the doorknob and pressing their eyeballs right up to it. There seemed to be a bit of metal stuck inside the keyhole.

"Looks like something broke off," said Delaney. "Looks like someone picked it." They both looked at me.

"Not me."

Delaney spoke up. "The old bird on the first floor says you went up the stairs at 10:10 and didn't come banging on her door until 10:20. A real clock-watcher, that one. What were you doing in here for ten whole minutes?"

"It didn't seem like ten minutes. I—I guess I was dazed. I made myself go over to her to see if she was dead. I guess I stood there a minute or two, trying to think what to do next. I didn't know anyone in the building. I didn't kill her. She's cold. She's been dead a good while."

"Yeah? You a doctor?" snapped Brickles. He didn't expect a reply, and I didn't give him one. "You didn't look around the place? Touch anything? Take anything?"

"No, sir."

"A detective'll be here soon and see about fingerprints," said Brickles. Then he looked at Delaney and jerked his head toward me as if to say, Your turn. Delaney stepped closer and asked, "Mind if we search you?"

I minded. So what? They were going to feel me up anyway.

For an answer, I held my arms out and braced myself. Delaney had the grace to look embarrassed. His face reddened as he brushed my clothes with his hands, felt my skirt pockets, and asked politely for my hat to see if I had hidden anything there.

"You lived in Hollywood long?" He didn't realize his partner had already asked.

"Just three months."

"Have a job?"

"Yes, I work for Douglas Fairbanks."

Next time I'll mention that sooner. The atmosphere in the hallway changed the second I said it. The Fairbanks name carried authority, respectability, and just a little intimidation. Brickles stood up straighter, Delaney pursed his lips and gave a solemn nod, and the two men exchanged a meaningful look.

"Whaddya do?" Brickles continued.

"I'm an assistant script girl. Sort of a girl Friday."

"You said you met the deceased last night. Where?"

"At a party."

"Whose?"

"Bruno Heilmann's. She was serving—" I almost said champagne but caught myself just in time. No point adding kindling to the fire. "Beverages. She recognized me."

"She recognized you from twenty years ago? That musta been some trick."

"I'm twenty-five. I'd have been five or ten when she knew me. But I think it was really my mother that she recognized. I look a lot like her."

"You know of any reason anyone would want to kill her?"

"No, sir."

A doctor puffed up the stairs, followed by a man with a stretcher. He didn't waste a word on us, but headed straight to Esther. I couldn't bear to watch. A few minutes later he came out into the hall, wiping his hands on a towel.

"Death caused by a blunt instrument," he told the policemen. I rolled my eyes. Brilliant deduction, Sherlock, with the bloodied horse statue lying beside the body. "About nine or ten hours ago, I'd estimate."

I breathed a sigh of relief. That ought to be enough to get me off the hook.

Brickles started knocking on every door on the third floor. It being Sunday, most of the tenants were home, but no one had heard anything alarming in the middle of last night.

"Where were you last night at two o'clock?" Delaney asked me.

"Home in bed. I left the party at quarter past midnight to catch the last Red Car. I don't know how long it went on, probably a couple more hours." I realized that Esther must have finished working the party and just gotten home when she was attacked.

"Is there anyone who can support your story?"

"My friend Myrna Loy was with me. We went home together." Delaney asked for the spelling. I hated to get Myrna involved in this mess, but I needed an alibi.

"There's something that puzzles me. There's no telephone here. After you discovered the body, you went all the way down to the first floor to knock on doors looking for a telephone. What's wrong with these doors right here?"

I hadn't thought how odd that would look. But years on the stage had trained me to think fast under pressure and to ad-lib in a confident manner without fumbling for words.

"I don't know. I wasn't thinking very clearly, I guess. I saw the old lady in her window when I came into the building and instinctively went back to someone I knew was home. She wouldn't open the door, so I went across the hall. Look, if I had killed Esther in the middle of the night, would I come back the next day to find her and call the police?"

"Let's go," Delaney said, motioning me toward the stairs. My heart galloped. I wasn't sure if he meant he was taking me to jail or the front door. And I worried about the letters in the tray that wouldn't be picked up until tomorrow. Delaney followed as I led the way down the stairs, and I gave a sigh of relief as he passed the mail tray without checking its contents.

Out on the sidewalk, the inevitable crowd had gathered. Lots of people come out on a Sunday morning when an undertaker's car pulls up. A man with a Chaplin moustache spoke for the throng, "What's wrong, Officer?"

"Anyone here know Esther Frankel?" People looked at one another as if they were deciding how to respond. "Fifties. Gray hair. Heavy build."

"I know her. What happened? Is she dead?" asked a big-breasted woman holding a baby on her hip.

"I'm afraid so. Murdered. Anyone see or hear anything in the middle of the night? Doc says it happened about two o'clock. She was just getting home after working a party."

More murmurs and head shaking and nervous glances.

"No one was up at two or three o'clock? No one saw anything unusual?"

"I was letting my dog out at about six this morning and I saw a stranger leaving this building," said an ancient man with a bent back and a bald head. "I remember it because he had a droopy mouth like my Edna. Hey, Edna, come here and let the officer see your face."

Before poor Edna could be put on display like a carnival freak, Delaney shook his head. "Too late. Doc says it was about nine or ten hours ago." The old man looked dejected.

No one else in the crowd spoke until a thin boy wearing an

undershirt and dungarees volunteered, "Yesterday I saw a red McLaughlin circle the block three or four times. It was a touring car. Not from around here."

"Did you get a license number?"

"Naw."

Delaney jotted down the description anyway. A couple others mentioned having seen it, too. Such a creature would be easy to find—red McLaughlins weren't exactly dime a dozen, even in Hollywood.

Then a woman separated herself from the crowd and approached Officer Delaney. She was about forty, dressed in a beige suit with a matching hat and gloves, and I guessed she had just come from church. "Officer," she said in a low voice. "There have been two break-ins in my building just in the last month." She pointed to an apartment building across the street and a little east of Esther's. "In both cases, no one was home. The burglaries were reported to the police, but no one's been caught yet."

"And you're wondering if this could be the same burglar who was robbing Miss Frankel's home, thinking she was gone for the night?"

"Exactly. He thinks the place is empty because he doesn't know she works late. She comes home, surprises him in the act, and in a panic, he kills her."

Several residents were close enough to overhear the exchange, and three chimed in with more information.

"The thief took money and jewelry," volunteered one.

"He picked the locks," said another. Officer Delaney scribbled furiously, then asked for their names and addresses.

He was wasting his time. Even I could see that the three crimes were not related. Esther was not killed by a thief who had broken in to steal valuables. Esther's killer had stolen nothing. Her apartment hadn't been ransacked. He hadn't been surprised in the act; he had surprised her. Judging from the blow and the location of the body, Esther had been absorbed in her playbills and hadn't even heard the man come up behind her. But I kept quiet.

"If anyone remembers anything from the middle of the night, call the station," said Delaney, then he turned to me. "Do you want a ride home, Miss Beckett?"

"No, thanks, Officer. I'll go home the way I came, by streetcar."

"I insist. You've had a bad shock."

Further arguments might have looked like I had something to hide, so I climbed into the Buick touring car and directed him across town to my house. He probably wanted to check the address and my alibi with Myrna.

Wrong. He wanted to ask me to dinner.

"I been thinking . . ." he began as we pulled up in front of my house. I should have sensed what was coming, but Esther's death had knocked the intuition clean out of me. "When this investigation is over in a day or so, would you like to have dinner with me?"

"Um, I . . . uh . . . geez, I guess that means you don't think I did it?"

"I never did. Women don't kill like that. Besides, small as you are, I don't think you could have reached the top of her head if you'd tried. We're looking for a man, that's for sure. Someone strong. I knew right away you weren't the type to kill someone."

"Honored, I'm sure, Officer." I gulped, thinking fast. Seeing a policeman, even for dinner, sounded like a tiptoe through a minefield considering the life I'd led. On the other hand, offending a policeman—especially the one investigating this particular crime—might be worse. The only policemen I ever wanted to see were those slapstick Keystone Cops.

"The name's Carl, by the way. Carl Delaney."

"Right. Honored, Carl. But I, uh, feel a little awkward about this, considering the murder and everything."

As if on cue, Myrna stuck her head out the front door and

yelled, "Jessie? Jessie, Mr. Fairbanks is on the telephone. Says it's urgent. What shall I say?"

Rescued in the nick of time by Douglas Fairbanks—just like in the pictures. I scrambled out of the police car. "Tell him I'm coming."

"Never mind, you go on," said Carl, convinced now, if he hadn't been earlier, that I really did work for Fairbanks. "Only I hafta tell you not to leave town until this is cleared up."

"Right. And thanks for the ride home!" I dashed up the walk and into the house, so relieved to have sidestepped the invitation that I wasn't even wondering why Douglas Fairbanks, who had never telephoned me once during the weeks I worked directly for him, would do so on a sleepy Sunday afternoon.

Men who install telephones mount them too high. I held the receiver cone to my ear and stretched up on my toes to get my lips near the mouthpiece. "Hello? Jessie Beckett speaking."

"Jessie," he said tersely. "Thank God you're home. I need your help. There's been a murder."

I nearly dropped the receiver. "How on earth did you know about it already?"

"Zukor called me."

"Adolph Zukor?" I repeated stupidly. The head of Paramount, the largest studio in the world. "Why?"

"Fear. He can't afford another scandal. His people, his company, hell, the whole film industry will suffer from this. He wants to keep it out of the newspapers until he can figure out how to minimize the scandal, so almost no one knows about it yet—"

"Yes they do! I called the police."

"You *what?* How did you—"

"I found the body. I've just come from there. One of the cops brought me home."

"You were there?"

"Yes, I had gone to see her, and when I arrived, the door was ajar and her body was on the bedroom floor. It was horrible. So I called the police."

"What are you talking about?"

"The murder!"

"Whose murder?"

"Esther Frankel, of course."

"Who the hell is Esther Frankel?"

The spiraling tension at both ends of the line snapped as we reached the same appalling conclusion at the same moment.

"Esther Frankel was murdered last night after the party," I explained quietly.

"So was Bruno Heilmann."

7

The cop guarding the Heilmann house watched as a short, brown-skinned washerwoman made her way up the middle of the walk, a gimpy leg giving her steps the cadence of a slow heartbeat. Her baggy clothes were faded and worn, and a hank of black hair had escaped the yellow bandana that wrapped her head. In one hand she carried a tin pail full of rags and scrub brushes. The guard must have expected her to veer right or left at the fountain toward one of the other houses, because when she continued around it toward the center house, he stood up from his chair on the porch and peered down at her with a suspicious squint.

"I come to clean the blood," I said, looking at his shoes so he wouldn't wonder why my blue-green eyes didn't go with my dark complexion.

For an answer, he drew a last, long lungful of cigarette smoke and threw the butt at my feet. Then he swaggered down the stairs, planted his boot heel on the butt, and ground it against the flagstone walk. Subtlety was not his strength.

I stood my ground. "The manservant, he send me. He say he not going back in till the blood is washed up."

"I don't give a goddamn about any servants. No one's going in there until the detective comes and says so."

"But he tell me—"

"Beat it," he said, drawing back one arm to backhand me. It was not an empty gesture. I ducked out of his reach, retreated, and hobbled away. At every step I could feel his hostile eyes burning into my back.

Once out of sight, I lost the limp and circled around to the back of the houses on the service road until I reached the rear of the Heilmann home. Last night the adjacent houses had appeared empty. Today the two I passed were occupied, but while I heard voices coming from one and a radio blaring at the other, I saw no one. If anyone had glanced out a window, they'd have seen nothing but a Mexican servant on her way to work. The residents didn't worry me. The guard did.

"There was only one guard when I drove by a little while ago," Douglas had told me over the telephone, "and he was hugging the front porch shade." It had given me an idea.

Douglas's plan for a frontal assault hadn't worked—bluffing cops isn't easy, even for an accomplished actress like me—but I had a backup plan of my own. I thought I could sneak inside through one of the rear windows.

At last night's party, all the windows had been open. Most people around here leave windows open, day and night, or else the house heats up like a bake oven. If Bruno Heilmann had been killed last night at the conclusion of the party, the murderer would certainly not have gone about afterward closing windows before he fled. Nor would the shocked valet have thought to do it that morning after he arrived; nor would the policemen who first reported to the scene. I figured there was a good chance I could climb in an open window without being seen.

The patio looked smaller in daylight than it had last night. Dead torches still ringed the edge; paper lanterns still bobbled in the breeze . . . and I had badly misjudged the police. They had closed all the back windows on the first floor, leaving open only those on the second floor. I gave one of the ground-floor window sashes a push but it was locked from the inside. No doubt the rest were, too.

"I know this is a huge thing to ask, Jessie," Douglas had said on the telephone, "and I want to make it clear that your job isn't on the line if you refuse. I'd do it myself but I can't go to a damned drugstore without attracting photographers. Neither can Mary. And Lottie is hysterical. All she does is huddle in the corner and whimper about her career. I couldn't care less about Lottie—the press can drag that little tramp through the mire with my blessing—but I'd do anything to protect my Mary. If the newspapers get hold of Lottie's affair with Heilmann, she'll be caught up in the murder scandal and ten minutes later it will spill over to Mary. Mary's always protecting Jack and Lottie from their own idiocy, and she takes the brunt of it. It's only been five years since Olive's 'accidental' death in Paris . . . My God, a second Pickford scandal coming on top of Fatty Arbuckle's rape trial and Wallace Reid's drug overdose! The public is fed up with the wild lives of Hollywood, with the Pickfords in the fore."

Douglas was not exaggerating. Fatty Arbuckle had descended into a severe depression; his career, friends, and fans had vanished during his trial, never to return, even after the second jury found him innocent and apologized for the whole ordeal. The scandal caused serious financial panic in New York, with Paramount's stock dropping to less than half its value. Studios went bankrupt. Actors were thrown out of work. And not long afterward, the public read about the death of popular young Wallace

Reid from a drug overdose. Fans were livid when a superficial investigation into the illegal dope trade failed to identify any of his suppliers. Reputations were fragile commodities, and even Little Mary Pickford, "America's Sweetheart," was vulnerable.

Beneath an old oak tree at the edge of the patio, I made up my mind. Examining the drooping branches, I found the one I wanted. I had not spent a year of my life in the Circus Kids act for nothing. Although I hadn't swung on a trapeze or dangled from a rope in a dozen years, I was still quite limber, and I had always had a good sense of balance, so it seemed the most natural thing in the world to step out of my baggy skirt, kick off my shoes, and scramble up that tree as if it were a stage prop. Climbing from branch to branch, I soon reached the one closest to an open second-story window.

The branch was as high as the roof, but it was slender. I tested it by inching out toward the tip until I could see how far down it would bend with my weight. Hanging from both hands put me at eye level to the windowsill—lower than I would have preferred, but from there it was a simple maneuver to jackknife my legs to the sill and arch my back until I slid inside.

The branch swooshed back as I let go.

I found myself in a sparsely furnished back bedroom. There was no time to waste. Douglas had told me what to look for.

There were four bedrooms, all with beds neatly made, of course, since Bruno Heilmann had been killed last night before he'd had time to tuck in, alone or with companions. I didn't have many details about his death, but I gathered from what Douglas said that the valet had arrived for work this morning to find Heilmann on the living room floor, dead from a single bullet wound in the back of the head. The horrified valet had the sense to call Adolph Zukor, Heilmann's boss at Paramount, rather than the police. Zukor hadn't attended the party but he knew Douglas Fairbanks and Mary Pickford had been there, so he called Douglas to ask what the hell had happened, who could have done such a thing, and did he think it could be covered up somehow or passed off as a heart attack? Zukor was terrified of bad publicity. All three of the sensational Hollywood scandals in the past few years had involved Paramount actors. There was a limit to the public's loyalty, and Zukor figured he'd finally reached it with Heilmann's murder.

"I convinced him there was no way to cover up the death of an important director like Heilmann," Douglas had said to me, "and that the police chief, while generally under Zukor's thumb, was unlikely to turn a blind eye to murder and pretend it was a heart attack. Zukor was thinking to stall, to keep it out of the papers at least until the killer could be apprehended and the whole mess could come out at once rather than dribble out day by day. He finally called the police."

It wouldn't be long before the police connected the two murders and wondered, as I already had, whether Esther Frankel's death was related to the director's party. Two people who had been at the same party and were killed at roughly the same time could not be a coincidence.

"Working there at the house until after the last person had left, she would have been present to see or hear something," said Douglas. "Perhaps she came away knowing something about who was there at the very end. Perhaps she witnessed something that would have allowed her to identify the killer."

And had been eliminated before that could happen? It seemed logical.

I crept on bare feet into the largest bedroom, the one that overlooked the fountain. This was a man's room, decorated with the same Prussian angularity as the downstairs with a bare minimum of personal touches: a photograph of an older couple I took to be Heilmann's parents, a picture postcard of a cathedral stuck in a mirror frame, and a book in German and half a chocolate bar on the nightstand. Shoes were lined up in soldierly precision on the closet floor; even his clothes hung at attention.

There was not a speck of dust or an item out of place in the entire room.

I could not see the cop on the porch below, but I could smell him. The air was still and I heard a match strike and a loud exhale, and the smoke from his cigarette wafted up. He was maybe ten feet below me on the other side of the open window and I heard every cough, every creak of the chair, as clearly as if we were sitting side by side on a porch swing.

"What Zukor doesn't know," Douglas had informed me, "is that wretched little Lottie has been sleeping with that arrogant Kraut. Lottie's husband, Allan, doesn't know, either, naturally. Hell, I didn't know until she blurted it out today. In any case, her monogrammed negligee and some other personal things are still in Heilmann's house, waiting for the detectives to discover them and bring the scandal right to our front doorstep."

And he wanted me to try to get them out of the house before the detectives arrived to search the place.

How could I refuse? Douglas Fairbanks had been nothing but kind to me, and Mary Pickford was my idol. They needed help. I had said yes. And now I was inside the director's house, searching through bedrooms.

If Lottie hadn't been so crazy for having her initials etched, painted, embroidered, or stamped on everything she owned, it might not have mattered that her personal belongings were spread about Bruno Heilmann's bedroom. I came across her pink lace negligee, monogrammed *LPF*, hanging on the bathroom door next to the largest bedroom. I eased open the bureau drawers and found some silk underwear with dainty *LP*s stitched on the edges. On the dressing table were her sterling silver brush and comb set with large *P*s engraved on the backs. A quick check of the bathroom revealed some jars of makeup, all thankfully unmarked, and a sterling-handled toothbrush, engraved. I snatched the toothbrush and left the rest.

A quick tour of the other bedrooms, just in case Lottie had

left something identifiable in them, turned up nothing of hers, but I did make one unexpected discovery. The guest bedroom in the front of the house had been set up last night as a dope bar. Several beautifully carved Chinese opium pipes lay on the table. The large drawers of a clothes bureau were full of folded paper packets containing heroin and cocaine and many boxes of what I was certain were more drugs. I'd seen it all before but never so much in one place. It was more than one person could possibly carry. No wonder so many guests were going upstairs last night. Obviously the policemen had reported the body and left the search of the house for the detectives—if they had found this stash, they would surely have confiscated it for themselves.

As I was stuffing Lottie's clothing beneath my washer-woman's blouse in preparation for my departure, I heard the sound of chair legs scraping on tile. The guard was getting up.

Unhurried footsteps traveled across the porch, the doorknob turned, the front door creaked open and closed tight, and he entered the hall downstairs. I could hear him so clearly it was as if I were standing beside him. If he'd walked around the outside of the house, he'd have seen nothing, since I'd made certain my skirt and shoes were well hidden under a bush. But I hadn't counted on him coming inside. Had I made a noise?

Instinctively I looked for a place to hide. I couldn't imagine he was going to search the place, maybe just take a peek in each room to see how the rich director lived, but I couldn't duck into a closet on the off chance he'd open it to nose around. Under the bed would be safer, and I judged I could fit.

The silence told me he was walking over the living room carpet. The creak of the swinging door said he was going into the kitchen, not toward the stairs, and I let out my breath. Maybe he wanted to raid the icebox or get himself a drink. I heard some faint rattles and clinks, then running water, then the swinging door again. An interminable silence followed when all I could hear was my blood pounding in my ears as if my heart had moved up to the middle of my head. *Don't come upstairs*, I willed with all my might.

The sharp sound of liquid streaming into liquid brought a thin smile to my face in spite of the danger, and I thanked my lucky stars there was a water closet on the ground floor. The toilet flushed and the front door opened and closed again. I didn't breathe easily until I heard him settle into his chair and scratch another match on the sole of his shoe.

I took one last glance out the front window and did a double take. Coming through the gate, walking briskly toward the fountain in my direction, were two men in dark suits and fedoras. Two detectives. *Cheesit, the cops!*

Crossing back to the rear of the house, I peered out to make sure no one was on the service road. The semicircular layout of the houses meant that the adjacent ones were not visible from the patio, so there was no worry that a neighbor would glance out a window and see me crouched there on the sill, gripping the edge with my toes. With all my strength, I sprang up toward the branch that had brought me here, rode the bounce until it settled, then worked my way hand over hand to the nearest sturdy limb and climbed down. Retrieving my skirt and shoes, I made my way along the service road past the other houses, limping in a tired manner toward the main street.

8

yrna pounded on the bathroom door. "Jessie! Jessie!" I
was standing in front of the mirror in my underclothes,
slathering cold cream on my face to remove the brown
makeup. The shapeless peasant costume was bunched around
my ankles. Lottie's belongings were on my bed. "Jessie! A very, very
awful thing! Bruno Heilmann's dead! The police are here! They
want to ask us questions about the party guests! Come quick!"

I felt guilty that I'd left Myrna in the dark about the murders
but reasoned that it was probably better for an ingénue like her
to face the police without knowing any more than she did. There's
no substitute for honest surprise. And frankly, there hadn't been
time to tell her. I had stepped out of the police car to Douglas's
telephone call and gone from there to my costume trunk and
makeup kit for the disguise. After returning from Heilmann's
and sneaking back into my house, I needed only a few more

minutes to resurrect wide-eyed, earnest Jessie Beckett who would be more than happy to answer any questions the policemen cared to ask. I whipped off the bandana and rinsed the black dye out of the lock of auburn hair I had let escape.

"I'll be right there!"

There wasn't time to report back to Douglas Fairbanks. I would have to wait until the police had gone.

I put on a blue dropwaist dress with a pleated skirt and a pair of smart shoes, composed my face, and joined Myrna who was standing in the center hall with two cops—did they always work in pairs?—wringing her hands and looking up at the ceiling as if the names of the party guests were written on the plaster.

". . . um, Raoul Walsh . . . and Gary Cooper. Let's see . . . Catherine Hays was there. Laura Frances, Robert Alexander, Lottie Pickford—oh, but of course Mr. Fairbanks has already given you that name. Have I already said Sara Rutherford? Oh, Jessie, thank heavens you're here to help me remember!" The policemen turned to me as I came down the stairs. "Officer Giles and Officer . . . I'm sorry, oh, Blackford, yes, they are working up a list of every single person who was there last night, and I can't remember very many. One of the guests killed Bruno Heilmann and they're trying to figure out who was the last to leave."

"I'll do my best," I said, squeezing Myrna's hand for reassurance.

"Where did you run off to after Mr. Fairbanks called?" she asked me.

I was hoping she wouldn't pose that question in front of the policemen, but Myrna was the sort who had nothing to hide and so was incapable of thinking anyone else did, either.

"He wanted me to meet him to go over the party list. He's eager to help in any way he can to solve this monstrous crime," I said piously. Then it was my turn to tell the police who had attended the party, and I was able to add several that Myrna had overlooked. Douglas Fairbanks had given them my name and Myrna's, and as soon as they received the go-ahead from on high, they would follow up with each person on the list, asking them to recall who else was there. Eventually they would re-create the entire guest list.

"And what time did you girls leave?" asked Officer Blackford, who seemed to be doing all the talking.

Myrna spoke up. "That's easy. It was twelve-fifteen because we had to catch the last Red Car at twelve-thirty."

"Who was there when you left?"

"Gosh, everybody, just about. We left pretty early."

"The Fairbanks left before we did," I added, "but Myrna is right. There were maybe two hundred people there at midnight and the party was going full swing. If you don't mind me asking, were you the officers who were called to Heilmann's home this morning?"

Both Blackford and Giles nodded. So these were the men who had checked the body and called the detectives but had not gone upstairs. They'd be sorry if they'd known what they missed. Blackford continued. "This isn't for public consumption yet. Captain said we could question you since Mr. Fairbanks had already told you, but they want to keep this death quiet for a while. They think it will help flush out the killer if fewer people know." He lifted his shoulders as if to ask, *Who knows where they got that dumb idea?*

The number of people who knew about the murder was growing larger by the hour. Officers Giles and Blackford knew. So did the police doctor who had come to examine the body—was he the same one who had been at Esther's? The guard out front knew. So did the valet who found the body. The two detectives who were probably still at Heilmann's house knew. And Zukor, of course, and Douglas Fairbanks, and Mary and Lottie Pickford. And now Myrna. And me. A secret with that many people in on it wasn't much of a secret.

When they finished their questions, Blackford said, "We need to call headquarters and the nearest call box is a couple blocks away. You got a telephone?" Myrna pointed him to the back of the hall and both men went to report in. We slipped into the kitchen.

"Isn't it awful?" said Myrna softly, now that we were alone. "A famous man like Bruno Heilmann murdered! Who could have done such a thing? I guess they'll figure it out pretty quick. As soon as they find out who left last, they'll know who did it."

"Not necessarily. Someone could have waited outside in the bushes until the last person had left and gone back inside to shoot him. Or one of the servants or cooks could have done it. Whoever it was knew how to shoot straight. He was killed with one bullet in the back of the head."

"I told you so."

I looked at her blankly.

"The bird hitting the window."

"Oh, Myrna, that's just coincidence."

"It's not. It happened before." I sat motionless as she struggled to decide whether or not to tell me about it. Finally she took a deep, fortifying breath and plunged into her story. "It was in 1918 when the Spanish flu came. I was thirteen. Mother and David caught it first. You couldn't get nurses. I mean, there weren't enough. One would show up and then disappear into the night. Father and I nursed them. When they were half recovered, it struck me. Father made up the couch for me in the dining room. He used to come and wrap me in frozen sheets every night, trying to get my temperature down. He sat there—I can remember him sitting right over me—and he went through the agony with me, afraid I was going to die."

She paused and shivered, although it wasn't cold. Without meeting my eye, she swallowed hard and continued. "Finally I passed the crisis, and Mother and David recovered. Then one night, I heard terrible noises from upstairs. He was hemorrhaging. He had the flu probably a long time before it showed itself, not knowing it because he'd been so busy taking care of everybody else. And particularly of me. Well, I became hysterical, and to get me out of the way, they sent me to one of my mother's friends. While I was wandering around the house, a bird hit a window. A minute later, the telephone rang and I knew what it meant. I took off up the stairs, running as far away as I could. They called me but I wouldn't answer. When I finally went downstairs, my mother's friend was crying. I knew my father was dead."

"I'm so sorry, Myrna," I said, giving her a hug.

She thanked me with a weak smile. "So you see, it's not an old wives' tale. It's true."

I thought of poor Esther. "Yes, maybe it is."

A noise from the hall drew my attention. The two policemen were standing in the doorway, both of them looking at me. I didn't know how long they'd been there.

"You'll be coming to the station with us, Miss Beckett."

I stood up. No need to ask why. It had always been just a matter of time before someone at the police station connected me to the other murder, Esther's murder.

I was the only person who had been at the scene of both crimes. It didn't look good.

9

S it there."

The police sergeant pointed at a wooden bench that looked as comfortable as a Baptist pew, and I sat with my hands clasped in my lap so no one would see my ink-stained fingertips, waiting to be questioned again about the two Hollywood murders.

Hollywood is not really its own town—it was at one time but nowadays it's part of Los Angeles, so the cops were Los Angeles cops and the police station was one of that city's network, Division Six on North Cahuenga next to the fire station. In my experience—and I have some experience—small-town cops are stupid and mean; city cops are every bit as mean but not nearly as stupid. So I sat still as a rock and tried not to look scared.

I knew what they were doing—letting me stew a while to lower my resistance—but knowing didn't make the clock tick

any faster. I tried to distract myself by watching the noisy sym-
phony that played in front of me. Clerks banged file drawers, secretaries clattered away in triplicate on Remingtons, telephone
bells jangled, sergeants barked orders, detectives argued, and the
swinging gate that divided the public from the police added an
unsteady percussion to the whole. Division Six was a crowded
place, even on a Sunday. Crime doesn't take a day off. One officer adjusted the western blinds to let in more of the bright daylight; another, standing on a desk to change a lightbulb, kicked
over a full coffee cup and cursed it. A drunk was processed at the
counter and hauled through the door marked JAIL; two sullen
prostitutes were fingerprinted, just as I had been earlier, and
taken in the same direction. It made me think of a vaudeville
stage with a dozen acts rehearsing at the same time and no stage
manager to impose order. Meanwhile, I waited in the wings for
my cue, my stomach churning as it always did when I was unsure
of my lines.

I had plenty of time to think.

Everyone in vaudeville steered clear of the police, and I was
no exception. Itinerant performers were often accused of crimes
they hadn't committed, and just as often the evidence consisted
of one sentence: "You ain't from around here." It was totally un-
fair, except when it wasn't. In my younger years, after my mother
died and left me orphaned on the circuit with a kiddie act, I
became a pretty good thief, thanks to the sleight-of-hand skills
I'd learned as a magician's assistant. My targets were mostly large
department stores and grocers, and I seldom got caught. On those
rare occasions, I'd act younger than my years and get off with a
scolding or a few slaps. Except when I ended up in jail for the
night. That experience, plus getting a steady job with a reputable act, made stealing less appealing, and I mostly gave it up. I
knew the police here had nothing on me from those years—
those cities were too far away and it had been some time ago.
And I was pretty sure they didn't know about the role I'd played

as a shill for a shady Indian mystic. But last fall, I'd been roped
into a scheme to impersonate a dead heiress—a bit of acting
that got tangled up in murder and came out a lot worse than
I'd expected—and while the family dropped all charges against
me, it had been a front-page story in several states. I'd changed
my name before moving to Hollywood, but I couldn't be certain
that someone, somewhere, wouldn't put the pieces together and
decide that a girl who'd been involved in murders in Oregon
might well be involved in murders in California.

I had already told the police everything I knew about Esther's
and Heilmann's murders. Of course, they didn't know about the
items I'd taken from the two crime scenes, but those had nothing
to do with finding the killer. And yes, I thought there was one
killer.

I had never figured Esther's death as random. It was too much
of a coincidence, and coincidence always makes me suspicious.
For one thing, there was no apparent motive—no robbery, no
rape, no vandalism, nothing taken or disturbed. The break-ins
that had occurred in her block, as reported by the neighbors,
bore no resemblance to the break-in at Esther's. In those, no
one had been home or harmed, and robbery had been the
motive. No, the person who killed Esther was out to kill Esther.
The question was, why?

Bruno Heilmann's murder had answered that, for me anyway.
Someone shot him. Esther must have seen the killer, not actually
doing the deed—if that had been the case, she'd have rushed
outside and called for help or telephoned the cops or been murdered herself on the spot. Supposing the caterers had remained
in the kitchen while she gathered up the dishes—a likely conclusion since they had stayed in the kitchen throughout the party—
then she'd have been in place to see the killer, perhaps to speak
to him while she picked up the last of the dirty glasses or wiped the
water rings off the lacquered tabletops. She would have noticed
who was last to leave the party and would have identified him

the moment she heard about the murder. The killer couldn't let that happen, so he shot Bruno Heilmann then somehow tracked Esther to her apartment. What begged for an explanation was how he'd found her, and why he'd used a gun the first time and a statue the second.

A curly-haired officer came through the main door. Carl Delaney. He caught sight of me, and his eyebrows arched with surprise. I thought he would come over and ask what I was doing here, but he pretended he hadn't seen me and banged through the gate without a word. Well, who could blame him? At least my dinner-invitation problem was solved. He'd keep his distance now that I was a genuine suspect.

He didn't, though. A few minutes later he was standing beside my bench, a neutral, watchful expression on his face.

"They think you had something to do with both murders," he said carefully, dispensing with the polite preliminaries. I nodded glumly. "Did you?"

"Nope. It's just a coincidence that I was at the scene of both. I left the party long before Bruno Heilmann was killed, and arrived at Esther's long after her death. The only crime I committed involved champagne."

"Don't mention that. They'll use it to charge you."

I nodded. My stomach gave a fierce growl to remind me I hadn't eaten since breakfast and it was going on toward dinnertime.

"Some detectives want to talk to you," he continued.

"When?"

"When they're ready."

That could be next week, but there wasn't much either of us could do about that. Someone at the far end of the room shouted for Delaney. "I'll be right back," he said.

He threaded his way through the forest of oak desks until he reached the man in the corner. Their conversation was punctuated with many gestures. I assumed they were talking about me, but I could have been wrong. It was sixteen minutes before he came back. I know; I watched every tick go by.

"Here," he said, dropping two Clark bars into my lap. "They used to give us these during the war. They're pretty good."

I was taken aback by the unexpected kindness. "Thanks," I said, putting one in my purse and biting into the other. "I mean it, thanks a lot." He reddened, so I changed the subject. "You were in France, huh?"

"Yeah. With the 28th Infantry Regiment of the First Division, the 'Fighting First.' We saw a lot of action—Cantigny, Soissons, the Argonne Forest. It was pretty bad. I hope we never see another war like that one. Anyhow, chocolate bars were one of the good things that happened to us." He gave me half a smile, and I thought that he'd have been an attractive man if he'd been wearing something other than that intimidating blue uniform.

"What are some of the others?"

"A two-day pass to Paris." A wistful note crept into his voice and he gazed out the nearest window as if hoping to see the fabled City of Light. "Me and some of the boys went up to the top of the Eiffel Tower and could see the whole city. It felt so good I didn't ever want to come down. And I remember once when—"

Two men in suits interrupted the travelogue. "Miss Beckett? Come with us."

Carl Delaney ducked away as I rose from the bench. We made our way through the door marked JAIL, one man leading me and the other following, as if they thought to prevent the prisoner's mad dash for freedom. We filed into an airless room that contained one bare table and two wooden chairs and was nasty with the smell of sweat and coffee. One of the plainclothesmen pointed his thumb at one chair and sat himself down across from me. The other leaned against the wall and glared as if he were mad I had interrupted his dinner. They wore no badges and did not volunteer their names.

They shot rapid-fire questions at me, alternating between

them so there was no pause for me to rest or reflect. I was certain they already knew the answers, but they argued with me on nearly all of them as if everything I said was a lie. I made sure to throw in that I worked for Douglas Fairbanks. The name didn't flicker an eyelid.

After what seemed like hours of questions about Esther, they turned to Bruno Heilmann and worked their way through the time I had spent at the party, accusing me of sleeping with Heilmann and every other man at the party, demanding to know who I'd spoken to, what I'd seen, whether I'd been upstairs, and when I had arrived and departed. I soon learned not to pause to think, or one of them would snarl, "Just answer the question, sister, don't think up lies." When we reached the end of the questions, they started over. Same questions. And then a third time. I figured they were trying to fluster me into giving different answers that they could twist into some semblance of guilt, but someone accustomed to repeating the same act on stage three, four, or five times a day is not going to get rattled by repetition. I got slapped several times by the standing detective—not much harder than a stage slap—and finally he said, "Okay, sister, we'll see how smart-alecky you are after a night in jail."

They led me out of the miserable little room and there, at the door that led to the cells, stood Carl Delaney. It felt wonderful to see a friendly face, even if it was a cop. "I'll take her in," he said. They handed me over with no comment and left.

We stood in the hall for a few minutes, saying nothing, waiting for I didn't know what, until Carl opened the door to the main room and looked about. "They're gone. Come on. Can't let you go home, but you don't have to spend the night in the pokey. Sit here." He pointed to a beat-up leather chair in the corner by the main door.

"Who are those guys?" I asked him.

"Tuttle and Rios. Detectives assigned to the Heilmann case."

Tuttle and Rios. I stored the names in my head, then dropped onto the chair like a marionette whose strings had been snipped. Carl brought me a cup of water that I drained so fast, he said, "Slow down, Miss Beckett. There's a whole reservoir full waiting for you."

He had just gone to refill the cup when the main door burst open and Don Q, Son of Zorro, strode into police headquarters. He was not in costume and he did not crack his rawhide bull-whip or brandish his rapier, but Douglas Fairbanks looked every inch the proud Spanish don on a rescue mission. I could almost hear the stirring music accompanying his entrance. He saw me at once and rushed to my side.

"Jessie! Thank God you're all right!" He turned to two officers standing openmouthed behind the counter and commanded, "Get me Captain Marchetti at once!"

The entire room went silent. Secretaries stopped, their hands raised mid-stroke above typewriter keys. Clerks paused in the middle of their file drawers. Officers set down their telephones. All eyes were on Douglas Fairbanks. For him, it was no different than any other day.

He turned to me and spoke, projecting his voice to the far corners of the room. "I only just learned you were here. I called your house and Myrna said you had been arrested. I came directly here. Don't worry; I'll take all the blame."

I saw the danger immediately.

"Mr. Fairbanks," I interrupted. "Wait a minute, this isn't about—"

"Where's Captain Marchetti?" he snapped when he noticed neither officer had moved. Douglas Fairbanks was accustomed to people scurrying to obey his orders.

"Off duty, sir," stammered one of the men. "Sergeant Yates is in charge—"

"Then get Marchetti at his home."

I made another bid for his attention, standing up and pulling on his sleeve. "Mr. Fairbanks!"

He shook me off. "Don't worry, I'll handle this." Then in a stage voice, he boomed to the room at large, "I demand this girl be released at once, do you hear me? I can explain everything."

"Douglas!"

He plowed on without another glance in my direction. "I'm the one who told her what to do. She isn't responsible for—"

"Duber!"

That stopped him cold. At last he turned to look at me, his face registering surprise and confusion at hearing his pet name from the lips of someone other than his beloved Mary.

"I beg your pardon, Mr. Fairbanks, sir. I meant no offense but I had to get your attention." I dropped my voice but privacy was impossible. I chose my words carefully. "I'm here to answer questions about the two murders. *That's all.* As soon as I'm released, I'll fill you in on that errand I was doing for you. You needn't worry about me. I've done nothing wrong."

"Oh." He seemed to shrink a couple inches. "I thought . . ."

I was absurdly touched. He thought I'd been arrested for breaking into Heilmann's house and stealing Lottie's things. His sense of honor did not permit underlings to take the blame for him, and he had come to set me free with a confession that could well ruin the Pickford-Fairbanks empire.

I became aware of Carl Delaney standing at the edge of our little drama, holding a cup of water, taking it all in with bright eyes.

Douglas regained his composure. "That means nothing," he blustered theatrically. "I demand this girl's immediate release. Get Captain Marchetti in here and we'll settle this between us, man to man. I'm not leaving unless she comes with me."

An officer picked up the telephone to call his boss.

"Do you know the captain?" I asked hopefully.

"I should say I do. I play tennis with him on Wednesdays."

Ten minutes later, Douglas and I left police headquarters in the backseat of his Rolls-Royce Silver Ghost, the most gorgeous car I'd ever seen in my whole life. The chauffeur saluted like we were generals, closed the door behind us, climbed in front, and eased away from the station in the direction of Beverly Hills. I heaved a sigh of relief. Douglas had promised Captain Marchetti I would be available again if anyone had more questions, but I doubted that would be necessary now that the Fairbanks spotlight was shining warmly on me. I persuaded Douglas that I would be fine at my own house, and the driver turned left at the next corner.

"You can pick up your belongings when you drop me off," I hinted carefully, uncertain of the driver.

He pulled on his thin moustache. "Good idea. So everything went smoothly? I imagined the worst when I heard you'd been arrested."

"It was a breeze."

He waited in the Silver Ghost as I ran into the house to gather up Lottie's belongings. I wrapped them hastily in old newspaper before handing them through the car window.

Douglas's dark eyes looked straight into mine. "Thank you for this, Jessie. You'll have to tell me the details tomorrow morning. See you on the set."

It's not every girl who gets rescued from prison by the dashing Son of Zorro.

10

J essie? There you are, run get some aspirin from my office for Lottie."

"Oh, Jessie, find DuCrow's bandana. He says he left it in his dressing room."

"Quick, Jessie, get another camellia for Miss Astor—this one's wilted. And we aren't using the dog in this scene after all—get rid of him."

It was Monday morning, business as usual for the *Son of Zorro* assistant script girl. No camellias left in Costume and a rose wouldn't do—the fair Dolores had worn a camellia in her hair yesterday and we could no more change flowers mid-scene than we could actresses—so I grabbed the dog's leash, deposited him with his handler, hopped into one of the studio's Ford flivvers, dashed to the florist, and picked up two camellias just in case Frank demanded multiple takes into tomorrow. That was a critical part of a script girl's job, maintaining continuity of clothing, props, and makeup from scene to scene.

As long as I was out, I stopped at a drugstore for a newspaper to see if Heilmann's death was mentioned—it was not, but Esther's was, page two, brief, upper right-hand corner—and I had just pulled onto the road when a small truck passed me, going in the opposite direction. Painted on its side were the words CISNEROS BROTHERS CATERING.

"That's it!" I cried aloud to no one.

Those two charmers at the police station had grilled me mercilessly about Esther's employer, certain that I was withholding their identity, but I honestly couldn't remember the name that had been stenciled on the caterers' aprons. And none of the other guests had been crass enough to enter the kitchen during the party, so I was the only person still alive who had come into contact with the Cisneros brothers.

A sharp U-turn put me a block behind their truck. I chased it half a dozen blocks until it turned onto a side street and pulled up alongside a one-story stucco building with a couple of spindly palms out front. A sign over the door proclaimed CISNE-ROS BROTHERS KITCHENS.

I halted abruptly, my hand on the doorknob. There were three possibilities for the killer: he could have been a guest, a random person off the street, or a caterer. If these caterers had been the last to see Esther alive, mightn't one of them be her killer? And by extension, Heilmann's? It was possible, but it made no sense. Why would caterers kill their employer and then their employee? If they had, surely they'd have fled across the border rather than go meekly about their work the next day.

There was no way to answer these questions from the front step, so I told myself to be careful, took a deep breath, and went in.

Passing through an unoccupied office, I came to a large kitchen where two familiar-looking men were squeezing sugar icing onto a tiered cake as tall as they were. Absorbed in the detail of their work, neither noticed me watching from the doorway. From an adjacent room, a thin young woman I hadn't seen before wheeled in an empty cart and began loading trays of canapés, ready for tonight's affair. Every night was a party night in Hollywood.

Nothing looked suspicious.

"Excuse me," I said. The men looked up from their pink icing squiggles. "Could I interrupt a moment? I'm Jessie Beckett, Esther Frankel's friend from the Heilmann party Saturday night."

The younger of the two nodded and gave an eager smile, probably imagining he had a prospective customer. His manner reassured me—it was not the suspicious behavior of a guilty man. Wiping his hands on his apron as I approached his table, he said, "I am Raoul Cisneros. This is my brother, Miguel."

"I guess you haven't heard about Esther?"

Their blank looks answered that question. As gently as possible, I told them that she was dead, showing them the newspaper as proof. Esther had worked for them for several years, and they were clearly stunned by the news. The older man, Miguel, crossed himself and, kissing the crucifix around his neck, sank heavily onto a nearby stool. When I went on to tell them about Heilmann's murder, their eyes widened and their jaws dropped in disbelief.

"Do you mind if I ask you a few questions? What happened when you left the Heilmann house? Did Esther send for a cab?"

Miguel Cisneros pulled his bushy moustache. "No, we thought it was safer to take her home ourselves, and it saved money, too. It was after two o'clock. We were headed in her direction anyway."

"I think she was killed because she saw the man who killed Heilmann. Did she say anything when she got in the truck? Anything about seeing a last guest or a suspicious person?"

He ran his fingers through his hair, leaving the gray strands streaked with pink. He exchanged a few words in Spanish with his younger brother, as if to check his memory before saying something to a stranger he might later regret. "No, Miss Beckett. Nothing of importance. She was tired. We all were tired. Her back ached. She looked forward to Sunday off and would be ready to work tonight." He shook his head, dazed at the realization that she was gone.

Raoul spoke up. "She said the last guest had left. I remember her saying that."

"Whether he was the last guest to leave or the second-to-last," I said, "someone stepped back into the house and shot Bruno Heilmann when he was alone, and that person was afraid Esther could identify him. Otherwise he would not have needed to follow her and kill her, too. Did you hear anything that sounded like a gunshot as you were cleaning up? A backfire? Fireworks?"

"No. But packing up the truck is noisy work. And the motor was running. Maybe we missed it."

A gunshot on a quiet night would be hard to miss. I wondered whether the police had found any of Heilmann's neighbors who had heard anything. An idea was forming in my head.

"You say she saw the killer?" asked Raoul.

"I think so. I think the killer waited until all the guests were gone, and came back to shoot Bruno Heilmann, and he thought the caterers were gone or outside packing up. He didn't expect to run across Esther. She probably smiled at him and finished wiping the tables, and joined you in the truck." The two men nodded soberly. "He must have followed you to her house. How else would he know where she lived?"

"I was driving," Raoul said. "It was late and the streets were empty. I remember another car behind our truck, because I was surprised when it turned into Esther's small street with us. But when I pulled over to the curb, it passed us, so I didn't think anything more about it. Do you think that was the killer?"

"I think it's very likely. You didn't see anyone outside at her apartment building?"

"No one."

I know enough Spanish to recognize a few words but not enough to catch the sense of what the men were saying to each other. I could understand gestures, though, and their rapid-fire exchange and hushed tones added to a sense of mounting alarm. I thought I knew the reason for their fear.

"The police . . . they have no idea who did this?" asked Miguel.

"Not yet," I said. "They'll probably be along soon, to question you."

"You told them—"

"No, I only remembered your name a few moments ago when I saw the truck, and I followed it here, but they asked me about you yesterday at the police station. I imagine they will be contacting every caterer in Los Angeles until they find the one who worked the Heilmann party."

"We would be suspects?"

I had to admit they would.

"Or the murderer, he could think we saw something, too. He killed Esther. He could think that we saw him or that Esther told us something about him."

More Spanish. I didn't have to understand the words to figure out they were considering leaving town. Frankly, I thought it was a good idea.

"Thank you for coming, miss," said Miguel Cisneros, taking off his apron and showing me the door.

"Check the newspapers until you read they caught the killer," I suggested. "Then you'll know when it's safe to come home."

His eyes widened with surprise. "You speak Spanish?"

"I speak common sense."

When I got back to Pickford-Fairbanks with the camellias, my boss said Douglas Fairbanks wanted to see me in his dressing room, pronto. I scurried across the lot and rapped on his door.

"Come!"

Dressed in black, the Son of Zorro was pacing the small room like a caged panther. The air was thick with cigarette smoke and heavy with tension. I sat on the edge of the extra chair as bidden.

"Lorna McCall's dead."

"Oh, my God, she is? Um . . . who's Lorna McCall?"

"A very pretty, very talented actress. One of the WAMPAS Baby Stars of 1923." I knew what he was referring to: Myrna aspired to this annual list of up-and-coming young actresses believed to be on the threshold of success. As the supposed next generation of film stars, Baby Stars were lavished with parties and attention—and parts.

"I take it she was at Heilmann's party, too?"

"Yes." He ground out the cigarette and lit another. "Her maid found her this morning, drowned. Her head in the toilet."

I winced. "Is she with Paramount?" Or, *was* she?

He gave an affirmative grunt. "Zukor and the police are calling it an accidental drowning for the time being. Of course, they're still holding off on Heilmann's death announcement. Neighbors who saw the ambulance think he was taken to the hospital Sunday morning instead of to the morgue. And meanwhile, the police have started questioning a few party guests, asking who left when, so rumors are flying. It's no use; I don't know why Zukor's so determined to delay the news. He has convinced the police to hold off until Heilmann's relatives can be notified. That's a laugh! The man doesn't have any relatives except for a couple ex-wives. Zukor's fooling himself if he thinks it will be less damaging to have an announcement of an arrest appear at the same time. This isn't the Hungarian Empire, where you can order newspapers around."

"Maybe Lorna was the last to leave the party, except for the killer, and she could have identified him when the police reached her. Like Esther. So he had to silence her too. Or maybe Lorna *was* the killer and she committed suicide in remorse." I thought of the guest list that the police were compiling, with approximate departure times on it so they could figure out who left early and who stayed till the end. Those at the end of the list might have seen something they didn't realize was significant; they could be in danger without knowing it.

"What if the killer isn't finished?" said Douglas. "What if there are others who noticed something or figured something out?"

I was already there. "If they saw or suspected anything, they'd go to the police, but not if they don't know Bruno Heilmann was murdered."

A bell signaled the end of break. For once, Douglas ignored it.

"I'm calling Zukor right now and telling him this has got to get in tomorrow's papers, come what may. All of the party guests could be in danger and not realize it. I've got to protect Mary."

"You and Miss Pickford left so early, neither of you could have seen anything significant. I'm sure she's in no danger. So did Jack and Marilyn. But Lottie was still there when I left around midnight." I thought again of that guest list and how useful it could be. I thought of my erstwhile suitor, Carl Delaney, and said, "I think I know someone who'll show me that guest list. And I sure would like to know more about Lorna McCall's death."

"Have at it. I'll tell Frank Richardson you'll be doing some more work for me. Someone else can hold his megaphone today. Maybe you'll learn something—anything—that will help end this nightmare."

"I'll try. Tell me this: who would want to kill Bruno Heilmann?"

"Who wouldn't? The man bullied staff, insulted actors, and demanded sex from every actress he worked with. And I've always suspected he was the one who supplied the dope that killed Wallace Reid a couple years ago. Zukor put up with him because he was a brilliant director. The best in the business. But I'd guess half the people at the party would have cheerfully shot him if they thought they could get away with it."

I had to ask. "Including Lottie?"

He gave me a sharp stare. "Lottie was home with us."

"I hate to say it, but she was awfully upset that night, and I wasn't the only one who heard her threaten to kill him."

"Just talk. Just an expression. We all use it without meaning it."

12

arl Delaney was sitting in a back booth facing the front door and stirring his coffee when I walked into Lucky's, a rundown diner catty-corner to the Cahuenga police station. Spotting him before he could signal, I made my way past the counter and slid into the opposite bench. On the radio, a pianist was tearing through "Dizzy Fingers." I ordered coffee. It wasn't yet lunchtime, and the place was empty except for a few cops at the counter.

"You said you wanted to swap," he prompted me in a cold voice. There was no one near, but we kept the volume down.

The stony stare from his once-warm brown eyes warned me off the approach I'd taken. My proposal to swap information had offended him. Carl Delaney had been helpful to me yesterday at the police station—at some risk to himself—and I was repaying him by trying to dicker. I couldn't afford to lose his support, even if it meant showing all my cards without getting anything in return.

"Only in a manner of speaking." I beamed, purposely misinterpreting his frown. "I have some information I know you'll like, and I was hoping you'd be able to share some things with me, but here's my news: I remembered the name of the caterers who worked the Heilmann party. It was the Cisneros Brothers."

He visibly relaxed. "Oh, yeah? Cisneros Brothers. Swell. That'll save lots of footwork. We'd have found them sooner or later but sooner's better. You just wake up and remember?"

"I was out early this morning buying flowers for the studio and a Cisneros truck happened to drive by. It sparked my gray cells. And, um, I may as well confess, I followed the truck to their kitchen and talked to the two brothers."

"And?" he asked warily.

I squirmed a little. "I'm thinking they won't be there when you arrive. I don't speak Spanish, mind you, but I had the impression that . . . well, between the police taking them for suspects and the murderer taking them for witnesses, they decided they'd be better off out of town. The truth is, Esther said nothing to them on the ride home. They were shocked that she was dead. They don't know a thing. They didn't see anyone after the party. She was the one who cleaned up the living room and patio while they did the kitchen. I think the killer followed her home in the Cisneros truck after the party. The brother who was driving thought he might have been followed."

Carl played with his coffee before meeting my eye. "That's good to know."

"They didn't hear any gunshots."

"There was only one shot, far as we know. We'll question the neighbors as soon as we get the go-ahead. Maybe they heard something. I'll tell you one thing, the killer was a good shot. He put a single bullet right in the back of Heilmann's head, and from a distance, according to the doctor. No powder burns. No stray bullets, either, not in the walls or anyplace."

"There isn't any reason to suspect he was killed during a robbery attempt, is there?"

Carl shook his head. "Not with seventy-eight dollars in his wallet, an ivory toothpick and a Waltham pocket watch in his trousers, and a two-carat diamond ring on his hand."

And a truckload of dope upstairs. "There was hooch at the party. And dope."

"Tell me something I don't know."

"Oh, so the detectives found the drugs when they searched the house?"

"A couple opium pipes, some traces of dope. Several cases of hooch, although after they finished passing it around the precinct, the evidence turned into empties."

So they hadn't noticed the huge stash in the bedroom? Inconceivable. Even a cursory search of the upstairs would have turned up that bedroom full of dope. There was only one explanation: the detectives themselves had stolen the stash and made no mention of it in their report. Can't say I was shocked. Crooked cops far outnumbered honest ones. Or had the killer taken the dope? It made a darn good motive.

I was right about one thing. The nothing-to-hide approach melted Carl's defenses. I continued candidly, "I was wondering if you've finished compiling that guest list."

"Just getting started. We got about a hundred names from you and your friend, the Pickfords, and a couple others Mr. Fairbanks mentioned, but we haven't been allowed to work the list yet. It's kinda awkward asking people when they left a party and not telling them why we want to know, but . . . officially, Heilmann's murder isn't public information. Someone thinks keeping quiet for a while will help catch the killer. Not sure why. Anyway, as soon as we get the go-ahead, Chief wants us to question every single person who was there, and that'll take a few days. We'll work the list backward, since the important names are the ones who left last—the ones who might have seen something— and we've got that much pretty firm. We'll start with them."

"Could I see the list?"

He gave it some thought. "I don't know why not. You provided some of those names yourself. There's a copy across the street. Order me another coffee when the gal comes by. I'll be right back."

A few minutes later he handed me a four-page typed list. It was a carbon, probably the bottom of seven with letters like fuzzy caterpillars, but still legible.

"Mind if I copy the last page?"

"Suit yourself. Maybe you'll think of some more to add."

I used his pencil and the back of a Lucky's menu, and finished in a few minutes. As I suspected, Lorna McCall fell toward the end of the list. So did Lottie Pickford, despite what Douglas had said about her being with them that night, and several others I knew. They had been among the last to leave. Among the last to see Bruno Heilmann alive. Among the ones who saw his killer? Had one of them killed him?

"Did you answer the call to Lorna McCall's apartment?" I asked, handing him back his pencil.

Carl shook his head. "Bates and Marconi did. They brought in the maid. The detectives are questioning her now." He saw me grimace and said, "They won't be hard on her. They don't suspect her of anything, like they did you. She's just some middle-aged foreigner who had the bad luck to walk into the girl's apartment first. She'll be released shortly."

That gave me an idea. A few pointed glances at the clock on the wall and hints that I needed to return to work eased Carl out of the booth and back to his beat. But instead of catching the next streetcar to the studio, I settled down on a bench in the full morning sun where I could see the front door of the police station, and I waited.

It was only a half hour or so before she came down the steps, a brown-haired woman dressed in the gray garb of a domestic. She came across the street and headed for the bus stop. I fell in behind her.

"Oh, they let you go, too?" I said to her as I caught up. Naturally, she looked puzzled, and I quickly gave her the impression that I had just come from the police station. "I saw you inside. They were questioning me, too. These murders are so horrible!"

After a few minutes of comparing stories—Carl was right; they treated her much better than they had treated me yesterday—I noticed aloud that it was nearly lunchtime and wondered if she was as hungry as I was. I said I'd be honored to treat her at Lucky's.

Her name was Magda Szabo. A solid woman and big-boned, she had the appearance of a sturdy Old World peasant that needed only a scarf tied under her chin to complete the image. She asked me where I worked. Turns out her husband was a cameraman for Vitagraph Studios. Their children were grown; she had been working as a domestic for young actresses for five years, ever since she and her family came to Hollywood from Hungary. Same country as Adolph Zukor, and no, they didn't know him. Hungary is a big place, it turns out. Her English was pretty good . . . better than my Hungarian anyway. By the time our meat loaf and potatoes arrived, we were old friends.

Food is a good antidote for shock, and Magda had been quite shocked to find her young employer dead in the bathroom that morning. She needed little encouragement to spill the beans.

"Only three months and one week I work there," she said, shaking her head in sorrow. "Such a pretty girl and so kind. Like angel she was to look at, but . . ." She made tsk-tsk sounds with her tongue and sighed. "Too much men, too much hooch, too much dope, too much party, but I am so sad for her to die like that, her head in the toilet."

"What do you think happened?"

"First I think it is accident—that too much hooch make her sick after ze party, so she go to throw up in ze toilet and pass out, fall front face into ze toilet and drown. Because when I come this morning, there is no broken lock, no looking like a fight, no broken things all over. Looks nice everywhere."

"So you found her body in the bathroom?"

"And I call ze police right away. Two police come fast. They bring me here to ask questions. Then I understand maybe it is not accident that she is dead. The police say she maybe kill herself"— and she made the sign of the cross at the thought—"or maybe someone kill her. Then I remember—oh, no! Two cups with coffee and two plates on ze coffee table were there! But I wash them first thing this morning and clean kitchen. Then I go to clean bathroom, and then I see Miss McCall. Too late."

Magda's efficiency had robbed the police of their chance to find fingerprints that might have identified who had been visiting Lorna.

"Zey very angry at me but . . ." She shrugged her shoulders helplessly. "I just come in today and do my job. I never think Miss McCall is dead in ze bathroom. Ze doctor say she is dead ze day before."

"Since Sunday?"

"Sunday." She nodded. "Ze doctor say late afternoon."

With some relief, I realized I had been in police custody during those hours. Finally, a death they couldn't connect to me!

"But suicide?" Magda continued. "No. There are easy ways to do suicide. Miss McCall have bottles of pills in ze bathroom, rat poison in ze cupboard, gas in ze oven. If a girl want to do suicide, she never choose suicide in ze toilet."

That made sense to me. "Were the coffee cups empty when you picked them up?" I asked.

Magda frowned. "One was empty. One was half full."

"Was there any lipstick on either cup?"

"On one cup, yes."

"Which one? The empty one or the half-full one?"

"Half-full."

"And the plates?"

"One big plate with breakfast cake. I put it away. Two small plates with crumbs."

There had been someone at Lorna's apartment Sunday afternoon, someone she trusted enough to let in, someone she knew well enough to serve food and drink. It could have been a friend who had left after eating and didn't know Lorna would accidentally pass out in the toilet. Then again, it could have been the same person who killed Bruno Heilmann and who realized Lorna, like Esther, knew too much to leave alive. If that were the case, though, he was disturbingly versatile, with a different manner of killing each time.

Eliminating suicide left two possibilities: accidental death and murder. I staged both in my head.

A friend—man or woman—drops in and finds Lorna suffering the effects of the previous night's excesses. She is staggering about, confused and ill. The friend makes coffee, cuts some cake, urges Lorna to drink up and eat something, and advises her to go to bed. If the friend is a man, he empties his coffee cup, the one without lipstick, and Lorna sips a little from the other cup. If it is a woman, she drinks some from the lipstick cup and Lorna, who has not yet put on her face, empties the other one. The friend leaves. Lorna feels sick, goes to the toilet to vomit, passes out, and falls forward to her death. For this story to be true, the honest, innocent friend would step forward as soon as he or she heard about Lorna's death and tell the police, "I was there moments before the accident, and Lorna was in a bad way," or something like that. Lorna's death was not yet widely known, but we would soon see if anyone stepped forward.

In the alternate version of my imaginary scenario, a person drops by and finds Lorna still woozy from the party. The person makes coffee and cuts some cake, or maybe Lorna is able to do it. The person is not a stranger to Lorna. The lipstick on only one cup could mean that the guest was male and Lorna had, indeed, put on her makeup that morning. If it is the man who killed Heilmann, he wants to find out how much Lorna saw or knows, and he will kill her if need be. Or he has come purposely to strangle her or hit her on the head with something heavy—surely he wouldn't risk the noise of a gunshot on a Sunday in a busy apartment building. Too ill to be suspicious, Lorna goes into the bathroom. The person follows and seizes the unexpected opportunity to make her death look like an accident. If it is not the man who shot Heilmann, who else would want to kill Lorna? I'd have to ask around to see if Lorna had any serious enemies.

When I got back to Pickford-Fairbanks after lunch, I didn't see Douglas Fairbanks—they were filming the scenes in Don Fabrique's headquarters that didn't include him, and he was somewhere rehearsing whip tricks with that Australian fella, Snowy Baker—so I slipped back into my role as assistant script girl, helping make the set exactly the same as it had been the last time we had worked on this sequence. Douglas reappeared in mid-afternoon and called me aside.

"What have you learned?"

Briefly, I told him.

"Well, I've learned a few things myself. For one, the news will be in tomorrow's papers. By the way, do you have plans for this evening?"

"Plans? No."

"Good. Then you must come to dinner with us. Very informal. There will be a few others there. Mary enjoyed meeting you Saturday night and told me to invite you."

"I'd be delighted." Giddy was more like it, although I knew very well the reason I was included. They wanted to talk about the murders. By tomorrow, all of Los Angeles would be talking about the murders and those immoral "movies" whose dissolute lives would have embarrassed the sober citizens of Sodom and Gomorrah. Now, for a while longer, I was one of the few who knew the score.

"Good. Come at— Oh, you don't have an automobile, of course. I'll send my driver to get you at six."

13

F rank Richardson kept us running long beyond the finish of
the scene with the barefoot dancer in the cantina, and I
barely had time to take a quick bath and change into the
blue and gold frock I had decided to wear to Pickfair.

To Pickfair! The utter impossibility of someone like me actually being invited to this legendary Hollywood mansion gave my
preparations a dreamlike quality. I handled it as if I were preparing for the stage, choosing the appropriate makeup, costume, and
hairdo for my role as a young woman going to dine with royalty.
Since Douglas had assured me that the evening would be neither
formal nor late—they liked to be in bed by ten—I took care not
to overdress the part.

On the stroke of six, Melva, Helen, and Lillian gave a collec-
tive whoop as the Fairbanks Rolls-Royce pulled alongside the
curb. They hung shamelessly about the door, whistling as I

minced my way along in my very high heels and allowed myself to be handed into the backseat by the same solemn-faced driver who had driven me home from the police station yesterday.

We drove down Sunset Boulevard, a wide street split down the middle by a bridle path and lined on both sides with pepper trees. Turning right at the high school, we motored past the Moorish splendor of the Hollywood Hotel, continuing north on a route that afforded a glimpse of the great white HOLLYWOOD-LAND sign in the distant hills.

"A real eyesore, isn't it, miss?" said the driver, noticing the direction of my gaze. "Rich fella by the name of Chandler put up those letters a couple years back. You know who he is, don't you? The *Times* publisher? I went up to see those letters when they had the dedication and lit up the whole thing for the first time, you know. They say there's forty thousand lightbulbs in that sign, can you believe it? And those letters don't look too big from down here, but each one of 'em is fifty feet tall, no fooling. And what's it all for?"

I admitted I had no idea. The far-off letters were part of the Hollywood landscape I had accepted without question.

"Advertising. All that money to advertise his housing development there on the old Sherman and Clark Ranch. Well, there was a ruckus when he lit it up, I don't mind telling you. Spoils the scenery, I say, and so did a lot of others. Chandler promised to take it down as soon as all the lots had sold, so the fussing went away. And when that happens, I'll say 'Good riddance!'"

"Are the lots selling well?" From my vantage point, the scrubby hills looked pretty barren.

"Well, they laid down some roads and brought over some Eye-talian masons to build stone walls. I think the first houses are going up now. They'll cost a pretty penny, I'll say that."

We motored along North Highland, passing the Hollywood Bowl, and continued into the hills until the macadam turned to a dirt road that led up San Ysidro Canyon. Winter rains had turned last fall's drab landscape into a spring paradise with vast swaths of sand blossoms and desert gold. The rush of our tires frightened a few brown rabbits into showing us their white cottontails as they scampered away from the edge of the road. In the distance, several deer stopped grazing long enough to fix curious stares on our car before they returned to foraging.

"Well, miss, here we are, safe and sound. That house across the way is Mr. Charlie Chaplin's. It's new."

I didn't give Chaplin's mansion a second glance. Who would, when Pickfair loomed ahead? There, at the road's end sat Douglas Fairbanks's wedding present to Mary Pickford, remodeled and expanded the year they married. Not a soul in these forty-eight states could fail to recognize the Tudor mansion, not after pictures of the house and gardens and swimming pool and stables and pond had been featured in every magazine on the newsstand, indeed, at newsstands all over the world. Pickfair was Mr. and Mrs. Fairbanks's retreat from the pressures of Hollywood—no one but cactuses lived in remote Beverly Hills, so they could ride their horses, run along desert paths, take walks, and live like normal people, away from prying eyes.

A butler met me at the top of the stairs and escorted me through a pale lime living room with lemon floor-to-ceiling curtains. To my left was a fireplace the size of a small cave; to my right, a gleaming white grand piano. "This way," he said, indicating the open doors that led to the patio where, as I knew from publicity shots, you could see the Pacific Ocean on a clear day. Beyond the patio, lit by cheerful gaslights, lay the famous out-of-door swimming pool edged with white sand. The scene nearly took my breath away.

"Welcome, Jessie." Miss Pickford rose from her rattan chaise to greet me. I said hello to Stella DeLanti, who was playing the queen in our Zorro picture, and to Douglas's brother Robert, the film's general manager, both of whom I knew from the set, then I was introduced to Ernst Lubitsch. I had heard the name.

Miss Pickford had brought him, and his wife, Helene, to Hollywood from Germany a couple years ago to be one of her directors, and he was well-known in film circles. Last, Miss Pickford turned to a plump girl with a round, pretty face whose baggy frock did little to disguise her fat stomach. She appeared to be about fifteen and was clearly bored by the adults around her. I assumed she was someone's daughter.

"Jessie, this is Lillita Chaplin. Lita, dear, Jessie Beckett works on the Zorro picture with Douglas. Charlie and Douglas will be along as soon as they finish their tennis game. Do have a seat and some lemonade, Jessie. I know it's been a long day for you."

Geez Louise, the kid was Chaplin's *wife*! His second, married just a few months ago in Mexico under somewhat mysterious circumstances. And she wasn't fat. She was pregnant. Now I believed those rumors about Lita being underage. Even malicious gossip is true sometimes: Charlie Chaplin had an itch for young girls. His first wife, too, had been little more than a child. I felt sorry for Lita and tried without success to engage her in conversation.

A shout from below signaled the end of the tennis match, and fifteen minutes later, Douglas Fairbanks and his best friend, Charlie Chaplin, sauntered up to the patio, no longer in tennis whites but wearing linen knickers, trim V-neck sweater vests, and matching bow ties, and still arguing amiably about the score. At that same moment, Jack Pickford and his wife, Marilyn Miller, arrived, and behind them came two seasoned performers I had seen at Heilmann's party, Paul Corrigan and Faye Gordon, the woman who had lost her temper and slapped the young actress. I took a close look at Faye, Miss Pickford's friend. Tonight she looked poised and confident, as if good news had come and carried her away.

"And he was a fine director, too." Ernst Lubitsch's voice carried over the others. "Zukor asked me to finish the film he was working on but I had to refuse because I have already promised . . ."

". . . but do you really think the same person killed all three?" That was Marilyn Miller.

"It could be three unrelated incidents, couldn't it?" asked her husband, Jack Pickford. "I mean, one of Heilmann's scorned lovers shoots him—or maybe a jealous husband, God knows, there were enough of them. Then Lorna McCall accidentally drowns in the toilet. And the other woman . . . some waitress, wasn't she? . . . is killed during a robbery. I don't understand all the fuss."

Stella DeLanti chimed in, "There wouldn't be any fuss if all three hadn't been at the same party. Both women must have seen something that could have identified the murderer. That means he was at the party. I was at the party, too, so maybe I talked to him! But I didn't see anything suspicious."

"You'd better hope not!" Jack said, sneering. "You could be next!"

She gave him a dirty look.

"Jessie, tell us about poor Esther," said Douglas in an effort to deflect a spat. "You found her body."

All eyes were on me. "Ooooo, how awful! Do tell," gushed Helene Lubitsch, and out of the corner of my eye, I saw young Lita inch closer and tilt her head toward me.

"Esther Frankel's death was in today's paper. At first, no one connected her with the caterers at the party. I had the misfortune to find her body when I visited her house on Sunday morning. She was a vaudeville friend of my mother's, and I was just paying a call for old times' sake. Her door was open a crack, so I let myself in."

The image of Esther's body was so vivid I had to pause. Here I was, talking about her like she was the entertainment at a party. I hardly knew the woman, but this seemed callous and gossipy. In that instant I decided to leave off the details of her death out of respect for her life. But when I remembered what a vaudeville stalwart she had been, I figured maybe she wouldn't

mind being the center of entertainment once more. I cleared my
throat and continued.

"She was dead. I called the police, of course. It seems to me
that she must have seen Heilmann's killer while she was cleaning up, although she didn't realize it at the time. Maybe he shot
Heilmann and then followed the caterer's truck to Esther's
apartment, picked the lock, and surprised her. If he hadn't killed
her, she would have remembered him the moment she learned
of Heilmann's death."

Stella DeLanti said, "Then the killer murdered poor Lorna
McCall for the same reason, I'm sure. What if he's not finished?
What if others at the party saw him and could figure out who
he was?"

"Oh, there you are, David," Miss Pickford said, looking past
me into the house where I saw the outline of another guest standing in the doorway overlooking the patio, methodically surveying
the gathering before joining it. "How good of you to come tonight. Come in, or should I say, come out!" Her pleasant laughter
made me think of a melody. "Everyone, this is David Carr."

My stomach lurched at the name. It couldn't be. I looked
closer. It was.

The newcomer stepped out of the shadows onto the flagstone with the confidence of a man who had seen the world and
found it everywhere agreeable. He was not tall, but he carried
himself in a way that added several inches to his height. A cool
gust of wind coming off the ridge tousled his hair. He carelessly
pushed it back off his forehead and smiled. It took every ounce
of my theatrical training to keep from gasping with surprise.
Different but familiar last name, and a face I would never forget.

"You've met Douglas already, of course, but you haven't met
the others, I think," Miss Pickford was saying to the group. Her
gentle voice sounded miles away, drowned out by the blood
drumming in my ears. "David is new to Hollywood, and he's
collaborating with my current film, *Little Annie Rooney*."

David's eyes swept the guests' faces until they found me. They crinkled in recognition. Then he winked as if we shared some private joke. He wasn't at all surprised to see me.

David. The man who had rescued me after my terrible injury in Oregon last fall and saved my life at great risk to his own. The man who possessed more good looks, charm, and money than a fairy-tale prince. The man who was kind to children, attentive to old ladies, and beloved by dogs.

The man who was certainly not a film collaborator, but Portland's king of crime, a gangster boss with ties to bootlegging, gambling, prostitution, bribery, and probably worse. The man whose every word to me so far had been a lie.

14

You're a hard person to find," said David, drawing me aside at the first opportunity. "Hey, you're covered in goose bumps. Want my jacket?"

"No, thank you." It was not the cool night air that made me shiver.

"You changed your name, Jessie Beckett," he said, pointedly emphasizing the last name.

"So did you, David Carr." It had taken only seconds to steel myself to play this cautiously. I would be cool but polite, treating him like a new acquaintance until I figured out what he was up to.

"I needed to be hard to find. I decided to take my real father's name. So did you, I see."

"At the risk of sounding dramatic, I should thank you for saving my life. You left before I could say it."

"Aw, shucks, ma'am," he drawled in his best cowboy lingo, "'twarn't nothing." Then he dropped the show and stepped back a little. "Let me look at you good and proper. How's the leg?"

"All mended, good as new. The arm, too." In spite of my resolve, his concern made me feel warm inside.

"You look like a million bucks. Ten million. I don't mind saying, though, you had me scared stiff. Honest, you were beat up pretty bad back there, and I was afraid I would never see those turquoise eyes sparkle up at me again. It tore me up leaving right after I'd found you, not being able to stay and make sure you were going to make it, but I had about twelve hours before the cops would be on me. Did you get my message?"

"Your mother's locket? Yes, it's safe, back at my house."

"I knew you'd take my meaning. I wanted to tell you that I'd find you after life settled down, but I was afraid anything written would find its way to the cops, and they'd know to watch you until I showed up. Then your old granny wouldn't say where you'd gone, so I had to run down some of your vaudeville friends and worm it out of them."

"Who?"

"Zeppo Marx."

"How long have you been in Hollywood?"

"A few weeks. I wanted to get established before I looked you up. Jessie," he said, lifting my chin with his fingers and looking anxiously into my eyes, "I had feelings about you from the first time we met. I can't—"

"I didn't realize you two knew each other," said Miss Pickford, joining us, her eyes gleaming with matchmaking ambition.

David beamed and saved me the reply. "Jessie and I met last fall in Oregon. It's a pure pleasure to find her here and renew the acquaintance."

But she was looking past us both. "Oh, Lottie, I'm so glad you decided to come downstairs tonight," she said, turning toward the house where her sister had appeared. Lottie seemed not to hear her.

"Ladies and gentlemen, attention please. I have a request!" Everyone turned. Framed in the doorway and swaying gently on her feet, Lottie Pickford stood in her gauzy white frock as if she were on a stage waiting for silence from her audience before she continued with her act. "I don't want to hear any talk tonight of . . . of . . . *him*." Tears squeezed from her big brown eyes and she motioned with her hands that she was too choked up to continue.

The tightening around Douglas Fairbanks's mouth told me he wasn't pleased to see his sister-in-law at dinner, and far less so to have her dictate the scope of the conversation. Mary Pickford, however, couldn't have been more solicitous.

"Of course not, dearest," she crooned. "I'm so pleased you're feeling well enough to join us. Perfect timing. We are going into the dining room in a few moments." And she linked her arm through her sister's and led her onto the patio.

I surveyed the guests with mounting anxiety. Was David to be my dinner partner? And sit beside me all evening? If he did, would I be able to keep my wits about me and swallow my food?

I'd've bet money that even the king of England didn't eat every night like we ate at Pickfair that night. I had to pinch myself as I looked about the room. Here I was, seated at the table with the three most famous people in the entire civilized world. We sat according to place cards, Mary Pickford presiding and Douglas at her right. I was at her left, with Paul Corrigan on my other side and Helene Lubitsch nearby. Relief battled disappointment when I saw that David had been positioned at the other end with Lottie Pickford and the Chaplins. Right away I noticed his efforts to draw out young Lita Chaplin. If anyone could do it, he could. Give the devil his due; he was charming.

Dinner began with printed menus at each place, and it included things I had never before experienced, like rose-water finger bowls, lace-trimmed napkins, and flavored ice between courses. The china and glassware gleamed in light cast by three crystal chandeliers. Instead of an overgrown centerpiece that would have blocked conversation with people on the opposite side of the table, there was a small bouquet of violets in front of every place. Alcohol was conspicuously absent. Douglas's well-known aversion to liquor meant all Pickfair dinners were dry—not even wine was served.

"No, I couldn't be there," Faye Gordon was saying to Marilyn Miller, and I dragged my attention back to my own end of the table. "But I heard his yacht was lovely. I had to be in Bakersfield last weekend to see my sick mother and so, sadly, I couldn't attend."

Next to me, Paul hissed, "The only reason she went to Bakersfield was to cover up the fact that she wasn't invited to Hearst's party." His rudeness made me wonder as to their relationship. Had they come together, or merely arrived at the same time? He wasn't finished. "You were at Heilmann's that night. When did you leave?"

I glanced in Lottie's direction, but she was too far away to hear us mention the painful name. "My girlfriend and I left early. Shortly after midnight."

"What did you think of Lorna McCall's final performance?"

"Excuse me? I wasn't introduced to her, and I guess I didn't see whatever it was—"

"Sure you did. Everyone saw. She and Faye here practically had a knock-down-drag-out."

"Oh, so *she* was the girl who was slapped. I didn't make the connection until now." So Lorna had been the girl in the fountain, minus her undergarments and wet to the skin. Now that the dead actress had a face, her loss seemed more real.

"Weren't you close enough to hear their spat? Lorna had had too much to drink—so had Faye, naturally—and Lorna made one too many catty remarks about Faye being too old for leading-lady parts. In the past couple years, Faye has lost roles to younger actresses like Clara Bow and Mary Astor, who's only seventeen, for God's sake, and then two parts she wanted went to Lorna, and Lorna was queening it over her when Faye pulled back and slapped her."

"That part I saw. Or the aftermath." No wonder Faye was in such good spirits tonight—she'd lost a rival.

"Maybe Faye will get that role now that Lorna's dead," remarked Helene Lubitsch from across the table.

"Not a chance," said Paul. "She's too old." He glanced down at Faye to make sure she wasn't listening, and confided sotto voce, "Says she's twenty-nine but she's thirty-five if she's a day. She won't get another decent role at her age. She's washed up."

I winced but it was too late. Mary Pickford, age thirty-two, had heard. She wasn't an actress for nothing—her face betrayed not a flicker of emotion—but I could feel the dismay radiating from behind the mask. "I think the entire profession would benefit if less attention were paid to one's age and more to one's abilities," she said sweetly.

Douglas, equally stung, chimed in. "Nothing replaces maturity and experience," he said, punctuating each word with his fork.

Incredibly, Paul didn't take the hint. He blundered on. "Nonsense. Faye's not going to attract anything but older women's parts and those are all minor roles. But did you see Lorna later that evening? She lost a bet with Heilmann and had to sit in the fountain out front. That really was her last performance, poor girl. Who'd have thought she'd end up like she did? It's enough to give a fella the creeps."

At the other end of the table, Lottie's need to be the center of attention trumped her earlier plea. Dabbing her eyes with a monogrammed handkerchief, she was prattling on about Bruno Heilmann, the party, and the police investigation. She was clearly drunk—she must have had a stash in one of the upstairs bedrooms—and I hoped she would not blurt out anything about me retrieving her things from Heilmann's house. Then it dawned on me that she probably didn't know what I'd done. Douglas would have too much sense to tell her.

Now that the gloves were off, the rest of the group entered the fray.

"It's amazing that Zukor has kept the whole thing out of the newspapers," said Marilyn Miller. "Secrets in this town are impossible to keep." Several people nodded ruefully, suggesting that some indiscretion had turned the spotlight their way in the past.

Lottie knocked over her water goblet. Douglas frowned.

"It won't be a secret for long," he said, as a maid scurried over to mop up the mess. "The news will be in tomorrow's papers."

Robert Fairbanks spoke up. "I heard the valet called Zukor and Zukor called you, right, Doug? That's how they kept it quiet— only two men knew and they didn't tell any women."

But that was wrong, I thought as smug laughter rippled down the male half of the table. Lots of people knew. Lots of women. I knew on Sunday. Myrna knew. Had she told the other girls? And Lottie Pickford had to have known on Sunday, or she wouldn't have panicked about her monogrammed belongings. Miss Pickford knew. Had Zukor told anyone? Obviously the police chief, several policemen, and the detectives knew, and Heilmann's valet who found his body. Had any of these people told anyone?

To my left, the tactless Paul Corrigan started to speak again, then caught himself. I turned just in time to see him looking at Lottie, then at Faye, then back and forth between them. He closed his mouth tightly and found something interesting about his beef Wellington. I didn't hear a peep out of him for the rest of the meal.

"Well, it seems likely that the waitress—what was her name?— was killed because she could have identified the man who shot Heilmann," said Charlie Chaplin. "Lorna McCall's death might have been an accident, but it seems far too pat for that. She must have seen or known something, and someone did her in for it. Now my question is this: Is the murderer finished? Or are there others who saw something? God, Doug, you and Mary didn't see anything, did you?"

Douglas waved his hand dismissively. "You will not be surprised to hear that Mary and I left early in the evening. We had other obligations—a good night's sleep being one of them! Nonetheless, I've persuaded Mary to put up with a bodyguard for the next few days, just until the police capture this madman."

"I want a bodyguard, too." Lottie's petulant voice rose above the rest. "I was at Bruno's right up until he made me—well, never mind—but what if the murderer wants to kill me like he did Lorna!"

"Of course you shall have one," said her sister. "I was planning to ask you that question tonight. And you can count your lucky stars Bruno did make you leave, or you might have been there when he was murdered." And been killed with him. The unspoken words hung in the air.

Lottie struggled up from her seat, knocking her fork to the floor, and wobbled out of the room. Douglas's eyes narrowed. Miss Pickford didn't seem to notice anything amiss. I glanced at the other end of the table and saw Lita laughing at something David had said. She was a fetching little thing when she dropped the pout.

A few minutes later, Lottie tottered back into the room carrying something in her hand. "Look what I bought today," she said. "I've got to protect myself, too!"

She held up a small pearl-handled pistol no more than five inches long and waved it gaily about, pointing the barrel carelessly around the table.

Everyone froze.

Everyone except David, who had been seated next to Lottie. David knew his way around guns. In one sinuous motion, he slid out of his chair and over to her elbow. "Let me see that," he said, taking it gently from her. The entire room exhaled in one giant breath. "It's lovely, Lottie. Belgian make, isn't it? Wherever did you get it?"

"From that store downtown. Allan has guns at home but they're so heavy I can't shoot them. The man at the store said this was a lady's gun. Just my size."

As she spoke, David took the magazine from the handle and opened and closed the slide. A cartridge was ejected, answering everyone's question. The gun had been loaded. "Look here, Doug. Isn't it nice?" he said, passing the gun to our host who quietly set it on the mantel. Thinking quickly, Chaplin launched an impromptu pantomime of a rubber-legged waiter holding a chair for a lady, getting laughs from all of us as he clumsily fell to the floor and bounced back up in his efforts to reseat the giggling Lottie. Distracted by the antics, Lottie was drawn further under the Chaplin spell as he told a long, naughty joke about a man and an alligator, and soon the tension melted away. Conversation turned to sex and Communists, and sex with Communists, and the pearl-handled pistol was forgotten.

15

T he Pickfair evening concluded with everyone gathering in
the living room to watch an unreleased picture. Jack Pickford and Marilyn Miller scooted out the door—"another
dope party," muttered Lubitsch under his breath—while the butler passed cigars and chocolate-covered cherries, Douglas's favorite. Douglas and Mary held hands on the sofa. The Chaplins,
who hadn't exchanged a word the entire evening, sat in opposite
corners of the room and walked home as soon as the film ended,
missing the lively analysis of the acting, directing, lighting, and
editing that followed. As the ten o'clock curfew loomed, Douglas
came over to my chair.

"I'll call the Rolls whenever you're ready."

David stood. "Let me save your driver the trip. I'm going back
to town and would be honored to escort Miss Beckett home."

Perversely, the offer both thrilled and dismayed me. There

was no way to refuse gracefully, and anyway, half of me couldn't wait to be alone with David. The other half needed time to think. But David's gesture brought the group to its feet, everyone remarking on the lateness of the hour and their early obligations the next day.

I thanked Douglas profusely for the invitation. "You have no idea how much this evening meant to me," I told him before turning to my hostess. Our eyes met and held, and I saw that words were unnecessary; Mary Pickford understood exactly how much this evening had meant to me. She had come up the way I had through the harsh, vagabond life of itinerant performers, passing straight from infancy to adulthood in her role as family breadwinner, forever terrified that this would be the day the applause died. Ironic, really, that both our careers hinged on portraying children when neither of us had any experience being a normal child. Those moments on stage and screen were as close as either of us would ever come to childhood.

We understood each other, Mary Pickford and I. We had taken the same road, and while she was miles ahead of me today, she knew the ruts and potholes all too well. *Look how far I've come*, she seemed to say in wonderment. But it was never far enough. The specter of poverty always hovered near, ready to snatch everything away the moment she relaxed, so she had to get to the studio at daybreak and drive herself hard and harder, acting, directing, and personally managing every aspect of her business, demanding perfection from herself and her crew because only the sound of applause could keep the specter at bay.

"Good night, Jessie, dear," was all she said, but the way she said it made my heart soar.

David and I drove out of the Pickfair driveway in his brand-new Packard, past the Chaplins' house, and down into the valley. A full moon hung in the night sky, raising a coyote chorus of mournful howls. Now that we were alone together, I felt self-conscious, and I silently vowed to keep the conversation as impersonal as I could.

"That was quick thinking at dinner," I said. "You probably saved at least one of us from getting shot."

"There was never much real danger," he said modestly. "Those small pistols are wildly inaccurate. With a short barrel like that, even Annie Oakley would have trouble hitting her target. And Lottie's a rank amateur."

"I wasn't worried about her aim. I was worried about a wild shot. She was pretty zozzled."

"So was Jack Pickford. He just holds it better. And every time they get into trouble, they wave Mary like a flag. It's a wonder Doug can stand those two."

"He loves Mary too much to banish them."

An awkward silence descended as David navigated the canyon road curves toward town. Finally he cleared his throat. "I'm glad to meet the real Jessie at last. I am meeting the real Jessie, aren't I? I mean, this isn't another role you're playing in another swindle?"

"No, this is the real me. That stint in Oregon made me realize I didn't want to go back to the vaudeville life of bad food, cheap hotels, and a different city every week. Some friends got me a job training to be a script girl at *Son of Zorro,* then understudy's luck got me a couple weeks as Douglas's assistant. You can say I'm no better than the hundreds of other silly girls coming to Hollywood every year trying to get into show business, and you'd be right, but I've got a steady job, and I'm feeling like I fit in here. Yeah, this is the real me. I know who I am now."

"I hear you're a detective in your spare time. You've only been here a couple months and already you're mixed up in murder. Must be your perfume."

"Well, I couldn't help that I was at the party where the first murder happened. Or that I knew the woman who was killed later that night. I didn't set out to find the killer. Douglas just asked for my help, and I came into it through the back door."

"You're smart. You notice things others miss. And you have a way of sensing things, almost like a mind reader."

I thought about that. After a lifetime on stage watching for subtle cues, making decisions based on someone's tone of voice, picking up on a raised eyebrow or the lift of a chin, and absorbing the audience's mood through my skin, it was probably inevitable that I would become sensitive to details, especially the human kind. "I think maybe I read people, not minds."

"You need to be careful. People who kill people don't mind killing people, if you get my point."

"I'm careful."

"I cared a lot about the old Jessie back there in Oregon, even when I didn't know who she really was, but I think—I'm sure I'm going to care even more for the real McCoy here in Hollywood. I look forward to getting to know you better."

Truth was, I was afraid to get to know David better. He came from my former life, the deceitful life I'd left behind, and I didn't want to get sucked back into the old ways. Besides, I was through with broken hearts, especially when it was my own.

"And what role are you playing in Hollywood, Mr. Carr? Just what is a collaborator, anyway?"

"In this case, it's a fancy word for investor. United Artists hasn't enough ready cash to finance all its films, so backers put up dough and come in for a cut of the profits, if there are any. Legal gambling, I call it, although with names like Pickford, Fairbanks, and Chaplin, the dice always come up seven or eleven. Even their worst clunker should break even. Douglas wants to make color pictures, and he's very interested in sound, and all that new technology costs a lot of bucks."

"Pictures with sound? You mean talkies? I heard about making a color feature next year but didn't know he was thinking about sound, too."

"Sure he is. So are Warner Brothers and Fox. So are a lot of people. But Douglas is real smart about it. He knows the motion picture business upside down and inside out, and he's crazy about tinkering with the mechanics. Although he keeps it pretty quiet."

"Why?"

"Before I got involved with Pickford-Fairbanks, I used to think everyone was on the edge of their seats waiting for talkies, that as soon as the right inventions came along, talkies would flood theaters all over the world. Now I know better. There's serious resistance from every layer of the industry. Talkies will bring a revolution in filmmaking, and like any revolution, blood will run in the gutters."

"Just adding sound wouldn't cause—"

"Yes, ma'am, it would. You ask any actor what he thinks about sound. Most hate the very idea. For one thing, a lot of them are foreigners—you know that because you're in the business, but the public doesn't—and their accents won't be accepted. Others have working-class accents or unappealing voices. Most don't have theater training, and they don't know how to project. Most think sound would ruin them. And they're right."

I couldn't argue with him there. I had been surprised to see what a large percentage of the film industry, and not just actors, was foreign born. Sometimes it seemed like the world had come to Hollywood to make pictures. And off the top of my head, I could think of several famous actors whose voices were harsh or high-pitched or nasal sounding or too breathless to carry.

"Directors are against the change, too," he continued. "You've been on sets when they're filming. You've seen how noisy it is. Most scenes are shot outdoors where the sun is strong, but listen to the wind and other background sounds and think how they would be picked up on microphones. And those Mitchell cameras! They sound like machine guns."

"I see what you mean. Directors couldn't continue to direct by talking actors through each scene as it's being shot. They'd have to do endless rehearsals and shoot in silence, like they do for the stage."

"That would double or triple the production time for every picture. And the cost."

"I guess so."

"Douglas is afraid the fluid, natural quality of films will be lost when actors have to hover around a microphone to be heard. Studio producers are wary about the high cost of recording equipment and the loss of their best stars. And as far as theater owners are concerned, installing sound equipment will cost thousands of dollars for each theater, forcing up ticket prices when they're already running more than twenty-five cents apiece in big cities. Those who couldn't afford to upgrade would go belly-up."

I was thinking about all the musicians who made their living playing in theaters who would lose their jobs. Then I wondered how talkies would be received internationally. Now it was easy to subtitle the original titles. How would foreign audiences understand dialogue spoken in another language?

"To put it bluntly," said David, "most people are scared to death of talkies."

But he wasn't. I could see fire in his eyes as we talked. "So you're going to collaborate with Douglas on making talkies and color?"

"Doug wants to be the first to star in a feature-length color film. He's already chosen the story—something about pirates. There's no holding back progress, Jessie. Color is here. Talkies are coming. They'll ruin a lot of people, but those who can weather the storm stand to make a fortune. Both Doug and Mary have had years of experience on the stage—they'll make the transition."

"You're not bootlegging anymore?"

"Hell, no, kid. I don't have a death wish. There's a nice, tight operation here in Los Angeles bringing Mexican liquor across the border, like the one I had in Portland with the Canadians, and no one muscles in on an established business unless he's looking for a bullet. No siree, Bob. I'm in the picture business now. I put up half the money for *Little Annie Rooney*."

It was a statement, not a boast, and it dropped my jaw. Making a major motion picture like that could cost two or three hundred thousand dollars.

"I guess you got out of town before the police caught up with you."

"You're looking at me, aren't you? I got away with my cash and my toothbrush."

He didn't volunteer further details, but I knew enough to doubt his story. Everyone knows bootleggers do more than smuggle hooch. The business leaches naturally into speakeasies, protection rackets, and police bribery, and often into drugs, prostitution, numbers, and other gambling rings. I'd fallen for David's aw-shucks honesty and boyish enthusiasm last fall before I knew he was mixed up in the underworld. Only once had I seen a glimpse of what lay beneath the guileless mask, and that was the night he had calmly promised to kill a man with his bare hands.

We pulled up in front of my house and stopped the car. He was about to ask if he could come up to my room. I spoke quickly.

"Look, David, I appreciate what you did for me back in Oregon. You saved my life and it cost you your, um, livelihood."

"I'm not looking for gratitude." His voice turned velvety hard. "Can I come in?"

"It's late and . . . I've got to be at work early . . ."

A single nod told me he wasn't buying a word of it. "Can I see you tomorrow for dinner?"

I turned to face him squarely. "Look, David, I don't want to get mixed up with anyone right now. I've made a clean start here and—"

"And your future doesn't include consorting with former criminals, is that it?" When I did not reply, he went on. "That's rich, coming from one of the world's great swindlers, or are you going to claim that little episode in Oregon was the only time you've ever run afoul of the law?" A split-second hesitation on my part brought a twist to his lips. "Just as I thought. Face facts, Jessie, you and I are scoundrels. We understand each other the way others never will. I'm not sure what you're up to here in Hollywood, but you can trust me not to give it away."

He was wrong. I wasn't a real criminal. I had always meant to make my own way with honest work; it was just that honest work was sadly shy about introducing itself while shady opportunities came on bold as brass.

"What I'm up to," I said tartly, "is a law-abiding way of life with friends who aren't looking over their shoulders for the cops."

"Well, if it isn't Miss Goody Two-shoes! Sworn off the hooch, too, have you?"

"That doesn't count! It used to be legal."

"So did gambling. And a few years ago you could buy cocaine from the druggist, no questions asked. It was only the stroke of a pen that made those illegal."

It wasn't just that. I knew enough to recognize an onrushing train. Twice before I had been in love, and twice before the outcome had not been pretty. At least I had salvaged something from the wreckage: the realization that I was attracted to the wrong sort of man. When I let myself fall in love again, it was going to be with some decent, steady, upright citizen. A banker, maybe.

"David, I—"

"What a little hypocrite you are." His soft, calm voice sounded more menacing than if he had shouted.

Stinging eyes made me fumble for the door handle, but I found it at last and yanked hard.

16

A man with a droopy mouth? No, miss, can't say as I do."
The ticket seller looked over the top of rimless glasses and
shrugged helplessly. "With hundreds of people through
this train station every day, no particular face is gonna stick in
my head 'less he's got antennas coming out his skull."

"Was anyone else working the ticket booths last Sunday afternoon?" I pressed.

"Now, let me think. There's usually two of us here early, then
a third comes in at noon. Sammy Alvarez over there usually
works the noon shift, but he wasn't . . . Oh, right, Sunday. It was
his daughter's birthday and he switched with Stitch Owens.
Stitch is in the back. If you want, knock on that door yonder
and ask for him."

Thanking the clerk, I moved out of the way of the people in
line behind me and scanned the station floor, breathing in the

familiar mix of leather, cigars, and coal smoke. Train stations smelled like home. Sometimes I thought of my life as one long train ride punctuated by glimpses of the real world whizzing by my window. For twenty-five years, I had dragged trunks and valises from one town to another, usually on the weekends, spending most Saturday nights on the train to save the dollar for a hotel. I'd been through a hundred stations like La Grande Depot, maybe not as large or as nice as La Grande, which was one of the main depots for the Acheson, Topeka, and the Santa Fe, but train stations have much the same smells and sounds, large or small, wherever you go. This one had been built back when the fanciful Moorish style ruled the imagination of urban architects everywhere and Los Angeles was being flooded by Easterners lured by the promise of a healthy climate. Back then it had been one of the most modern and luxurious stations in the country; this afternoon it bustled with overdressed matrons, serge-suited businessmen, rough cowboys, shabby Mexicans, and a couple Indians with their long black hair tied back with leather thongs. Who would remember a man with a droopy mouth in this colorful cast of thousands?

I hadn't slept much last night, despite my bedtime glass of sherry. Thoughts of murder pushed sleep clean out of my head. Seemingly small details kept elbowing their way upstage, demanding consideration, putting me in mind of the throngs of extras that showed up at every open casting call trying to be noticed among so many. *No thanks, not today, not you, no thanks. Yes, you.* I had been pestered by the image of a man with a droopy mouth—a man no one in the neighborhood knew—and the sound of a single gunshot—a sound no one in the neighborhood heard.

I knocked on the door that the ticket vendor had indicated and asked for Stitch Owens. About three minutes later, a man with a blotchy face and a bulbous nose stepped out.

"You looking for me?" he asked as he scratched a match for his cigar. His voice was rough, as if he didn't get much chance to use it.

"Yes, sir. You were working the ticket booth Sunday afternoon, two days ago?"

"Might've been." He pulled on his cigar to get it going, not bothering to turn aside when he exhaled.

The smoke burned my nose and throat, but I didn't flinch. I put on my youngest voice and mannerisms and rocked from my heels to toes like a girl. My stylish bob lessened the effect, but I had no time to create this part properly. "I know it's a long shot, mister, but I was wondering if you sold a ticket to a man with a droopy mouth on Sunday afternoon."

"What sort of man?"

I played the odds and improvised. "Middle age. Average height. Dark suit. The droopy mouth is the only part anyone would remember."

He let his eyes travel slowly about the station before returning to me. "Why do you want to know for?"

I gave a worried sigh. "It's my auntie who sent me, sir. My uncle left Sunday afternoon and hasn't arrived yet. She asked me to check and see if he ever left the station."

"Sorry, kid. I don't make it a habit to remember passengers. Now scram."

He slammed the door. I surveyed the station again. The departures-and-arrivals board shuffled around letters and numbers like cards at a poker table until they snapped at the right place. Brakes squealed as a train eased into its platform. Steam hissed as another pulled out. Redcaps hurried to and fro. At the far end of the station, tucked under a sign for the Harvey House, was a newsstand.

What would a man do after buying a ticket? I took my younger self over to the newsstand where an array of morning papers had been stacked on the floor. With a glance at the headline that blared PARAMOUNT DIRECTOR MURDERED, I reached for the *Los Angeles Times*, the *Examiner*, and the *Daily News*.

"Excuse me, mister. Was this newsstand open Sunday, two days ago?" I asked, handing him six cents for all three.

"Sure was, little lady. Every day from six-thirty sharp."

"Were you working here that day?"

"I was indeed."

"Do you happen to remember seeing a man with a droopy mouth?"

"What do you mean, droopy mouth?"

"The corner of his mouth sagged a good bit." I pulled the corner of my mouth down, the way poor Edna's had looked that morning outside Esther's apartment.

"I'm afraid not," he said, then he cocked his head to one side. "Mind me asking why you're asking?"

"I'm looking for my uncle. He was supposed to take the train east on Sunday afternoon, but he didn't arrive yesterday, so my auntie asked me to make sure he left. I hope nothing happened to him."

"He probably just got off for a stretch along the way and missed his train. Happens all the time. He'll arrive on the next one."

"I'm sure you're right. Thank you, sir."

Our director, Frank Richardson, had sent me to La Grande Depot to meet a new makeup artist he had hired to replace one who had jumped to Warner Brothers a couple weeks ago. I had come early to test my theory about the man with the droopy mouth. The fact that no one in Esther's neighborhood recognized the description made me think he could be from out of town. If so, he must have come and gone by train. Someone at the station might remember a man with an unusual physical characteristic like that. The hands of the giant clock high on the opposite wall told me I had another hour and a half before the makeup artist's train pulled in. Plenty of time for a little investigating. I carried my newspapers into the Harvey House.

There is a Harvey House restaurant in every Santa Fe railroad station worth its salt, and those who didn't eat Harvey House food in the restaurants ate Harvey House food in the dining cars. I was darn sure I'd eaten more Blue Plate Specials in my lifetime than Fred Harvey himself, and I could have recited the menu and prices with Harvey Girl precision.

The Harvey House at La Grande Depot was situated in a long room designed to resemble a dining car. Inside, some forty swivel seats were fixed around a single racetrack counter so spanking clean that the light from the globe fixtures above bounced off its surface like a mirror. The breakfast crowd had moved on, the lunch crowd had not yet assembled, but for Harvey Girls, idleness is sin. One was mopping the floor, another was watering the ferns that grew in wall planters, and two more worked in the middle of the racetrack, setting each place with a complement of silver utensils, a blue china plate, a glass cruet of water, and a linen napkin.

I sat at one end of the counter and ordered coffee. By the time it arrived, the two men at the opposite end had paid their bill, and I was the only customer in the place.

The explosive *Times* headline left me with no doubt that by tomorrow every daily in America would have followed its lead. By the time William Randolph Hearst and Joseph Pulitzer resumed their never-ending duel, the scandal would escalate—as it had with poor Fatty Arbuckle—into the realm of international melodrama, until no one who had actually attended Bruno Heilmann's party would recognize the event.

I read through the story. Bruno Heilmann, Paramount director extraordinaire, had been killed at dawn in a hail of bullets after a decadent orgy in his Hollywood mansion. Witnesses described seeing a suspicious man lurking about the house during the party, and several identified him as the husband of one of

Heilmann's paramours, as yet unnamed. Zukor was said to be pressuring police to find the killer fast. There was no mention of Esther, aside from the original article, nor of Lorna McCall.

Nearly every word the reporter wrote was wrong. If the subject hadn't been so serious, I would have laughed out loud. Surely all newspaper stories were not this far off the mark? Had the scrambling of facts been accidental? The others carried the same hokum under the headlines: WHO KILLED BRUNO HEILMANN? and FILM DIRECTOR'S SLAYING LEADS TO PROBE.

I motioned to the Harvey Girl who had brought my coffee. "I wonder if any of you girls worked this past Sunday?"

"Sarah did," she replied, cocking her head toward the floor mopper. "She opens on Sundays and was off at three. I came in then for the late shift."

"Only one girl on duty on Sundays?"

"No, two, plus the cook of course. Rebecca was here on morning shift, too." She indicated the girl with the watering can.

The morning shift girls didn't interest me. The killer, if he wasn't local, would have left after Lorna McCall's death which, according to the doctor, had occurred Sunday afternoon. "Do you happen to remember a man with a droopy mouth who came in for a bite to eat that afternoon?" I illustrated the affliction by pulling down the corner of my own mouth.

"Can't say as I do. Has he gone missing?"

I gave her the uncle routine and a large tip, then made my way to the far end of the room where Sarah was bent over a bucket of suds. She was dressed in the standard Harvey Girl uniform—a long-sleeved black dress with a stiff Elsie collar, black shoes and black stockings, with a white wraparound apron that was so starched it would have broken before it folded. Never mind modern skirt lengths, Harvey Girl hems measured eight inches from the floor. And the heavens would crack if they ever wore jewelry or makeup. Poor things, they all looked like nuns to me.

Sarah's eyebrows arched expectantly as I approached, and
she looked happy enough to stop mopping.

"Excuse me," I began. "I wonder if you can do me a great favor.
I'm trying to trace the whereabouts of my uncle, who's gone
missing. You were here Sunday afternoon, were you not?"

She nodded. "My shift was over at three."

"Do you remember a customer whose mouth drooped on one
side, like this?"

"Oh, yes, miss, I do," she said with no hesitation. A friendly
young woman, maybe twenty years old, she seemed happy to
catch her breath and oblige a customer at the same time. "I remember him because, well, it's not so usual to see a person with
such an affliction, is it?"

Thankfully not, I thought, elated at the news. My hunch was
correct. The droopy-mouthed man was from out of town. I was
betting that this man had killed Esther and probably Heilmann
and Lorna McCall, too. "What time was that?"

"Six-thirty on the dot. We always open at six-thirty."

"In the morning?" That was impossible. Lorna had died in
the afternoon. "Are you certain?"

"Yes, miss. He was waiting outside for us to unlock the door.
That's how I remember."

"Did he speak to you at all?"

"He isn't a talker, your uncle, is he? He sat there." She pointed
at the end of the racetrack counter. "Next to where you were
just sitting. He was almost the only one in here. Sunday mornings aren't busy for us. There aren't many trains leaving till late
morning."

"Did he mention where he was going?"

"He took the Chicagoan."

"He told you he was going to Chicago?"

"Not in so many words, but it seemed likely. He ordered a
cooked breakfast and nursed his coffee until seven. The first Chicagoan that day leaves at seven-ten. The next train out doesn't

leave till almost eight. And he was dressed in big-city clothes, a striped suit and a swell hat, so that made me think he was city-bound. Of course, he could've gotten off any place along the route, but the seven-ten goes all the way to Chicago."

Well acquainted with the Chicagoan from my vaudeville days, I knew its stops nearly as well as its conductors did. The route headed west from Los Angeles, and after passing through Albuquerque, split in two, the northernmost section passing through Dodge City, the southernmost through Amarillo. The tracks joined up again at Newton before continuing through Kansas City to Chicago, a journey that lasted two and a half days, start to finish. The eastbound train was called the Chicagoan. The same train going west was known as the Kansas Cityan. If Droopy Mouth had gone directly to Chicago, he would, I calculated, arrive at about five this evening.

I thanked Sarah with a silver dollar and interrupted Rebecca, who by now was wiping chair seats with a damp rag. She, too, remembered seeing the man early that morning but had nothing to add to what Sarah had told me.

I returned to my coffee and considered what I'd learned. If I was right, the droopy-mouthed man seen leaving Esther's building had killed her, but he had come to Los Angeles to kill Heilmann. If he had left on Sunday morning's train, he had definitely *not* killed Lorna McCall. It looked like Lorna's death really was accidental.

Having arrived in Los Angeles, probably sometime Saturday, the killer would have needed transportation to and from Heilmann's house. With taxis, he ran the risk of being remembered. He couldn't take a bus or a Red Car—they didn't run that late at night. He couldn't walk all the way—Heilmann lived miles from the train station. He couldn't rent a car or he'd leave a trail. Under the circumstances, what would I do?

I'd steal a car.

I flipped the pages of my *Times* until I came across what I was looking for: a woman's name among the bylines. Ida Overstreet. Sounded good to me.

Nellie Bly excepted, female reporters had been around for only about ten years, ever since the Great War siphoned off so many young men for service in Europe that the newspapers were forced to hire women to do a man's job. After the war ended, most were let go, but a few stayed on at the larger newspapers to write up weddings and recipes. I had hoped to find a woman's name in the news section of the *Times*, but no such luck. The society reporter would have to do.

"Where's the nearest police station?" I asked the Harvey Girl, setting a nickel on the counter for my coffee. She told me. I walked back to the newsstand and bought a notebook and some Wrigley's gum. With another glance at the clock, I left La Grande and climbed into the Ford flivver. I had plenty of time.

17

Ten minutes later, a hard-nosed newspaperwoman marched up the steps of the Central Division police station at First and Hill, a notebook under her arm, a pencil behind her ear, and a chip on her shoulder.

"Good morning, Officer," I said briskly to the uniform manning the counter. "I'm Ida Overstreet of the *L.A. Times*, and I'd like to speak with your captain, please."

He looked me up and down. "What for?"

"I'm doing some research for an article on car theft and need a little information." I spoke firmly, without the slightest hint of a smile, and stared him down until he slid off his stool and disappeared into a back room.

Tapping my foot, I tried to look blasé, as if this were my hundredth interview at a police station. In truth, I was thanking my lucky stars that this place was miles away from the Hollywood station, where they knew me all too well. No one was likely to recognize me here.

From the inside, the place looked much the same as its Hollywood counterpart, although it was half again as large. More blue uniforms going and coming, more plainclothesmen working the telephones, more secretaries and clerks typewriting in triplicate. More noise, more cigarette smoke, more jangling telephone bells. More crime downtown, no doubt about that. Four great ceiling fans did their best to distribute the smoke evenly, but despite the open windows, the room smelled stale.

Officer Rowe returned with a short, middle-aged man who used too much shoe polish on his hair. He'd been eating.

"I'm Captain Stanley," he said, wiping his mouth with the back of his hand.

"Ida Overstreet, *L.A. Times*," I said, thrusting my hand out for a firm shake—a mannish gesture I thought suited my Girl Reporter character to a T. He was so surprised at the gesture, he actually took my hand and shook it. "This won't take long; I just need to ask you a few questions. Shall we go into your office?"

"Here's good enough." He hitched his pants up over his belly.

"Fine and dandy. I want to know about stolen cars. Has there—"

"I never heard of you."

"No reason you should, unless you read the *Times*." I flipped today's paper to the fashion story with the Overstreet byline, and held it out. He looked down his nose at the story, then brought his squinty eyes back to my face. I chewed hard on my gum and examined my fingernails, praying he wouldn't ask for real credentials.

"I thought you dames worked the society beat."

"This dame also does the news when she's told to. And the boss told me to dig up some information on recent car thefts. Have you had any cars reported stolen in the past week? Or don't you know, Captain Stanley? And what was your first name?" I took my pencil from behind my ear and held it poised over my notebook while I waited.

That got him. "Rowe, get the log." We stood glaring at each other without blinking as the younger cop went behind the counter and fished up a large bound ledger. The captain ran his finger down the page until he came to what he was looking for. "Friday night we had a couple tough kids steal a Packard Single Eight. They were picked up near the river a few hours later. Same night a woman on Hunter Street reported her Hudson Essex stolen but it turned out her son took it and she didn't want to press charges. Saturday noon someone pinched a Cadillac Phaeton . . . that one's probably in Mexico by now. Saturday night a man reported his Dodge stolen from the La Grande lot; turned out it was there on Sunday."

Officer Rowe sniggered. "I remember him. He just forgot where he parked it. Swore he left it in the first row on Thursday, and it wasn't there when he got home Saturday. We sent a man over Sunday morning and he found it in the back corner."

Bingo.

The captain continued. "Two cars reported stolen Sunday—a Buick and a Franklin. No trace. Nothing since." He snapped the book closed, silently daring me to continue.

Never having known a real reporter, I had no idea how they talked during an interview, but I imagined they asked a slew of snappy questions. I improvised as convincingly as I could. "Has there been an increase in car theft in this part of Los Angeles recently?"

"No. It's been about the same as usual."

"About the same as usual," I repeated, recording his words in my notebook. "And what do you recommend the public do to prevent car theft?"

"Keep their cars at home locked up in the garage." The Master of Sarcasm sneered.

I sensed my audience had reached the limits of its patience. Time to bring down the curtain. "Thank you, Captain Stanley. And you, too, Officer Rowe. You've been a great help. You can look for your comments in my article in this Sunday's *Times*."

"I can't wait."

Returning to La Grande, I visited the newsstand a third time. "You're getting to be a regular here, young lady," joked the vendor. Smiling my response, I handed him the money for a copy of *Variety*. Eagerly I flipped through its pages until I reached the section that listed which acts were playing in which Midwest theaters this week.

Chicago is an important vaudeville town, second only to New York City in number of theaters, so the list in *Variety* was long. I had heard of perhaps half the acts playing there this week and counted many as friends. But when my eye fell on the Cat Circus, I let out a cry of joy. Pay dirt. Angie was in Chicago.

For about four years, I had played in a family song-and-dance troupe called the Little Darlings—Jock and Francine Darling (yes, that was their real name) and their three children, plus four of us who played the older kids. We were like the Seven Little Foys, except they were all real Foys. I played Janie Darling, the second oldest, although I was in my twenties. Angie played my older sister because she was taller. In kiddie acts, height trumps age. She was seventeen when she left the Little Darlings for Walter, the love of her life and the man who managed the Cat Circus act. Angie and I had palled around a lot during the time she was with the Little Darlings, and I missed her. I hadn't seen her in about a year. But the Cat Circus was playing Chicago this week, and all I had to do was contact Angie for help.

According to *Variety*, they were booked at the Majestic on West Monroe, a theater I knew from my Little Darlings years. I could send a telegram to Angie in care of the Majestic, but chances were she wouldn't receive it until right before the first performance, and that would be too late. Walter and the Cat

Circus would have rehearsed as usual on Monday morning, and there would be no reason for them to be at the theater on Tuesday morning. Experienced acts seldom showed up more than thirty minutes before showtime. But when Angie and I were with the Little Darlings, our act stayed at a gem of a hotel each time we played Chicago. Not far from the lake, cheap, clean, and serving decent food, the Riordin Hotel was a find that Angie would not forget. And knowing her take-charge frugality, I was sure that she, and not Walter, was handling domestic finances these days. I would eat my red cloche hat if Angie and Walter were not staying at the Riordin.

With my eye on the clock, I scurried into the Western Union office located in a corner of the train station. Two men were ahead of me in line. I tapped my toes while I composed the message in my head, making every word work for its pay. When I got to the window, I was ready to write it out.

HUGE FAVOR VERY IMPORTANT GO DEARBORN STATION TODAY MEET CHICAGOAN DUE AROUND FIVE NEED TO KNOW IF LONE MAN WITH DROOPY MOUTH GETS OFF DON'T SPEAK JUST LOOK OVER PASSENGERS LOVE YOU WALTER & CATS.

The operator counted up the words. "Two dollar forty," he said without looking up.

I gulped. Never mind the cost. "I need rapid delivery for this one, please."

"Two dollar sixty."

"And a backup address in case the first one doesn't connect."

"Two dollar ninety."

I paid as the man handed the paper to the clerk behind him. It would go out over the wire in minutes. A few seconds later, it would come out on the Chicago end printed on a sticky strip that another clerk would press on a yellow form. With any luck, it would be placed at the top of a stack and a boy would be waiting to snatch it up and head out on his bicycle; with really good luck, his route would take him by the Riordin first and Angie would be in their room when the desk clerk called. Angie might have this message in hand in thirty minutes. If I were wrong about the hotel, it would go to the Majestic Theater next but that would be too late . . . I shook my head. I couldn't be wrong.

Even without Fortune's favor, Angie would receive the message in a few hours, hopefully in time for her to get down State Street to the Dearborn Station to meet the Chicagoan. There was nothing more I could do but wait.

And I had a train to meet myself.

18

You'll love it here, Miss Young," I said cheerily as I wedged the last of Mildred Young's seven suitcases into the backseat of the company flivver, then held the front door for her. "It's one of the most beautiful places on earth and the weather's always divine. I hope your trip was pleasant?"

"Long, but tolerable," she replied, removing her hat and smoothing her straight brown hair with her fingers. "Thank you for meeting my train."

"Our director, Frank Richardson, didn't want you to fuss with a taxi. He sent me—I'm his script girl in training—to bring you straight to the studio so he can welcome you himself. Then I'll take you to the Hollywood Hotel—it's not far from the studio—and you can settle in before you start work tomorrow."

The makeup department had been short staffed ever since the assistant had been lured away by Warner Brothers. Miss

Young had been hired, sight unseen, to fill the important slot. Good makeup was crucial to a film's success, and it involved far more than making stars look glamorous. There were old actors to be made up younger, young actors to be made up older, and Caucasians to be made up Chinese, not to mention the Indian warriors, werewolves, ghosts, circus clowns, witches, and men from outer space that needed creating from scratch.

I stole another look at Miss Mildred Young. She was plain, dangerously thin, and middle-aged. No doubt she came highly recommended from the theater world, but she was not what one expected in a makeup artist. Her own appearance—hair that looked like it had been bobbed with a dull knife and a face unadorned with even the faintest dab of rouge—was a poor recommendation for her skills. I hoped Frank Richardson would not be disappointed.

She told me to call her Mildred and asked some polite questions about the *Don Q, Son of Zorro* cast as we motored out of the parking lot. On my way to the station I had taken Santa Monica east to Sunset Boulevard and jockeyed over to First Street, but going home I was too busy talking and missed a turn.

"Damnation! I'm sorry. I'm afraid I've only lived here a couple of months, and I'm not very familiar with the downtown part of Los Angeles." I thought it prudent to avoid mentioning that I had learned to drive only recently. I was heading generally west when I noticed I was on Beverly Boulevard, a street I recognized. Now I knew where we were.

"What is a script girl?" asked Mildred, who was busy taking in the scenery on both sides of the road.

"A script girl is the director's right hand, a liaison between him and the film editor. She monitors the script during shooting to avoid errors in continuity—you know, like having someone wear a dirty shirt in one scene that inexplicably turns into a clean, fresh shirt in the next shot. She tracks wardrobe and makeup, keeps notes on each scene, and takes each day's film and notes to the editor. Pauline Cox is Frank Richardson's script girl, but she's leaving to get married in a month, so I'm training to take her place."

"I see. So we'll be working together."

"At Pickford-Fairbanks, we all work together. Mary Pickford likes to say that no one works *for* her, we all work *with* her. I just wanted you to know that I'm new here, too, still learning the ropes, so if you need any help settling in, I'll understand. Any questions you have, I probably had myself a few weeks ago."

"That's very kind of you. You are probably wondering how I was hired in the first place. Theater requirements are so different from film."

"Well, I . . . to be honest, it did occur to me. I've been in vaudeville so I know something about stage makeup, and it's a lot heavier and more exaggerated than what people wear in the pictures."

. She gave a somber nod. "It has to be, to be seen from the balcony. But now that film directors are favoring close-up scenes, makeup requires a more subtle hand. I've made a study of film makeup, watching how the kohl eye shadow and dark lips have given way to a gentler palette. I've learned a good deal from Miss Pickford's pictures. The natural look gives her characters a more realistic appearance. I believe I can achieve that. Of course, I'm only the assistant . . ."

"Like me."

". . . but I'll learn."

"My plan precisely. At least, that's what I tell myself."

"What's it like, living here?"

I gave the question some thought. "Hollywood is kind of like a fancy casino full of flashy gamblers and ruthless cheats. No one has a past and the present is already over because everyone's busy living for the future—the next dollar, the next deal, the next love. A throw of the dice turns shopgirls into stars and princes into paupers. But here the jackpot isn't money—it's fame."

"And I suppose, like in all gambling dens, losers outnumber winners?"

I smiled my assent. "And that's why I'm holding back and watching the crowd to learn which games are honest before I go rushing in to place my bets. Oh, look! Up ahead on your right. Going this way wasn't such a mistake after all. It gives you the chance to see Paramount Studios. They're the largest in Hollywood, really, the largest in the whole world." I pointed to one of the entrances as we chugged along Melrose and turned right at Gower.

There we came to a complete stop.

A hundred people or more had spilled out of the Gower Street entrance into the road, blocking traffic. We crept forward a few yards until I could make out several men in police uniforms who were not behaving like madcap Keystone Cops—they were real policemen. I chewed my bottom lip nervously. As we waited, two ambulances inched through the studio gates and sped north toward the hospital. By then I'd guessed what had happened. I just didn't know who.

Someone else was dead. And it had been no accident.

I pulled the car over to the curb and leaped out, leaving it idling. "Wait here. I won't be a moment," I cried to Mildred, and before she could protest, I was hurrying toward the entrance, past cowboys, a princess, several women in bathrobes, a couple knights in armor, dozens of technicians, one director—you can always tell directors by their tall boots and riding breeches—and a handful of cops. Finally I spied a familiar face. Standing apart from the crowd in the shade of an orange tree with his hat on backward was a young cameraman I knew from a couple of parties.

"What's happened, Bob?" I asked him.

He shook his head. "I don't know. It was something over at the *Cobra* set. They're saying two people are dead." He looked above my head at someone inside the gate. "Look, there's Sylvie

Baxter. She's Henabery's script girl." Bob didn't have to tell me that Henabery was the director of *Cobra*. We all knew who was directing every film at every major studio in Hollywood.

Bob and I pushed toward her through the crush and, in the confusion, I got past the Paramount guards. Sylvie looked dazed. Tears had streaked her cheeks with kohl. Bob patted her shoulder in a brotherly way. "There, there, Sylvie. Buck up, girl. What is all this about? Who has died?"

At that moment, a black car rolled by us and I could see Rudolph Valentino and his wife, Natacha Rambova, in the backseat. The chauffeur tooted his horn until the guards at the gate parted the crowd enough to let them pass through it. Bob didn't have to tell me that Valentino was starring in *Cobra*. We all knew who was starring in every film at every major studio in Hollywood.

The sight of Valentino uncorked Sylvie's tears, and Bob let her sob a moment on his shoulder. When she regained her voice she said, "I told the police, I just walked in to get another cup of coffee for Mr. Valentino, and I saw them on the floor. I thought they were both dead."

"Who?" I asked.

"Faye Gordon. Paul Corrigan." She swallowed hard.

My hand flew to my mouth in dismay. I'd been eating dinner with them just last night! And both had attended Bruno Heilmann's party last weekend. I remembered that Faye had spoken about having a small part in *Cobra*, not the starring role she wanted—that had gone to twenty-seven-year-old Nita Naldi— but a part nonetheless. I wasn't aware that Paul Corrigan had had a role at all. At least, he hadn't mentioned it last night.

Sylvie claimed my attention again. "I screamed and everyone came running. The Paramount doctor rushed over and said Corrigan was dead, but Miss Gordon was still alive. She was able to tell them that the coffee tasted odd. The police took the coffee. It must've been poisoned. And I almost . . . I mean, I almost filled a cup for Mr. Valentino. Dear God, I almost poisoned Rudolph Valentino!" She swayed on her feet until Bob pulled her up against his chest. "I should have known!" she wailed. "I saw a woman wearing a hat with a peacock feather in it just this morning!"

Peacock feathers. The unluckiest of omens for theater folk. Worse than wild birds flying into windows. No actress would have worn a hat with a peacock feather into the studio; it had to have been a visitor. Why the gate guard hadn't stopped her, I couldn't imagine. Someone would lose his job over that.

Outside the gate, policemen and directors were urging everyone to return to their sets. I made my way back to the car where Mildred Young was waiting.

"Has someone been hurt?" she asked.

"Dead."

"Another Hollywood murder?" she said primly. "I've been reading the newspapers. No need to distress yourself telling me about it. Doubtless I'll hear more than I want to know soon enough."

I flashed her a grateful smile and steered the car left on Santa Monica toward the green gates of Pickford-Fairbanks Studios, my mind churning faster than the engine gears.

The moment I had delivered Mildred Young to Frank, I went searching for Douglas Fairbanks. He was not filming this morning, and I found him in his office in the long, low building that fronted on Santa Monica.

"I need to see Mr. Fairbanks at once," I said to his secretary, a capable matron who knew me well after my stint as Douglas's assistant.

"He's on the telephone, and he's expecting some—" she began, then, taking stock of my agitation, changed her mind. "Go on in."

Douglas set down the receiver and stared at me like a defendant waiting for a jury verdict. I blurted out the news. He paled.

"As far as I know," I finished, "Paul Corrigan is dead. I'm not sure about Faye Gordon."

Calmly he picked up the receiver and spoke into the mouthpiece. "Get me the hospital." In three minutes he had his answer. "Someone poisoned the coffee. Corrigan died. Faye is hanging on."

I had to ask. "Do they know yet what sort of poison it was?"

Our eyes met over the words neither of us dared voice aloud. "Not yet," he said finally. But we both knew what they would find.

Bichloride of mercury. The words fairly danced in the air between us.

A popular choice for suicides, bichloride of mercury was commonly prescribed by doctors treating syphilis. In such cases, it was taken in minuscule doses or by injection. I knew it was odorless and colorless and supposedly had a metallic taste, but that could easily have been masked by the flavor of strong coffee.

I also knew as well as Douglas what would happen after the laboratory had determined mercury bichloride to be the poison. Headlines around the world would scream, and all thoughts would leap to Jack Pickford and his late wife, Olive Thomas, who had died in Paris under such suspicious circumstances after drinking bichloride of mercury. Then they would speed straight to Mary Pickford. She was entirely innocent and uninvolved, but that counted for nothing. Fatty Arbuckle had been innocent, too, and he'd been ruined, his movies banned by his own studio. I felt sick to my stomach.

The secretary gave a discreet knock and cracked the door. "Excuse me, Mr. Fairbanks, but Mr. Schenck and Mr. Keaton are here."

"Mary . . ." said Douglas feebly. "Find Mary and let her know. She and Faye are . . . well . . . and tell her 'by the clock.'"

19

The gang fight was in full swing when I reached the *Little Annie Rooney* alley. As I watched America's Sweetheart leap on the back of a young tough and flail away with her fists, director Beaudine talked through the scene, a megaphone at his mouth so the actors could hear him over the grinding racket of the Mitchell cameras.

"Move in closer, Spec. Add a little more life there! Throw something else. Okay, Joe, pull her off now. Get ready for the cops—look left on three. One, two, three. Good. Cut." A man holding the tail slate recorded the scene number and the cameras stopped.

I approached Beaudine for permission to interrupt. When he learned I brought a message from Mr. Fairbanks, he nodded me onto the set. Miss Pickford motioned me over to a crate in front of a slapdash fence in the tenement alley. The gang children flopped to the ground for a quick game of jacks. As I picked my way over broken plaster of paris bottles, felt bricks, and balsa-wood clubs, someone turned off the fan, and the laundry above our heads, which had been flapping like pennants in the wind, hung limp.

She was dressed like a scarecrow in a pompom hat, with the usual whiteface makeup to prevent skin from looking too dark on film. I apologized for the interruption, told her what I knew about Paul Corrigan and Faye Gordon, and repeated Douglas's private code, "by the clock." I didn't know what it meant, but it meant something significant, that was clear. She sat motionless for a long moment, her face like alabaster, but I could feel her grief at the loss of her friend. Too much the professional to re-act publicly, she thanked me for bringing the information, then signaled to Beaudine that she was ready to resume filming. I stepped out of the way and nearly collided with the picture's collaborator.

"I just heard," David said grimly.

"Bad news always travels like fire in the wind."

"You look like you could use a stiff drink."

"I'll be fine."

"Come over to the commissary with me before you go back to work; I'll buy you some coffee—er, maybe something else." And before I could protest that I didn't have time, David had me by the elbow and was escorting me behind the tenement set through the back lots toward the studio commissary.

"They're going to be all over her by tomorrow," he said, or-dering two cherry crushes. "Tell me what you know."

I did. I was brief. Honestly, it wasn't much.

"Thanks for the drink," I said. "No hard feelings about last night?"

He shrugged. "Somehow a bruised ego seems pretty trivial

when people you just ate dinner with are getting bumped off. Besides, we're going to see each other now and then in this town. There's no sense in nursing grudges, is there?"

"None at all," I said, a little irked at how fast he'd recovered from my rejection. "But I have to go now, really. I need to drive the new makeup assistant to her hotel and then get back to work."

We left the commissary together. "You going to Heilmann's funeral tomorrow?" David asked.

"I thought I would."

"You were a friend of his?"

I listened for a note of jealousy in his question but couldn't hear it. "Only an acquaintance. I just thought I might learn something by being there."

"Can I offer you a ride to the cemetery? I'm escorting Mary and Lottie for Doug. He can't go."

"No, thanks, I'm going to walk over with one of the girls who lives with me. But what's your interest in all this, anyway? You didn't know Heilmann, did you?"

"You're kidding me, right? I got a hundred thousand clams sunk in *Little Annie Rooney* and you're asking why I care about the Pickford reputation? If the fickle public spurns this picture, I'll be joining the drugstore cowboys on the corner of Gower Gulch waiting for work."

He gave me a grin, and I couldn't help but match it. I could picture him strutting about in sheepskin chaps and spurs, chewing tobacco with the other hopefuls who congregated every day at Sunset and Gower, hoping to be picked up for a bit part in a western.

"You'd get work. You've got that cowboy look."

We worked late that night on the cantina scene, and when Frank finally dismissed the crew, I practically flew home. Would there be a telegram from Angie waiting for me?

Much was against it. There were many Chicagoans—eight, ten, twelve trains a day went in each direction, depending on the day of the week and the season—and Angie could have met the wrong one. She could have missed the telegram at the Riordin and received it at the Majestic Theater too late. She could have met the right train but missed Droopy Mouth in the crowd. By the time I reached the house, anticipation was eating me alive.

"Hi, Jessie," called Lillian when I came through the front door. "Boy brought you a telegram. In the mail basket."

Taking a deep breath, I ripped open the yellow sheet.

SAW DROOPY TAKE CAB SOUTH MARRIED
WALTER JULY ANGIE

Exactly what I needed to know! Finally, things were starting to make some sense. I counted the words and laughed out loud. Trust Angie to keep it under ten for the cheapest rate. And she'd managed to get Walter to marry her, had she? Good old Walter. I'd have to send them a present.

In all the excitement, I almost forgot about my mother's playbills. But there was the unstamped envelope I'd mailed from Esther's, safe and sound in the bottom of the basket, returned to sender for lack of postage. I ran upstairs to my room where I could open it in private. I didn't want the girls to see me cry.

A minute later, I heard quick steps on the front porch. The screen door banged open and slammed shut, and Myrna came pounding up the stairs two at a time. I smiled as she burst into my room.

"I got the part! I got the part!" she sang, throwing herself into my arms for a congratulatory hug. "I got the part!" Twirling on her toes, she chanted the magical words several more times before collapsing on my bed in peels of laughter.

I laughed just to see her pleasure. "Catch your breath, now, and tell me about it."

With a grin as big as a rainbow, she sat up and folded her shapely legs beneath her. Not for the first time, I was struck by her artless sexuality. No question in my mind, Myrna had enough of "It" to be an actress. Maybe even a star.

"The company is Western Compass Studios. It's small but decent. It's over in Culver City, and they've made a few pictures."

"Which ones?"

"I forgot to ask. This one's about Greek mythology, a story about Zeus. I'm one of his romantic interests named Io. There were a dozen girls testing Monday when I was there—and I don't know how many others on other days—but I got the part on the spot. Not an extra, a real part, with sixty dollars a week and my name in the credits!"

"In letters as big as the Hollywoodland sign, I hope! Seriously, sixty dollars? That's terrific, Myrna. I'm thrilled for you. What did your mother think?"

"She's very, very happy for me." Her grin faded. "Daddy wouldn't have been . . . all entertainment was burlesque to him. He didn't approve of California."

"Then how did your family come to move—"

"When I was a child, Mother got pneumonia, and Montana winters are so cold that Daddy sent her south with me and my brother to recuperate. Mother hated the cold, and she loved Los Angeles. We had a darling house in Ocean Park, and we moved back and forth between Montana and California for a few years, always wintering here. Then, after my father died, we returned to California for good and moved to the little house on Delmas Terrace."

"Will you go back there now that you're going to be working in Culver City?"

She shook her head. "Not if I can help it. I'm a grown woman; I don't want to be a burden on Mother. Besides, I haven't been signed to a studio contract or anything like that. This is just one part in one film. It'll be over in a few weeks. But Johnnie Salazar told me it could work into others if I'm good enough." She paused and gave me a sideways glance, as if to gauge my reaction to her next question. "How about you? What made you leave vaudeville and come to Hollywood?"

"Well, it's kind of hard to explain. I was staying with my grandmother in San Francisco last fall, recovering from a broken leg. San Francisco is a big vaudeville town, you know, with lots of theaters, so getting a job with another act was just a matter of time. With a roof over my head and three squares a day, I could afford to wait for the right act to come along. But something in my head kept urging me to give up the stage and go to Hollywood."

"You mean you heard voices?"

I shook my head. "Not real voices. Not even real words. It wasn't like my mother talking to me or a vision. More like a thought that someone kept putting inside my head again and again. You know how it is when a piece of a song won't leave you alone for days at a time?"

"Sure."

"It was like that. I couldn't get away from Hollywood. A friend of my grandmother's would come to tea and she'd mention something about Hollywood. My grandmother's cook would say something about Hollywood. I'd open a newspaper and my eye would fall on the word 'Hollywood.'"

"That sounds kind of spooky."

"Sometimes I'd wake up in the morning thinking about Hollywood because I'd been dreaming about Hollywood all night long. I finally started asking my vaudeville friends if they had any contacts in the motion picture business. Several of them did, and that's how I heard about the job at Pickford-Fairbanks. I figured it was a sign that I was meant to go. Mary Pickford had been my inspiration for years. And once I'd made up my mind to go, the music stopped."

"Gosh. Are you glad you came?"

"Very."

"Me, too. I was telling my mother about you and—oh, I almost forgot. Mother saw the newspapers. I told her you and I had gone to Bruno Heilmann's party. She was horrified."

"Everyone's horrified," I said, showing her the afternoon paper I had picked up and giving her the latest about Paul Corrigan's and Faye Gordon's poisoning. "I expect we'll see that in tomorrow morning's papers."

The afternoon editions tucked into the mounting scandal with the enthusiasm of a hungry man at a feast. WAMPAS BABY STAR DEAD shouted one headline, followed in smaller, quieter letters, *Lorna McCall, 22, Drowns in Toilet.* SECOND MURDER SHOCKS FILM WORLD said another, and DRUG-CRAZED FILM QUEEN IS MURDER SUSPECT.

The reporters had tracked down the Hungarian maid, Magda Szabo, and pumped the poor woman for all she was worth. Evidently no one in Hollywood really knew Lorna McCall, but that only gave the reporters more room for creativity. Lorna had appeared in bit parts in a few films, landed a couple good roles and the WAMPAS Baby Star designation, and died "on the cusp of the heavens as she reached for the stars," according to one enraptured inky wretch. A few of Lorna's girlfriends provided salacious detail about her recent social life. Her family remained unknown. Obviously her name, like most Hollywood names, was a recent fabrication, and no one knew where she came from or anything else about her past. The story of her last day on earth began at Bruno Heilmann's party where she consumed massive amounts of alcohol and dope and took a dip in the fountain. The dress she wore that night was described in detail . . . except she hadn't been wearing that one when I saw her in the fountain. An anonymous tipster confided that Lorna returned later that night and shot her former lover, Bruno Heilmann. Despondent, she then swallowed a bottle of pills and passed out in the toilet where she drowned.

I could almost hear Adolph Zukor saying, "Cut! Okay, now, let's move on to the next scene."

As it happened, Esther Frankel had a brother in Fredericksburg, Texas, who hopped the first train to Los Angeles as soon as he was notified of her death. I know because Augustus Frankel telephoned me Tuesday night and said he wanted to meet me while he was in town.

"The police gave me your name, Miss Beckett," he said. "I hope I don't impose on your time, but I would so much appreciate a few moments. They say you found poor Esther and I, well, I'd like to know whatever you can tell me."

So first thing Wednesday morning I went to Esther's. I hated going back into that apartment, but I figured her brother had a right to have his questions answered, at least as far as I could answer them.

"Thank you for coming, Miss Beckett," he said, meeting me at the door with a short bow.

An odder-looking man than Augustus Frankel would be hard to invent. He was in his fifties, I guessed, with a head of thick, wild, snow-white hair that sat like a crown on top of a face crowded with bushy eyebrows and an enormous handlebar moustache, all black as soot. It would have been a great gimmick for the stage, but I knew in an instant that this man had not the slightest bit of fakery in him. A trace of a German accent lingered about his speech, and his courtly manners betrayed an old-world upbringing I always find endearing. I liked him at once.

"My sincerest condolences, Mr. Frankel. This must be a very sad time for you and your family."

"Ach, yes. Such a shock. Little Esther . . . yes, it was a shock. She was always so full of life. Please come in. I hope it doesn't distress you?"

"A little, but I'll be fine," I murmured.

The apartment showed signs of disarray. Mr. Frankel had already begun sorting through Esther's belongings.

"Please sit," he said, indicating the sofa. "May I get you some coffee?"

I declined. Coffee had lost its appeal, at least temporarily. He poured himself a cup and occupied the chair opposite me. "Please. Tell me what happened. The police have so little to say."

So I told him about the party where Esther had spotted me, how excited we both had been to connect again after all those years, and how she invited me to come over on Sunday morning. Only three days ago? It seemed like a year.

There was a knock at the door and we rose.

"Excuse us," said a man's voice. "We're the Zimmers from across the hall. We heard Esther's brother had come and wanted to pay our respects."

Mrs. Zimmer had brought a chicken dish. They stepped inside, saw me, and declined to sit. "We didn't realize you had company," she apologized. "I just thought you'd like some home cooking for dinner." They stayed a few minutes and spoke kindly of Esther until Mr. Frankel's eyes brimmed full.

"We weren't too close," he admitted with a regretful shake of his head. "We sent cards at Christmas, and once, when her act came through Austin, oh, twenty years ago it was, Mother and Father and I went to see it. We were very proud of her. I wish now I had made more effort to keep in touch, but I thought . . . well, I guess we always think there's plenty of time for such things."

"Will there be a funeral?" asked Mrs. Zimmer. It was something I had intended to ask myself.

"Yes, but just for the family, back home in Fredericksburg. Little Esther belongs at home, in the family plot, with Mama and Papa."

The Zimmers offered to help in any way they could, and then excused themselves. I picked up my story where I had left off.

"I found her in the bedroom. She'd been dead several hours. I located someone downstairs with a telephone who called the police."

"And what do you think happened?"

"At the moment, this is what I think—I think she was returning to the Heilmann kitchen with the last few ashtrays, and she saw the killer coming through the front door. He must have figured the place was empty of guests, but hadn't realized the caterers were still there. Esther probably smiled at him, maybe thinking he was a guest who had forgotten something. But he knew she had seen him, and would have been able to describe him once the murder became known. Heilmann was in the living room, looking out toward the patio, his back to the entrance hall, and evidently unaware of the man. The killer took out a gun and shot Heilmann from across the room. At least, that's what the doctor said. Even if Esther hadn't been hard of hearing, she probably wouldn't have noticed the gunshot, because I think he used a silencer. No one in the nearby houses heard it and neither did the caterers. I've never heard a silencer myself, but I'm told it has a sound of its own, nothing like the bang of a gun. Then he probably went into the kitchen to shoot Esther, but she had gone out the back. The Cisneros truck was leaving by then, so he ran back to his car, which must have been parked nearby, and followed them. There wouldn't have been many cars on the road that late at night, so following would have been pretty easy. The Cisneros brothers hadn't seen him, only Esther, so when they dropped her off here, he followed her."

"How would this evil man know what apartment Esther lived in? There are more than a dozen in this building."

I nodded. "Eighteen. And he didn't know her name so he couldn't look on the mailboxes, like I did when I came the next morning. No, he probably watched from outside to see which window lit up. That's what I would have done."

He stared for some minutes at a spot on the wall behind me before heaving a sigh. "What a terrible way to die. I hate to think of her, alone and frightened, dying like that."

"To tell you the truth, Mr. Frankel—"

"Call me Gus, please."

"To tell you the truth, Gus, I don't think she ever knew what killed her. And I don't think she suffered. From the looks of it, she was standing by her bed, looking through the playbills that she was going to show me the next day, with her back to the door. I figure she didn't hear the man break in—he had some sort of skeleton key that snapped off in the lock—and she never saw him come up behind her. I think he didn't shoot her because of the noise. Even silencers make some noise, and you may have noticed how thin the walls are in this building. And her horse statue was right there. I think he picked it up and hit her over the head, and that she never saw it coming. I don't think she suffered one second."

Another knock at the door. Another neighbor. From where I

sat, I could see her, a young woman in a plaid dress holding a hot casserole dish with quilted mitts.

"You must be Mr. Frankel. I'm so sorry for your loss. I liked Esther. We all did. Why anyone would want to kill her, I don't know. It just doesn't make sense to any of us."

Gus invited the young woman inside. He introduced me as the person who had found Esther's body.

"Oh, yes, we all know that. We all saw you on Sunday when the police came. They weren't very nice to you, were they? I wish I could have been more help. I'm sure I nearly saw the man who did it."

"Really?"

She nodded importantly. "I told the police I probably missed seeing him by minutes. You see, I was in the hall after about three o'clock in the morning, talking to my fiancé. We just got engaged"—she held out her left hand as proof—"and Steve came straight here with this ring after his boat docked. He's in the navy."

Someone needed to say something, so I did. "Congratulations."

"Thanks."

"Why were you in the hall?"

"Oh, yeah. Well, we didn't want to keep my sister and my mother up. And well, it was more private."

"The hall?"

"That time of night, there's no one around. This is a pretty quiet floor."

"So you didn't see anyone come out of this apartment?"

"We were sitting right there"—she pointed—"so we couldn't have missed him if he'd come out. But he had already sneaked off by then."

Maybe not.

"Tell me something. Did you notice the door cracked open?"

She frowned. "No, I didn't. I wasn't really looking at the door or thinking about that sort of thing, but I think I'd've noticed if

Esther's door had been open, sitting right across from it like we were, you know."

I knew. "It's just as well you didn't see him. The killer was a man who didn't want to be seen. I think Esther saw him and that's what cost her her life."

"Gosh, you're right. I didn't think of that. It's scary living next to a murdered person."

"I don't think you have anything to worry about," I reassured her. "You didn't see anyone, and the killer is probably far away by now."

"Well, Mr. Frankel, I hope you enjoy the goulash, and just leave the dish beside the door across the hall whenever you're done with it. Mother will be over as soon as she gets home from work, to tell you how much we . . . well, you know. We're all pretty shocked, I don't mind telling you."

21

The mortal remains of Bruno S. Heilmann were laid to rest at the Hollywood Memorial Park Cemetery on Wednesday afternoon, April 15, 1925. A garden of funerary sprays and floral wreaths ringed the gravesite, and a flowery obituary appeared in the *Times*. Anticipating a large turnout of mourners and reporters, police cordoned off the area to keep the latter from pestering the former. Officers Delaney and Brickles were among those on duty, minding the reporters' manners. Carl Delaney gave a nod when he saw me.

"Myrna," I began softly. "I have an acting job for you. See that policeman by the rope?"

"The handsome one?"

"No, the older one. I need you to distract him for a moment while I speak to his partner. Ask him how the investigation is going. Act young and scared."

"That shouldn't be hard."

If I ever had doubts about Myrna making it in the pictures, they would have evaporated with her show that morning. Her lower lip trembling, she engaged Officer Brickles with a masterful performance, planting herself so he had to turn away from me to face her. I don't know what she was saying, but it did the trick.

"Good morning, Officer Delaney," I said, my back toward Brickles.

He touched his cap. "Miss Beckett."

"Getting any closer to finding the murderer?"

"I think so," he said cautiously. "Good news is there haven't been any more murders in the last twenty-four hours. Bad news is the newspapers' War of Words is scaring folks. We're flooded with calls about suspicious characters sneaking through the shrubbery."

"The papers are full of suspects."

"That's because reporters have nothing else to do but speculate. No one will talk to them. We have orders not to say anything. Same is true for the movie people."

I nodded. He was right; the studio bosses had threatened to fire anyone who spoke to the newspapers. With no reputable sources, reporters were going wild turning fantasy into fact.

"You, on the other hand, are likely to get a visit soon from your favorite detectives."

"Oh?"

"Your fingerprints were found all over Miss Frankel's apartment, specifically her desk. After you told us you hadn't touched anything."

I had been ready for that one ever since I'd been arrested and fingerprinted. I had lied with confidence at the time because I knew my fingerprints weren't on file, so there would be no match for the prints found on Esther's desk. Once that comforting anonymity was lost, I figured someone would match me up eventually and notice the discrepancy between what I had said and what I had done.

"I guess I forgot about looking for a telephone. It was after I found Esther. I did a quick look around the apartment, thinking she might have a telephone—"

"You searched her desk?"

"Some people keep telephones in their desks."

"Really?"

This wasn't going the way I'd planned. "Yes, really." It was quite adept as explanations went, and his skepticism offended me. Carl didn't reply, he just gazed steadily at me with those big brown eyes that looked like they could see a long way into things, past the surface and into the underneath parts, letting me know he knew I was lying. Affronted, I excused myself and moved away without picking up anything useful.

Myrna cut her scene and joined me.

"Thanks," I said.

"Nothing to it. Look around. There are more reporters than mourners."

"Well, we're early . . ."

I spotted Lottie Pickford near the coffin. She had hidden her face behind a dramatic black veil, but her theatrical gestures gave her away, at least to those who knew her. Mary Pickford was beside her. She hadn't come out of love for Heilmann, but for her sister. Like Lottie, she wore an ankle-length black dress and a hat with a net veil, and like Lottie, she wasn't fooling anyone. Her size would always give her away.

A few men stood near the two women. One was David Carr, looking impossibly handsome in a severe black suit of excellent cut. On the other side of Miss Pickford stood a man as tall as David and every bit as handsome, but twice his age, with short, dark hair flecked with gray, thin lips, and steely eyes. With a jolt, I realized it had to be Adolph Zukor, Heilmann's employer and the most powerful businessman in Hollywood. I had never seen him, but I had heard that Mary Pickford used to work for him when she first came to Hollywood, and, while they had their professional differences, they remained close personally. The third man hung back a little from the Pickfords, his eyes continually moving over the mourners and the larger group of reporters. The bodyguard.

My black dress had been too heavy for the warm day, so I wore a dark purple skirt with matching vest and jacket, a black hat, plain Mary Janes, and black gloves. Myrna and I moved a little to the side to take advantage of the shade of an old tree. The silence was such that we could hear the steady drone of bees attracted to the floral arrangements all around the gravesite. A young minister arrived in a black sedan and began shaking hands with the mourners. Probably looking for family members.

"The crowd looks very, very thin," whispered Myrna.

"Douglas Fairbanks said Bruno Heilmann had no relatives in this country other than a stable of ex-wives, and not a lot of friends."

"Hollywood friends," she scoffed. "The sort who come to your parties but not your funeral."

"To be fair, some of the people who were at his party Saturday have left town out of fear. They're thinking some madman is on a killing spree, trying to eliminate anyone who saw him. After what happened yesterday morning at Paramount, I can't say as I blame them."

"You and I didn't run away."

"We aren't in any danger. We left the party early."

"Thank goodness for that! Hey, look. There's my friend Coop." She pointed as the tall young actor joined the group at the gravesite.

Out of the corner of my eye, I saw David detach himself from the Pickfords and amble toward our shade. "Hello, ladies," he said in a quiet voice, flashing his teeth at Myrna before turning to me for an introduction. After a polite exchange, he divulged his news. "The latest word on Faye Gordon is encouraging. She's going to survive. One of the doctors from the hospital just told the Pickfords that Faye drank only a little of the poisoned coffee. He thought she'd be released soon."

"I suppose she is swamped with flowers and well-wishers," I said, trying to think of a way I could talk with her. But having attended the same dinner party didn't make me a friend. "I wonder if she had any information for the police that would help their investigation."

"The police have questioned her, of course, but she isn't seeing visitors. Even Mary Pickford was turned away at the hospital. Seems Faye doesn't want anyone to see her without her hair arranged and her makeup fresh. You know what they say: no one in Hollywood has birthday parties."

"Oh, that's silly," said Myrna.

"Not if you're worried about the wrinkles showing. Mary understood," continued David. "She sent her own maid over to the hospital with her own makeup kit so Faye could look her best when she is discharged tomorrow. You know there will be a crowd of photographers waiting for her, and one unglamorous picture can sink a career."

"How thoughtful of Miss Pickford," I said, wondering whether I had the effrontery to call on Faye at her home with some flowers or a casserole. I could always say I was there on behalf of Pickford-Fairbanks Studio. It was somewhat true.

"I hope the police are close to catching the killer," said Myrna. "Who could do such monstrous things? It's awful knowing that someone at that party—someone I might have talked to—is a murderer." She punched her palm with her fist. "They've just *got* to catch him!"

"And quickly," agreed David. "Before he gets to anyone else."

"I've been thinking . . ." I began. "What if the killer isn't someone we know? What if he wasn't a guest at the party?"

David looked at me sharply. "What do you mean? You think it was someone hiding outside until everyone had gone home?"

"Possibly. But here's what's bothering me. No one heard the gunshot. The police asked the neighbors and no one heard a thing."

"They were all probably asleep," said Myrna.

"The Cisneros brothers weren't asleep. They were outside behind the house, loading up the catering truck when Esther joined them. She had to have left the house just about when the killer fired the gun, yet she didn't say anything to them about hearing a gunshot. Of course, she was hard of hearing, but when I asked the Cisneroses about it, they'd heard nothing, either."

"Maybe they drove away and then the shot was fired," said Myrna.

I shook my head. "Possible, but not likely. If the killer had waited until after the truck left to fire, he wouldn't have had time to get to his car and follow them. And another thing. The killer shot Bruno once in the back of the head, and from a distance—I had this from Carl Delaney, that officer, over there. I keep thinking about that: one long-distance shot. That no one heard." I looked pointedly at David.

He followed my thoughts. "You think the killer used a silencer."

"And that he was a crack shot. Put those together and what do you have?"

"A torpedo."

"A what?" asked Myrna.

"A hired killer," explained David. "A paid professional. The sort who would carry a Maxim silencer. Those things don't really silence, you know. There's still a sharp noise, but it doesn't carry very far." The voice of experience.

"So some jilted girl or angry husband hired a killer?" asked Myrna.

"That's possible," I said. "Shhh. The service is starting."

I put my hand on David's arm to hold him back as Myrna

moved toward the tent. "There's something else," I whispered, "but I don't want to worry Myrna about it."

"After the service," he replied.

The minister opened his prayer book. "I am the resurrection and the life, saith the Lord: he that believeth in me, though he were dead, yet shall he live."

22

inisters are fine people to have at funerals. They can come up with nice things to say about anybody. The good reverend earned his pay that day, waxing eloquent on the noble life of a man he had never met, a man who, by all accounts, had done nothing more laudable than to create some first-quality pictures. A thin legacy, in my book. My gaze wandered from face to face, finding few that looked familiar. The majority of the mourners were the actors and cameramen who had been working with Heilmann on his last picture, a picture that was now stalled until Zukor could find a director with an undersized ego who would agree to finish another man's work. A tall order.

After twenty minutes, a splendid coffin bearing the remains of Bruno Heilmann was lowered into the ground with ropes, and the minister threw in the first handful of earth. Some of the more publicity-hungry mourners went over to the reporters to offer quotations for tomorrow's papers. The photographers fiddled with their flashes, waiting for the police to allow them access to the gravesite. Adolph Zukor escorted the Pickford ladies to their Rolls-Royce. When I saw Myrna engaged in conversation with her hometown friend, Gary Cooper, I seized the opportunity to pull David aside. I needed an expert.

"Look here, David. What if the motive wasn't jealousy or revenge, like the police think, but dope? I saw some at his house. In an upstairs bedroom."

"What sort?"

"I think it was mostly heroin and morphine, maybe some cocaine, too."

"So what? All the parties around here serve dope."

"But there was a lot of it. Drawers full. Big bundles, wrapped in blue paper. More than you would need for a hundred parties. And Douglas mentioned once that he thought Bruno was supplying Wallace Reid. You remember him?"

"The actor? Sure, I saw a few of his flicks. He died a couple years ago. It was in all the papers. Morphine, wasn't it? Everyone was shocked to learn handsome Wallace Reid was a hophead."

"What if Bruno's death involved dope? What if some hired gangster killed him for that?"

"Sounds likely. I'm sure the police are investigating all leads."

I winced. "No they're not. They don't know about the blue packages in the guest room. I asked Carl Delaney yesterday and he said there was nothing in the report about packages of dope, just that there were some traces around the house."

"So let me get this straight. You think a hired killer shot Heilmann with a silencer, searched the house, found the dope, took it, then followed the caterers to your friend's house and killed her?"

"No, the killer didn't take anything. He may have meant to,

but he wouldn't have had time to search once Esther had seen his face. He had to shoot and leave fast to follow her home."

"Maybe he came back after he'd killed Esther."

"I'm sure he didn't. A neighbor saw him leave Esther's, and it wasn't until the next morning. And he went straight to the train station."

"Then why didn't the police find the dope the next morning when they found the body?"

"The policemen who came first to the house didn't do a thorough search, you know, for fingerprints and traces of drugs and clues like that. Nowadays, they divide up the work and evidently that's a detective's job. I learned that from Esther's death. Two detectives came by Heilmann's later and searched the whole house, took fingerprints, that sort of thing. I think they found it—"

"And kept it for themselves. Happens all the time. That's why it didn't make the official police report. And so the investigators don't know to look for a torpedo."

"Right."

"One thing I don't get. What makes you so sure the stuff was found by the detectives and not by the policemen who got there first?"

I'll say one thing for David—he isn't slow-witted.

"That's a little hard to explain."

"Try me."

"I, well, I went into the house after the cops had left so I could . . . well, to get some things from upstairs that belonged to Lottie, so the police wouldn't find them, so they wouldn't link Bruno's murder to Lottie. Because, really, Lottie didn't do it. I'm certain of that. The detectives hadn't arrived yet, and the body was still downstairs. I wasn't looking for dope; I was checking quickly in each bedroom to make sure Lottie hadn't left anything there, and that's when I saw it. I have no idea how much. There were drawers full of the stuff, pounds and pounds of it."

"You broke in?"

"Well, I didn't actually *break* anything . . ."

"I can't believe the cops left the house unlocked!"

"They didn't. They just left the second-story windows open, and I climbed up a tree next to a rear window."

"There were no guards?" he asked incredulously.

"One, but he stayed out front."

"Jesus Christ! You did that for Lot— No, of course not. You did it for Doug and Mary." He was quiet for a while and I waited. Suddenly he chuckled. "Sure would be fun to let the police chief know about this and watch a couple detectives twist in the wind, but . . ." He sighed. "Hell, for all you know, the chief's in on it, too, and they'd cover it up. You'd get worse than they would. In fact, you'd be in serious danger, knowing what you know. Nope, there's nothing you can do but keep your mouth shut."

Except find the killer myself. I was the only one who knew where to look.

"There's more. On Sunday afternoon, outside Esther's apartment, the police asked bystanders if they saw anything suspicious during the night. One old man said he saw a stranger with a droopy mouth come out of the building around six, when he let his dog out. The cops weren't interested since Esther was killed in the middle of the night, not in the morning, and murderers don't typically hang around after killing someone. But it struck me as odd that no one in the crowd commented on the old man's remark." David looked puzzled, so I explained. "There were quite a few people gathered around, maybe three dozen, and when the old man described a stranger with a droopy mouth, no one said, 'Oh, that's just Hank,' or anything like that. It seems to me that a man with a droopy mouth is pretty memorable, and that someone living on the block would have known if a man with a droopy mouth lived around there and would have spoken up. But no one did."

"So the stranger with the droopy mouth was the killer?"

"I have reason to believe he did stay at Esther's after he killed her. And I think he took the early Chicagoan out of Los Angeles on Sunday morning."

"So he wasn't from these parts. But that's a long ride, almost three days. The train must make dozens of stops. Too bad you don't know where he got off."

"But I do know. I have a vaudeville friend playing Chicago, and I sent her a telegram asking her to meet that train when it arrived yesterday evening, and she saw a man with a droopy mouth get off."

He whistled again. "Have you told this to anyone?"

"I'm not sure who to tell, considering which detectives are handling the investigation. I don't know how high the corruption goes. Besides, it only recently fell into place, and there's still a lot I don't know."

"Such as, if that's the killer and he left town on Sunday morning, who killed Lorna McCall on Sunday afternoon and poisoned Paul Corrigan and Faye Gordon on Tuesday?"

"I'm not sure about that. Not yet. But it definitely wasn't the hired killer from Chicago. Even forgetting everything I've told you, think about the odds of a stranger getting through Paramount's gate unnoticed. If one did somehow talk his way past the guard, he'd have been logged in and remembered."

"So there are two murderers?"

"Maybe even three. There are really no similarities between the ways these people died. Nothing links them except Heilmann's party."

David left the cemetery with the Pickfords so I rejoined Myrna, who had taken refuge from the sun under a large oak tree where she was exchanging opinions on the murders with her Montana friend, Gary Cooper.

". . . that's when Jessie and I helped the police draw up their list of party guests," she was saying as I approached. Gary acknowledged me with a half-smile that dimpled one cheek as Myrna continued talking. "Have they questioned you yet?"

"Hello, Jessie." His voice was deep and rich. "Yes, Myrna, I had a visit from our boys in blue, asking me what time I left and who else was with me."

"We left early," Myrna said proudly, as if she and I had possessed the foresight to exit the stage before the final, deadly act.

"I'm afraid I stayed almost to the end. I didn't realize it at the time, but now I think I probably saw the murderer. I'm probably the only person still alive who did."

"What!" I exclaimed too loudly.

Coop would not be rushed. He looked around to make sure no one was within listening distance and nodded deliberately, relishing the story. "I was among a group of ten or so who left some time before two. That's what I told the police anyway. And it's true, as far as it goes. The others will vouch for it. But once we got near Hollywood Boulevard, everyone split up, a few to this or that club, a few home. I was trying to decide which way to go when I realized my hat didn't fit."

"You had the wrong hat?" Myrna asked.

"I should have noticed when that butler handed it to me, but, well, I'd had a bit to drink and wasn't paying attention. But I realized right there on the street corner that my hat was too big, practically on my ears."

"No one else noticed?"

"Let's just say they all had a little too much to drink, too. Anyway, I turned around and walked back to Heilmann's, hoping I could swap for the right hat. It was borrowed and I'd have to buy my friend a new one if I couldn't return his. But when I got to Heilmann's, the party was over. I'm a little fuzzy on the details, but I remember seeing a man leave by the front door."

"The killer?" asked Myrna.

"I think so."

"How do you know?"

"Well, he sure as thunderation wasn't a guest. He wasn't wearing a dinner jacket."

"What did he look like?" I asked, trying to sound casual.

"From where I was standing by that fish fountain, I couldn't make out any details. All I saw was a man wearing a business suit. He moved fast around to the back of the house where a truck was pulling out, and he jumped in a car and took off after the truck. I figured him for one of the staff, and when I noticed how quiet the house was, I realized the party was over and I wasn't going to swap hats then. So I headed home."

"Did you tell this to the police?"

"Nope. And I don't plan to. You know what they'll think."

I certainly did. If the police knew he was the last person to leave the party, he'd be their prime suspect.

Gary continued. "It's not like I'm holding back some important clue that would help solve Heilmann's murder. I wouldn't do that. But I can't describe the man."

Myrna reassured him that he'd done no harm to the investigation, then her hand flew to her mouth. "Oh, my gosh! Did the killer see you? He might think you could identify him and you'd be in danger, too!"

"I thought about that, but no, I don't think he knew I was there. It was too dark and the fountain was too far from the house."

"I don't think the killer is anywhere near Hollywood at this moment," I said. "There's good evidence that he left the state some time ago."

What Gary Cooper had seen contributed no new information, but it did confirm my theory about the killer following the Cisneros truck to Esther's apartment building. Evidently Droopy Mouth had parked behind Heilmann's near the service road while he waited for the guests to leave. No doubt he'd watched the Cisneros brothers packing up and assumed all the caterers were there by the truck, ready to leave. He hadn't counted on

Esther still being in the house. I sighed. It had been such a close call. If only Esther had walked out of the house one minute earlier, she wouldn't have been in a position to see him as he came in the front door and she would be alive today. The futility of it made me want to cry.

23

The cold clank of steel on steel greeted me as I approached Douglas Fairbanks's private gymnasium, located in the main building alongside his saltwater plunge pool, dressing room, and office. Inside the gym, he was practicing with his fencing master, Henry Uyttenhove, a Belgian import I had heard about but never met. An assistant pointed me to a wooden bench against the wall and, as the two men lunged, parried, attacked, and retreated, I settled down to wait for the lesson to end.

Douglas had no intention of waiting. "Ah, Jessie. At last," he said, without taking his eyes off his opponent for one second. "How was the funeral?"

"Heavy on reporters, light on mourners."

"Ha!" With his left hand raised behind him and his right leg leading, he executed three sharp steps forward and followed them with a thrust that lifted his teacher's foil out of his hand

and sent it sailing high above them both. With an ease that comes only from practice, he caught its handle with his own blade and slung it back to Uyttenhove with an exaggerated bow. It was only then that I realized this wasn't a lesson—it was a rehearsal for a particular fight scene. He was practicing the same way I would have practiced a vaudeville dance routine, over and over, until the intricate steps could be executed in one's sleep. Only then could the spontaneity be added. I watched in amazement as the two men worked the routine again, forgetting for a moment why I had come.

"Again," he said, and they resumed their *en garde* positions. "Go ahead with the details, Jessie."

"Faye Gordon's doctor was there," I said, jerking my attention back to the reason I was there. "He said she would probably be released in a day or two. Fortunately she hadn't swallowed enough of the poisoned coffee to kill her."

"I'm sure Mary was pleased to hear that. She's known Faye for years." He ducked a high sweeping stroke and leaped over the low one that followed, spun around, and tossed his sword from one hand to the other. Evidently it wasn't up to snuff. "Again," he said to Uyttenhove, and they repeated the dance. And to me, "Anything more?"

It wasn't the time to tell him of my other suspicions. "Only . . . well, I was wondering about Lorna McCall. I've asked around and no one seems to know much about her."

"She was a WAMPAS Baby Star."

"And she had some good parts. But that's all anyone knows about her. She doesn't seem to have had any family. A friend in the police department said her body is still in the morgue, unclaimed."

"I can hear an idea in your head, Jessie." He lunged, his back leg straight behind him as he leaned into the attack. Uyttenhove parried and gave ground.

"I just find it odd that Lorna's death didn't cause anyone to step forward. I wonder about her. Was she really killed as a result of that party, or was there something else?"

"Like a jealous lover, you mean? Hmm. It's possible. As for her family, they probably don't know about her death yet. Although it's been widely reported, Lorna McCall is undoubtedly a stage name."

"But the photograph in the newspapers—"

"Doesn't necessarily resemble some young girl from some small town in some Midwestern state several years ago."

I had to admit he was right. I thought a bit as the two men clashed. Gus Frankel popped into my mind. That gave me an idea. "I thought I might go over to Lorna's apartment and ask a few questions."

At that, he came to a complete stop and looked sternly at me, pointing with his foil for emphasis. "Listen here, young lady. Whoever killed Lorna McCall isn't going to take kindly to you rummaging around in her life, looking for clues. You be careful about who you talk to and what you say. And don't use your real name."

Douglas Fairbanks wasn't quite old enough to be my father, but his fatherly concern sure felt good.

F uneral clothes wouldn't do for the part I was about to play, so I returned home to change into my traveling suit, a sleek blue outfit with a matching hat and chamois gloves that were left over from the heiress gig last year, and then set out to find Lorna McCall's apartment. The newspapers had reported the address, and it wasn't but a mile from where I lived, so I walked out my front door—and smack into David Carr coming up the steps.

"What are you doing here?"

"I ran into Doug, who mentioned you were off investigating something, and I didn't have anything to do this afternoon so I—"

"I don't need a nursemaid, David."

"Don't get your back up, Miss Priss. Doug didn't suggest

anything of the kind. I just thought you might like company. I'm a swell guy to have around. And I make a fine chauffeur."

"I was planning to walk."

He fell in step beside me as I reached the sidewalk. "Good idea. I could use some exercise. Where are we headed?"

I gave in without further struggle. It would be nice to have the company as long as he didn't get in the way, and I was quite sure David, of all people, could handle himself in less-than-honest circumstances. And another set of eyes wouldn't hurt.

"I'm going to visit Lorna McCall's apartment."

"You don't look dressed for a break-in."

"This time I'm not going in through a rear window. I plan to talk my way in."

"What are you looking for?"

"I'm not sure. I'm hoping to learn something—anything—about her."

"She was a WAMPAS Baby Star."

I rolled my eyes. "If I hear that one more time, I'll scream. The problem is, no one has much else to say about her."

"Well, she was known to be . . . um . . . free with her favors . . . not that I would know anything about that."

"I've heard that, too. But she seems to have no past. No family. No hometown."

"She must have had friends."

"'Hollywood friends,' as Myrna calls them. The police talked with several young actresses who palled around in Lorna's set and a few of the men she'd known, but none of them recollected hearing her mention a hometown or any family. Seemed like she was born in Hollywood a couple years ago."

"And what would her past tell you, if you could discover it?"

"Why someone wanted to kill her. Whether her death was linked to the others. Or maybe nothing at all."

"What's the address?"

I told him.

"Good, we have plenty of time to discuss your game."

"I'm Lorna's older sister from Topeka. You can be our brother." He hadn't changed out of his suit since the funeral, so he was suitably dressed for the part of a man just off the train.

"I've been your brother before. It wasn't much fun. I'll be your husband this time. More possibilities."

"Nothing doing, I'm—"

"Besides, we don't look much alike. And neither of us looks like Lorna. I met her. She didn't have any freckles or your coloring. If I'm your husband, it doesn't matter about my looks, and you can always say you're half sister to Lorna if it comes to a challenge."

He had a point. But that word—husband—was sticking at me, pushing images into my head that were hard to shove out.

Fifteen minutes later we arrived at the address of the late Lorna McCall, a cozy cluster of two-story buildings shaded with flowering bushes and overarching trees that lent privacy and a look of self-satisfied prosperity to the complex.

"Lorna was young to have been this successful," remarked David approvingly.

Without much effort, we located the manager, a suspicious, hawk-nosed female with dark hair braided and wrapped around the side of her head like earmuffs. She gave me the silent hat-to-toe treatment when I introduced myself.

"I'm Lorna McCall's sister from Topeka, Kansas." I clutched a hanky in my hand in case I should burst into tears. "The police notified me about Lorna's . . . Lorna's horrible . . . death," I choked, "and, well, we came as soon as we could." Unmoved at the sight of my affliction, she turned her stare to David. "And this is my husband, David."

David whipped the hat off his head, put his arm around my shoulders, and gave me a husbandly squeeze. "Pleased to meet you, ma'am. And you would be?"

"Mrs. Patterson."

"Pleased to meet you, Mrs. Patterson. I hope we haven't come at an inconvenient moment, ma'am, but time presses on us cruelly. We have to leave your lovely town tomorrow to get home to our two babies. Meanwhile, we set aside this afternoon to have a look through Lorna's apartment, and if you would be so kind as to show us the way, we'll be out of your hair."

Now I'm usually pretty quick on the uptake, as you might expect after a lifetime coping with stage catastrophes. I've improvised my way through a theater curtain catching fire, a drunk barging into our act, Darcy Darling throwing up in the middle of a song, magic tricks that went amiss, and a minor earthquake, but for some reason, David rattled my composure. I could only blanch at the talk of babies—that certainly wasn't in my script. And I didn't like losing control of the script.

But it melted dour old Mrs. Patterson. David's endearing smile was worth the price of admission, and that farmboy manner of his would charm a snake. Producing a skeleton key from her pocket, the woman led the way to the rear of the complex and up the stairs.

"The police told me that no one saw any visitors to Lorna's on Sunday. I thought that mighty odd, but now I understand. With all these bushes, someone could come and go without being noticed."

She nodded. "Over there's the passageway to the parking lot, so a body could come through there, walk along here, and go upstairs without another soul laying eyes on him. We've always felt the privacy was an asset, but now some of the residents are wondering if we shouldn't cut back the shrubbery."

She unlocked the door and stood aside as David took my hand and led me in. "Take your time," she said. "Come get me when you leave. If you need boxes, I have a few."

I burst into tears.

"Excuse my wife, Mrs. Patterson. This has been hard on her.

She's normally not so emotional but what with Lorna's death and the new baby on the way, well . . ."

The what?

"I understand completely," she said, closing the door as she left us.

"You do that crying stuff pretty well," said David. "I'll have to remember that."

I rounded on him. "Dammit, David, what was that 'our babies' stuff? And I don't look pregnant!"

He shrugged. "I just thought it up. Kinda liked the way it sounded." He smiled disarmingly. I felt like clobbering him with my handbag but he moved out of range and flicked on an overhead light. "Let's get to work. What exactly are we looking for?"

Curbing my exasperation, I told him. "Any clue to Lorna's real name or family. You start in here." I indicated the living room and adjacent dining room with a sweep of my hand. Lorna had lived in fine style. The jade-green color of the sculpted Chinese rugs repeated in the drapes and in the scatter pillows on the white upholstery, giving an impression of cool sophistication that was marred only by the wilted flowers and drooping greenery. The apartment was scrupulously clean, but I suspected no one had been in here since the day of her death. "The detectives have been over the place, but I was told that the only thing they found was a bank book. Maybe we'll be luckier. Look through her desk for letters. Check any books to see if she wrote her name in them, or if there is an inscription, like 'To Betsy from Mother.' Go through the closet for names in her coats or hats and scraps of paper in her pockets. See if there are any keys with tags or grips with travel labels on them. I'll do the same in the bedroom."

Lorna had liked green. Her bedroom suite was done in a cool lime with yellow and orange accents that reminded me of the citrus groves that made this part of California famous. Everything was in pristine condition, seemingly new and untouched. Sterile. It gave me the creeps.

I rifled through a closet full of expensive clothes, drawers packed with lacey unmentionables, and a vanity, learning only that Lorna McCall had never felt the need, as Lottie did, to mark her stuff with her initials. On her bedside table sat an alarm clock, a pair of glittery earrings, and a glass of water. I went through the cabinets in the bathroom where she had drowned, hoping to find an old prescription bottle with her real name on it. Lots of pills, no names.

"Any luck?" David leaned against the doorjamb with his hands in his pockets.

I sighed and shook my head. "You?"

"A few recent postcards. I laid them on the desk for you. The usual bills. I checked the kitchen, too. Threw out all the spoiled stuff in the icebox and emptied the drip pan."

"All right, I'm done in here. Now let's switch and see if either of us missed anything."

Twenty minutes' searching confirmed what I already knew about David Carr—he was a man who missed very little. I found nothing in the living room, dining room, or kitchen that hinted of Lorna's personality, let alone told me anything about her past or her real name.

Dejected, I stood in the center of the living room and made a slow circle. No framed photographs on the walls, no snapshots on the bookshelves. No books on the bookshelves, for that matter, and no magazines or newspapers . . . seems our Lorna wasn't a reader. A few china knickknacks that looked new. A green glass bowl that might have been a gift. A silver cigarette holder full of Chesterfields. Mirrors on the walls where others would have hung paintings. More stage set than home. In fact, I'd seen hotel rooms with more personality. *Where in this soulless room was Lorna?* It was almost as if she had deliberately erased her past from her present.

I closed my eyes and listened hard, trying to absorb what the

room was saying. Little by little, I drew the room inside me, trying to picture Lorna at the table, on the sofa, in the bedroom,
trying to soak up the emotions Lorna had left behind. The clues
were there, tucked in the edges of awareness, hiding in the shadows. *Come out, come out, wherever you are. Ollie ollie oxen free!*

That's when I realized that the absence of information *was*
the clue. In fact, I knew more about the girl who called herself
Lorna McCall than anyone in Hollywood.

I opened my eyes to find David watching me from the doorway to the bedroom, his head cocked to one side, standing still as
stone. As I blinked back into myself, he came forward. "Where've
you been?" he asked gently.

"I was . . . thinking."

"For almost ten minutes."

"Was it that long? Seemed like a few seconds. Did you find
anything in her bedroom?"

"Nope. How 'bout you?"

"Yes . . . that is, no, but I know now why no one knew much
about Lorna. She had run away from home and was making sure
no one would ever find her. She suffered horribly growing up—
beatings, rape, violence, maybe all of those. She didn't have much
education, but she was uncommonly pretty, and that was her
ticket out. She took nothing with her when she left except
whatever money she could get her hands on and worked her way
to Hollywood where her looks could buy her a new life. Liquor
and dope dulled the memories. Sex bought affection." I looked
around the sterile room once again.

"Did you get all this out of some sort of vision?"

I shook my head. "It wasn't a vision. I just *understood*. I've
known a few girls like Lorna in vaudeville and burlesque. Mostly
burlesque. And there are more working in every brothel in every
town. Their stories are much of a sameness."

"What, now?"

"Now? Now we leave. There's nothing else to learn here. No one's going to trace Lorna's background, not now, not ever. She made sure of that."

An hour later, I was back at the studio taking notes on a scene that had just been completed. Frank kept us working late that night on an indoor sequence. I got home hungry and tired, made myself a tomato sandwich for supper, and went straight to bed. That night I dreamed I was an actress playing opposite Rudolph Valentino in *Cobra,* and when we paused between takes, Henabery's script girl was bringing me a second cup of coffee.

25

D on't be nervous; you'll do fine," I assured Myrna at the breakfast table the following morning. "Have some Cream of Wheat. You'll need something on your stomach."

"You sound like my mom."

"Mother knows best. It may be a long while before they let you break for lunch. I am surprised, by the way, that the filming started so quickly."

"Actually, they started a week ago, before the Io part had been cast. Geez, I hope I'm good enough. . . ."

"You're talented, agreeable, and hardworking. Trust me, they'll like you. There are so many prima donnas out there—so many like Lottie Pickford—that a girl like you will be a pleasure to work with."

"You think so? What's Lottie do that irritates people so much?"

I sighed. Where to start? "For one thing, she's often late, and that's inexcusable. Anyone else would be fired, but a Pickford? Untouchable. So don't be late. Allow some extra time in the mornings in case the buses are delayed. And she drinks so much she's usually hungover the next day, so she constantly has to take breaks for headache powders, coffee, water, bathroom visits, and so forth. And she thinks she knows more than the professionals and quarrels with them about how her costumes look, how she should be made up, how she should be lighted, and which camera angles are best."

"I wouldn't dare argue with those people. I don't know anything."

"You'll do great. I can't wait to hear about it when you get home tonight."

I wasn't following my own advice that morning about arriving late to work. I took last night's dream for a warning and decided to make a stop at Paramount Studios before reporting to my own set. If I left the house early enough, I could get to Paramount, see Henabery's script girl, and arrive only a little tardy at Pickford-Fairbanks. I knew Douglas had told Frank Richardson and Pauline Cox that I would be doing some work for him during the day, and neither one had said a word to me about my frequent absences, but I didn't want to seem to take advantage of the situation.

Two guards were working Paramount's main gate, and a short line had formed. When my turn came, I gave my name and asked to see Sylvie Baxter for a few moments. The guard spoke on the telephone and told me to wait. Miss Baxter was on her way.

She strode up a short time later, dressed in a chic brown suit with a mannish cut, her clipboard under one arm and a pencil behind her ear. She remembered me from Tuesday morning.

"What can I do for you, Miss Beckett?" Her voice was short, not curt, but all business—a far cry from the weepy young woman I'd seen after the poisonings. Her polite tone of voice clearly indicated she had no time to waste. I made a mental note to cultivate that manner in the future. It seemed admirably professional.

"It's Jessie, please. Thank you for seeing me. I'm grateful for your time and won't take much of it. Douglas Fairbanks sent me to ask you a few questions about the poisoned coffee. When I saw you on Tuesday, you said that you were on your way to get a second cup of coffee for Mr. Valentino."

If she was surprised at my mission, her face didn't show it. No doubt she had long since ceased to wonder at the unusual demands stars and directors made on their underlings. "That's correct."

"Had you brought him his first cup?"

"No."

"Do you know when he had his first cup?"

"No." She thought a moment, and added, "But it was at least an hour before that, since we had been filming without a break for that long."

"I see. Did Paul Corrigan have a part in *Cobra?*"

"No."

"In any Paramount picture?"

"No."

"What was he doing here?"

"Someone told the police he had come to pay a call on Faye Gordon in her dressing room. He had been logged in a half hour earlier."

Considering that Paul Corrigan had spent hours the previous night in her company, the early-morning visit seemed peculiar. He and Faye had barely spoken at Pickfair ... in truth, Paul hadn't spoken to anyone after his sudden freeze at the dinner table. He had shared a sofa with me during the film, and when I made an attempt at polite conversation, he was so lost in thought, he didn't hear a word I said. He must have remembered something urgent to tell Faye, something that came to him after the dinner party was over.

"Do you know anyone else in the studio who had coffee after Mr. Valentino?"

She shook her head. "The police asked us that, too. I don't think there was a satisfactory answer. They asked everyone to remember what time they had coffee. No one remembered. I had coffee, but I couldn't tell you what time. We were very busy, as always. It isn't something you think about, normally."

"But only people working on the *Cobra* set would have been helping themselves to that pot of coffee?"

"Not necessarily. Anyone passing through, a grip from another film or a secretary from the office, would have been welcome to help themselves. It's impossible to say."

And anyone passing through could have poisoned the coffeepot.

I returned to Pickford-Fairbanks, swapping the outdoor fragrance of pepper tree perfume for the studio scents of fresh-cut wood and wet paint, and reported to the *Son of Zorro* office. A glance at the schedule told me we'd be working that morning on a simple scene that was set in Don Q's chambers with his two loyal servants, Robledo and Lola. I hurried to the correct set, where I saw Charles Stevens, the actor playing Robledo, talking with the director. Charles was already dressed in his doublet and trousers. The dismay on his face was as plain as his makeup.

". . . so sorry, but we'll have to postpone it," Frank Richardson was saying. "I'm going back to the cantina since it's already set up next door." Catching a glimpse of me, he said, "Jessie will telephone you if we can shoot your scene tomorrow."

Charles threw me a furious look I knew wasn't meant for me. "Sorry, Charles," I sympathized as I whipped out my notepad and jotted down his number, Madison-0799.

"Yeah, yeah, me, too. Just shoot me if I ever accept a part in another film with Lottie Pickford."

"Lottie?"

"Didn't you hear what Frank said? You must have come in

after he made the announcement. Lottie is sick today." He mimicked her voice. *"I'm just too sick to come in, Fraaaank.* Sick, my
eye. Hangover's more like it. That dame would be a lot healthier
if she'd quit boozing all night long!" And he muttered his way to
the dressing room.

When I caught up with Frank, he and Douglas Fairbanks
were engaged in earnest conversation. I hovered at the edge of
the stage so as not to interrupt, but Douglas saw me and motioned
me over.

"Lottie's not coming in today," he began. "Her nerves are
shot. The police have settled on her as their prime suspect for
Heilmann's murder. They visited her last night, asking questions.
Mary and I weren't there, but I imagine her responses were less
than helpful, considering her state."

I took a deep breath, my mind racing. "Did they arrest her?"

He shook his head. "I am amazed that they didn't. They merely
told her to stay in town."

"Then they are suspicious but have no real proof. What evidence do they have? Did they say?"

"According to Lottie, who is admittedly not the most reliable
source, she was entertaining at her own house when the police
arrived. Evidently they heard from a number of people that
Lottie had been drunk Saturday night, and that she threw a
temper tantrum and threatened to kill Heilmann. Some of the
last to leave reported that he threw her bodily out the door
when she refused to go home."

"That's not much evidence," said Frank.

"They found a cigarette case on Heilmann's night table. Solid
gold, engraved with something blatant like 'All my love forever,
Lottie,' and their initials entwined. Someone tipped off the
police about their affair and said that Bruno had cut it off. And
someone else told them Bruno had been sleeping with Lorna
McCall, too."

Drat that cigarette case! If only I hadn't missed it. I threw

Douglas an apologetic glance. I hoped he wasn't too put out at my failure.

"Other women have been cast off," I said in Lottie's defense.

"Very true. I can mention several without even thinking. Faye Gordon was one, and now she's in the hospital. Lorna Mc-Call, and now she's dead. Looks like someone is removing the competition. And Lottie owns a gun."

"She didn't do it," I said. "For one thing, she was too drunk Saturday night to hit someone with one shot from across the room. For another, we all saw Lottie's new gun. She couldn't have hit anyone with that, and besides, she bought it after Bruno's death, and she can prove that."

"Her husband, Allan, has a room full of guns."

"I remember her saying something about that at your house on Monday night. Nonetheless, she isn't a good enough shot, whatever the gun. And have they thought about Esther? Lottie isn't big enough or strong enough to bludgeon a tough woman like Esther to death." I didn't want to mention my hired killer theory, not in front of Frank.

"I'm afraid there may be other evidence they haven't yet revealed."

He was thinking about the results of the tests done on the coffee taken from the studio. If those turned up traces of bichloride of mercury, fingers would point to both Jack Pickford, whose history with that substance had created an international incident, and Lottie Pickford, courtesy of her ties to her brother. A case could be made that she had both motive and ability.

"But surely she has an alibi for Tuesday morning." I had spent most of Tuesday morning at La Grande Depot, but Lottie must have been working at the studio.

Frank's grim expression said it all. "She didn't come in until noon. Said she was too sick." He took out a cigarette case and offered them around. I declined. He and Douglas lit theirs and smoked a moment while they reflected on the dilemma in silence.

"Is Lottie forbidden to leave her house?" asked Frank at last, probably thinking ahead to rearranging his filming schedule.

"They told her not to leave town, so she could come in. But believe me, Frank, she's in no condition to work. After the police left, she called Mary, hysterical, and then went back to bed."

More like back to the bottle.

"Never mind," said Frank gamely. "We can work around her for a while without much effort. We'll not need you on the set until tomorrow, Doug, for the dance scene with Juliette. Jessie, you can start calling the cantina extras to come in at noon and notify Costume and Makeup that they're on the way. Then report to my office and help Geraldine with some paperwork until everyone assembles."

"By the way," I said, "have either of you gentlemen heard of Western Compass Studios or a director named Johnnie Salazar?"

"I haven't," said Douglas.

"I have," said Frank. "At least, I've met Salazar once or twice. Why do you ask?"

"A friend of mine has landed a part at his studio, and I told her I'd ask around about his reputation."

"I'm not familiar with his work," said Frank, "and I don't know the studio, but he hangs around with Jack Pickford's crowd. Some people call him when they need liquor by the case."

26

ach day saw the rhetoric soar to new heights. Thursday's front page was inked with fresh allegations as reporters vied to write the most lurid stories, and editors crafted headlines so enticing that no literate person could pass a newsboy without buying a copy. PERIL TO NATION SEEN IN HOLLYWOOD SCANDAL screamed the big print atop a *Times* article that quoted Mayer, Zukor, and one of the Warner brothers on the damage these stories were doing to the industry. The reporter who penned THROBBING CODED LOVE LETTER FOUND babbled on about a mysterious love letter found in Heilmann's desk, a letter written in secret code. I think he made the whole thing up . . . or maybe it was a letter written in German. Would Heilmann's death be THE MURDER THAT MURDERED THE MOVIES? shouted Hearst's paper. FOUR DEATHS AND COUNTING warned another. Panic-stricken stars were said to be fleeing Hollywood, although I saw little to indicate that it was so. Police were baffled. Would they find the Hollywood Killer before he struck again? The biggest excitement came with the announcement that the poison in the coffee was bichloride of mercury, the deadly potion that had ended the life of many an unhappy person, including Jack Pickford's first wife.

There it was. Bichloride of mercury, out in the open.

And still, in all the hoopla, not a single reporter had linked Esther's death to the others. Or maybe they all had and just didn't care to write about it. She wasn't a famous director or glamorous actress, after all. She was a nobody, a former vaudeville player who served glamorous Hollywood its champagne and caviar.

But I cared about Esther. A helluva lot more than I cared about Bruno Heilmann. He had been killed for something he did. She had been as innocent as a child. Nothing would bring her back, but I could at least identify her killer. She deserved that much.

I was sorting photographs with Geraldine in Frank's office when a sharp rap turned both our heads. "Come in," she called. A sunburned errand boy with ears like pitcher handles pushed open the door. "Mr. Richardson's not here—" Geraldine began.

"Miss Beckett?" he addressed us both.

"That's me," I said.

"There's a policeman wants to see you. At the front gate. Shall they let him in?"

"Tell him I'll be right there."

The boy nodded and ran off.

I found Carl Delaney inside the gatehouse chatting with the security guard. His smile faded as I came up. Not a good sign.

"Where can we talk?" he asked with cold politeness.

I indicated an empty bench in the shade where secretaries sometimes took their lunch, and we sat down. I clasped my hands together so as not to seem fidgety or nervous. But I was. Carl was more perceptive than most cops. Than most people, period. I wasn't fooling Carl. Not much, anyway.

He didn't waste time on pleasantries. "Have you seen the newspapers?"

"Yes."

"Then you know there was poison in the coffee."

I nodded. "I also know Lottie Pickford is your prime suspect. She didn't do it. I'm certain of it."

Carl stared hard at the pavement while he listened. Finally he asked, "How about you tell me why you think so?"

"There are lots of reasons," I said evasively.

"Just for the record, I don't think she did it, either. But I'm not in charge of this investigation, and some of the boys think she looks mighty suspicious. Heilmann was breaking off their love affair, and he'd started sleeping with Lorna McCall. Lottie was jealous of her and angry with him. She was one of the last to leave the party that night, and she threatened to kill him in front of a lot of people."

"And I was one of those people. Look, Carl, she may well look suspicious, but it's circumstantial. She didn't kill Heilmann. Or Esther Frankel."

"Our new crime lab downtown tested the stomach contents of Mr. Corrigan and Miss Gordon. They both showed traces of bichloride of mercury. The detectives think that points to Lottie, too."

"Actually, it points to Jack Pickford, if it points to anyone."

"He's got alibis for everything."

He would, I thought bitterly. "Just because her brother used the stuff years ago doesn't mean Lottie has any." The irony of my vigorous defense of Lottie was not lost on me. I couldn't stand the woman and here I sat, arguing her innocence like she was my best friend in the world. "Look, Carl," I said, exasperated. "I don't know anything. I'm only trying to help."

"Help who, is what I'm wondering."

"My boss. He's trying to protect his wife's reputation and their studio. Another financial crash like the one after the Fatty Arbuckle scandal could wipe him out, not to mention ruin the whole film industry. They're all afraid that the Catholic Church will boycott or that those do-gooder women's groups will rise up and start calling for blood. Did you hear what the head of MGM said yesterday? 'If this keeps up there won't be any motion picture industry.'"

That earned me a long look. "You seem to know a lot more than anyone else about these things," he said in his careful way, "and I like to check in now and then to see if you're going to tell me something I don't already know. Besides, I was across the street at the pharmacy, looking at their poison book, so I didn't have far to come. We've been visiting every pharmacy in Los Angeles to see if anyone bought mercury bichloride in the past few weeks. That's 'anyone,' mind you, not just someone who looked like Lottie Pickford."

Everyone who has ever bought anything like rat poison at a pharmacy knows you have to sign a book saying what you purchased and when, just as a deterrent to crime. And Lottie's face was so well-known, she couldn't have gotten away with giving a false name. She could have worn a disguise, but I didn't think I needed to point that out.

"Any luck?" I asked him.

"Not yet. So why couldn't Lottie Pickford have done the murders?"

Unable to sidestep the subject any longer, I took a deep breath. "One, she isn't big enough or strong enough to have bashed in Esther. Two, she was too drunk Saturday night to stand up straight, let alone hit a man in the head from a distance with one shot. Three, she doesn't know much about guns. Said her husband's guns were too heavy, so she bought a tiny one for protection—a couple days *after* Heilmann was killed, by the way. And four, how do they think she got inside Paramount Studios without being on the gate list?"

"Sneaked in somehow. She has no alibi for Tuesday morning."

"She was home in bed nursing a hangover."

"So she says. And no one was there to corroborate the story. Same for Sunday afternoon, when Lorna McCall was killed."

I sighed. Had I been a juror, none of this would have sounded very convincing. Then again, the case against Fatty Arbuckle had been far weaker and the trial had still destroyed him. In the motion picture world, the truth never mattered. Only what the public found titillating.

27

I was making myself a late supper when Myrna crept through the front door. "Hey," I called, "I'm in the kitchen. How did it go?" One look at her pretty face answered my question.

Without a word I poured some orange juice into a tall glass. "Here, sit down. I just squeezed this. I'm making my famous Egg-on-Toast for supper. Two fried eggs on a piece of toasted bread, buttered. There's nothing better. How about I make you one, too?"

I took her silence for a yes, and in a few moments, placed my culinary masterpiece on the table. Handing her a knife and fork, I sat down across from her. I waited until we'd both cleaned our plates before leaning back in my chair and saying, "What did they want you to do—play the part naked?"

Her lips parted and she stared at me in frank astonishment. Finally she found her tongue. "How on earth did you know?"

How did I know? I'd been in show business my whole life. I'd seen acts go from vaudeville to burlesque and back again. I'd crossed that street myself. Myrna was young and she was pretty. It didn't take a crystal ball to know that men would want to work with the package unwrapped.

"I'm psychic."

"Really?"

"No, silly. What else would make you so upset?"

"Well, you're not quite right. They want me to wear two costumes. One's a net and the other's a cloud. Do you know the story of Zeus and Io?"

I confessed I did not.

"It's a very, very stupid story. Zeus comes down from the sky and sees this river nymph named Io and wants to, you know, and he doesn't want his wife Hera to find out, so he hides Io in a cloud and they, you know, then he turns her into a white heifer to disguise her. So Hera sends a vicious fly to sting the heifer, and Io jumps into the sea to get away from the fly, and comes out human again. That's the fishing net scene. We filmed some of that today."

"Wearing the net?"

She nodded glumly. "I told Johnnie I didn't like the costumes, and he said he understood but that I wasn't a child anymore and it was time for me to grow into adult parts. He's been very, very nice all along. He told me some really sweet things and said to just give it a try and then decide. All the other girls were wearing nets, and they said it was artistic, that film is art just like Greek statues and Renaissance paintings so I, well . . ."

"So you tried it. And how do you feel?"

"I don't know."

I knew.

"Listen, Myrna. Once when I was seventeen, I worked in an act that crossed the street, meaning it went burlesque. I was a magician's assistant. You probably know that magic is mostly misdirection—making people look at your right hand while your left hand is really doing the trick. Well, this magician wasn't very good, and I was the act's misdirection. The magician said the same things to me that Johnnie is saying to you: everyone's doing it, the female body is art, don't be a prude—"

"I'm not a prude! When I was sixteen I posed almost nude for the statue that's in front of Venice High School. That was art. This was different somehow. I didn't know what to do. I don't want a reputation for being difficult, like Lottie Pickford."

I cringed. "Myrna, that's not what I meant by being difficult."

"So what happened with your magician's act?"

"I tried it for a week and decided I didn't like it. I didn't feel like art; I felt cheap. So I quit. Found another job. Look, I'm not ashamed of myself, and I'm not saying it's bad to take your clothes off in a picture. I'm saying, don't let anyone push you into doing something you don't feel good about."

"Johnnie had to leave midday. He wasn't pushing me. He said give the part a try and he'd talk to me when he got back at five. But he didn't get back. He never showed up. We finished shooting at six, so I left."

"You'll see him tomorrow morning. If you don't want to continue, tell him so. He'll understand."

28

Before I had reached Pickford-Fairbanks the next morning, I'd passed two paperless paperboys.

"All sold out, miss. We'll be gettin' more in about nine," the olive-skinned lad told me. "I'll save you one!"

My day started at Makeup, reviewing the first shoot with Mildred Young to make sure we maintained visual continuity. She found herself low on a particular Max Factor undertone that she'd used the day before, and I offered to run over to the *Little Annie Rooney* set to borrow some from their kit.

Making my way through the rabbit warren of tiny workrooms, offices, and storage rooms behind the back lot, I found the makeup artist and coaxed a jar of undertone away from him by promising my firstborn child if I hadn't replaced it by early next week. Heading back to our own set, I caught a glimpse of David Carr making his way with jaunty steps across the lot. My heart skipped a beat, but I played coy and pretended not to notice him.

He saw me. "Hey, kid," he called. "You're just the one I wanted to see. Come here. I've got a present for you."

I looked pointedly at his empty hands. "Oh?"

"In here." He tapped his head. "You're gonna love it."

"I can't stop."

"I'll tell you over a cup of coffee."

"No time." I held up the jar of makeup. "Gotta run this back to *Zorro*."

"Sure. Fine and dandy. Just look me up when you're ready to learn the name of your droopy-mouthed gangster."

"What!"

He preened and sauntered closer. "Yep. How 'bout that coffee now?"

"I . . . I don't believe you. Yes I do. Who is it?"

"Commissary's thataway."

I know when I'm licked. Three minutes later we were sitting down at a Formica table with two cups of steaming java between us.

"All right, tell."

"Name's Sal Panetta."

"How on earth did you find that out?"

"You aren't the only one with friends in Chicago. I telephoned an old pal and asked if he knew of a torpedo with a droopy mouth, and he didn't hesitate a second before saying, 'Sure, that'd be Sal Panetta. One of Johnny Torrio's Outfit, only Torrio got gunned down a couple weeks ago and the Outfit got taken over by his second, a fella named Capone."

"Sal Panetta," I repeated. "Geez, who'd've thought I'd ever know his name?"

"No one. And now you can forget it, because that's the sort of information that comes back to bite you. Telling the cops won't do you a damned bit of good. Torrio used to boast that he owned the Chicago police, and this new boss holds the same hand."

"I understand. But why hire someone all the way from Chicago to kill a man in California?"

David shrugged. "Maybe somebody owed someone a favor. Maybe the local boys were too well-known to risk it. Who knows? I have the sense that it had something to do with the change in command in Chicago. Maybe somebody's proving what long arms he has."

"So I was right? It was dope and not revenge or jealousy that got Bruno Heilmann killed."

"You are one smart cookie." I was elated at my success—and David's praise. "Heilmann was importing the goods from Mexico, competing with the hometown boys. He was a fool. No one's gonna sit back and let some walk-on take money out of their pockets."

"You're telling me Hollywood has its own gangsters smuggling dope?"

"Not just Hollywood, all of Los Angeles. It's a vicious business down here, with competing gangs fighting for territory. A pity, really. There's plenty for everyone, if they could just organize and get along."

Was that how he ran Portland? By organizing and getting along? Or by eliminating his competition? I was reminded how little I knew about this man. I needed reminding.

"Well, thanks . . . I guess."

"You're welcome. Now I want you to forget about this. You were right. You solved Heilmann's murder. And the waitress's. But it's over. *Finito*."

Once at a state fair, I saw one of those big silk balloons with a noisy flame that filled the balloon with hot air until it rose into the sky. When it had returned to earth and the passengers had climbed out of the basket, the carny man turned off the flame, and just like that, the enormous bubble silently crumpled into a heap of silk that would fit in a suitcase. Right there, sitting in the studio commissary, I thought of that balloon. I should have felt triumphant—after all, I had figured out who murdered Bruno Heilmann and Esther Frankel. I had figured out why he had done it and how he had done it and when he had done it, but knowing was no good. Nothing was going to come of it. I couldn't tell the police without risking my own life. Even if I could, there was no chance of bringing the killer to justice. No one was going to charge a gangster who lived two thousand miles away and had alibis enough to stuff a Christmas turkey. I had wanted to avenge Esther's death, for her own sake and for my mother's, and I had failed. Her killer—and the local gangsters who hired him—were going to get off scot-free. It wasn't fair.

Life isn't fair, Baby, my mother used to say. Didn't everyone's mother used to say that?

"There's still Lorna McCall's death—"

"That was probably an accident," he said.

"And Paul Corrigan's and Faye Gordon's poisoning. Were they accidents, too?"

At that moment, David reached across the table and took both my hands in his. *Whoa!* I hadn't been expecting contact and my defenses were caught napping. My pulse pounded in my throat and my cheeks flushed hot.

"Jessie," he said in a deep, grave voice. "Look at me."

This was harder than I thought.

"Remember that time on the Portland train when we dished lies to each other for a couple hours?"

Indignant, I pulled my hands back. "I wasn't lying! I was acting. I was playing a part."

"My mistake. I, however, was lying through my teeth. But that's beside the point, which is: we know very little about each other. And what we *think* we know comes mostly from others. I want to know the real Jessie, the by-God honest truth about your life, straight from you, and I think you want to know about me. It's only fair that we take another train ride, one with no lies. And no acting. Don't you?"

I sidestepped. "A train ride?"

David shook his head and gave me that aw-shucks grin guaranteed to melt a girl's resolve. "Not a real train ride. I think we can do better than that. I propose a corner table at the fanciest restaurant in Hollywood, where you and I can spend a quiet evening together talking straight. No strings attached, just dinner. I thought tomorrow night after you got off work would be good. What do you say?"

David has dangerous eyes. Somehow, he locks those baby blues on you and pulls you inside and you don't even realize you've erased your own ideas and replaced them with his until long after it has happened. Not for the first time, I thought he'd have made a good vaudeville hypnotist. Or maybe he already was. I opened my mouth to say no.

"I—I guess there's no harm in that."

He took my arm as we left the commissary, his mile-wide smile beaming brighter than southern California's sun. "I'll come by your house at eight tomorrow night. Now scoot, before you're late with that makeup."

I passed the front gate just as the Fairbanks Rolls-Royce eased through with Douglas and Mary in the backseat. It must be nine o'clock already, I thought to myself with surprise. You could set your watch by Douglas's schedule: nine to four every day. No one considered these hours light duty—we all knew he exercised before and after work, running, lifting weights, fencing, swimming, playing tennis, riding, and practicing with his whip. Maintaining his superb physique was essential to his success. And ours.

The Silver Ghost slowed, and a rear window rolled down. Douglas leaned over and called, "Good morning, Jessie. My office in five minutes, please."

When I arrived, his secretary motioned me to a leather chair.

"Mr. Fairbanks and Miss Pickford are in with an unexpected visitor. They'll be with you in a moment."

I made myself comfortable and glanced over the newspaper collection on the coffee table. Alongside today's *Times* was the *San Francisco Examiner*, various trade weeklies, and dailies from the smaller cities of San Diego, Sacramento, and Bakersfield. Every front page blared Hollywood death and debauchery.

Today the *Examiner* went a step further, claiming that Bruno Heilmann had been homosexual. The accusation made my eyes pop. According to the reporter, Heilmann had been murdered and "disfigured" by his homosexual valet, who promptly skipped town. But it was not the ridiculousness of the story that shocked me; it was the bold use of the most terrifying word in the motion picture industry: "homosexual." The word simply did not exist in the Hollywood lexicon; one could be pardoned for thinking it had been deleted from every dictionary in town. The faintest whiff of sodomy would have turned actor into leper and driven legions of American families out of motion picture palaces forever. No, in Hollywood, every actor was manly and had chaste relationships with scores of lovely maidens.

I tossed the paper aside in disgust and picked up the *Times* where I learned the latest suspect was Mary and Lottie Pickford's mother, Charlotte. *Charlotte*, for crying out loud, was supposed to have been avenging her youngest daughter's honor. Seems someone saw Charlotte lurking about the Heilmann house that night. Another piece fingered the butler who had found the body—he had purportedly shot Heilmann and stolen a large amount of cash from a safe, then returned the next day to pretend to discover the body. I hoped no one would pay too much attention to this theory, as it came uncomfortably close to something I could be accused of at Esther Frankel's. I sighed. Sooner or later, everyone in Hollywood was going to be dragged into the mire of these murders.

I nearly missed the article at the bottom of the front page.

TWO DETECTIVES SHOT IN THE LINE OF DUTY, it read. Idly, I looked at the first paragraph, then gasped aloud.

"What is it?" The secretary looked up from her typewriter.

"Oh, I'm sorry. I was just shocked at this article."

Assuming I meant the one about Charlotte Pickford, she nodded. "Aren't we all, dearie? I ask you, what's the world coming to when innocent old ladies are accused just for meanness' sake?"

Quickly I scanned the piece about the shootings, then went back and read it again, slowly this time, trying to see through every word to the truth behind it. Details were few. Two detectives investigating a dope-smuggling ring had been ambushed Thursday afternoon—yesterday—in some remote desert gully northwest of Hollywood. The smugglers were bringing heroin into the country from Mexico, and the detectives received a tip that led them to the rendezvous point. A fierce gun battle had left the two detectives and three smugglers dead. An unknown number had escaped with the bulk of the dope.

The names of the martyred heroes were Tuttle and Rios.

29

S it down, Jessie," began Douglas Fairbanks. "I wanted you to see these newspapers that just came in from New York." On the desk were several back issues of Pulitzer's *World*. I said good morning to Mary Pickford, then breezed through the headlines. If anything, the East Coast stories were more scurrilous than the West.

"These are absurd," I said, glancing up from an article that screamed about a pink silk nightie found at Heilmann's home, tracing it to a young actress who hadn't even attended his party, and another that implicated the homosexual valet. "And I saw the *Times* story claiming your mother killed him," I said to Miss Pickford.

"Hearst would say his own mother shot Heilmann if it would sell papers," growled Douglas. "Publicity agents are working round the clock, trying to protect their clients. Still, New York is panicking." Most of the financial and business people involved in the motion picture industry worked out of New York, a five-day train ride from California. By and large, Hollywood liked the arrangement—it kept the big bosses at a safe distance where they couldn't meddle in day-to-day affairs. But today, New York seemed like the moon.

Miss Pickford spoke for the first time. "Most film company stocks have lost half their value."

"Has yours?" I asked, my concern showing plainly in my voice.

She gave a wan smile. "United Artists is owned by the three of us: Douglas and Charlie Chaplin, and me, with help from a few others like Buster Keaton and Joe Schenck. Our company isn't public so we don't sell stock on Wall Street. Nonetheless, this isn't good news for anyone in Hollywood." I'd heard it said that Mary Pickford had a head for business and now I believed it. My only brush with the stock market came from vaudeville joke books.

"Are the police making any headway?"

"They still have their sights trained on Lottie," said Douglas.

"Lottie didn't do it. I know who did now. At least, I know who murdered Bruno Heilmann and Esther Frankel. A hired killer from Chicago."

Douglas and Mary exchanged startled looks. "Go on," Douglas said.

I took a deep breath and plunged into my story. "First of all, did you know there was a dope bar upstairs at Bruno Heilmann's on Saturday night?" He and Mary said no, and I continued. "Well, that's why so many people were going upstairs. When I was searching for Lottie's things on Sunday, I came across a guest bedroom full of dope. Looked to me like cocaine and heroin, more than you would ever buy for a party. Drawers full. Many, many pounds of it. I remember you said you had long thought Heilmann was the one who supplied Wallace Reid, and I believe you were right. I think he had been selling dope to a lot of people in Hollywood. A friend of mine who knows about these things says the stuff crosses the Mexican border and goes to gangsters here that don't appreciate outsiders moving in on their territory. The gangsters wanted Heilmann out of their business, and they hired a professional from Chicago named Sal Panetta to handle the job."

"How . . . ?"

"Here's what I think happened. Panetta came to Los Angeles on Saturday, hung around the Heilmann house until the last guests had gone home, and then came in the front door to shoot Heilmann. Esther was gathering up the last of the glasses and ashtrays or wiping the tables, and saw him enter. He was wearing a striped suit, not proper party clothes like the rest of the men, and she would have noticed that and known he wasn't a guest. Heilmann was in the living room, alone—since he had thrown Lottie out—and was facing the patio with his back to the front hall. Esther saw Panetta, and that doomed her. She returned to the kitchen and went out the back door to the Cisneros Catering truck."

"And why do you think he was a professional killer?" asked Douglas. "Why not the father of some poor debauched girl avenging his daughter's virtue, like the newspapers are saying?"

"The newspapers haven't said anything true yet! Panetta killed Heilmann with one well-aimed shot to the head, and he used a silencer. Which is why no one heard the gunshot. Not a lot of fathers can shoot like that and no regular people own silencers. That's what convinced me it was a paid killer in the first place."

Douglas looked rather dazed.

"Panetta followed the Cisneros truck across town, watched Esther get out, and figured out which apartment was hers by watching for the lights to come on. He went upstairs and used a skeleton key or something like it to open the lock—it broke off. Esther didn't hear anything because she was hard of hearing, and anyway, she was back in her bedroom looking through her trunk. He came up behind her and hit her over the head with a metal statue that was handy."

"Why not just shoot her?"

"I guess he figured even a silencer was too noisy in the dead of night in such close quarters. I was in that apartment building twice and the walls are paper thin. I don't think Esther knew a thing. For that matter, I don't think Bruno Heilmann did, either. This man was a professional killer."

"Why haven't the police figured this out?" Miss Pickford took over the questions now.

"They assumed Esther's killer immediately fled the scene of the crime. I'm sure it's what criminals usually do, but not in this case. He didn't leave until about six o'clock in the morning, at least three hours later. A neighbor saw Panetta while he was letting out his dog. The neighbor noticed a stranger with a droopy mouth—he reported it to the police while I was there, but they dismissed it because the timing was off. I only remembered it because it seemed odd to me at the time that no one in the crowd spoke up to identify the man. The fact that no one knew a man with a droopy mouth who lived in that neighborhood told me he had to be a stranger. And a stranger sneaking around at six o'clock in the morning didn't sound right."

"Why would the killer stay put for more than three hours?"

"At first I thought it was because he didn't have anywhere else to go. The train station is closed that time of night, so he couldn't go back there. But I learned something on my second trip to the apartment that made me understand he was trapped at Esther's, because he couldn't get out without being seen again. There was a young couple sitting in the hall after about three o'clock, newly engaged so who knows what they were doing, but they were directly across the hall from Esther's door. The killer would have heard them talking. And Esther's door must have been closed tight at that point . . . I think the couple would have noticed if the door had been ajar like it was when I arrived the next morning."

"So the murderer sneaks up to the third floor, clobbers your friend, and gets ready to leave only to find this couple has settled in for the long haul," said Douglas.

"Exactly. He holds the door closed, maybe leans up against it to keep it shut, and waits until they leave."

"Which may have been a couple hours."

"It was really the safest place for him to be. He's not from these parts, and he doesn't have anywhere to go at three in the morning that wouldn't arouse notice, and he wants to remain unnoticed. He needs to get out of town as soon as possible. He was seen leaving Esther's around six. Do you know what opens at six-thirty? The train station. So I went to La Grande and found a couple Harvey Girls who remembered serving breakfast to a man in a striped suit with a droopy mouth, and I knew my suspicions were correct."

Douglas whistled quietly.

"There's more. One of the Harvey Girls thought he caught the seven-ten Chicagoan. So I gambled that he rode all the way to Chicago. That would have put him in the train station Tuesday evening. A vaudeville friend of mine is playing Chicago this week, and I managed to get a telegram to her asking if she could meet that train and see if a man with a droopy mouth got off. She did, and he did."

"And how did you learn his name?" asked Douglas.

"I have a friend with unsavory connections in Chicago who telephoned long distance and asked if there was a Chicago gangster with a droopy mouth. Bingo. Panetta."

"Who hired Panetta?"

"I don't know for sure, but my friend thinks the local gangsters must have been spitting mad that someone had barged into their drug business."

"Wait a minute," said Miss Pickford. "This Panetta must have had an accomplice. How else could he get around Hollywood in the dead of night, from Heilmann's to Esther's to the depot?"

"I asked myself the same question. He couldn't call taxis—they'd remember him. Red Cars and buses don't run that late at night, and it's way too far to walk. He stole a car at the station when he arrived on Saturday and returned it when he left on Sunday morning."

"How the dickens do you know that?" asked Douglas.

"I posed as a girl reporter and asked at the Central Division police station about stolen cars. A man reported his car missing from the La Grande station parking lot when he returned from a business trip on Saturday. When the police visited the station Sunday to check his story, the car was there, but not in the place the man says he left it. The police think he was drunk or forgetful or stupid. I think the man from Chicago stole the first car he found with keys inside, used it that night, returned it to a different parking place early Sunday morning, and left town on the earliest eastbound train."

Both Douglas and Mary looked at me with frank astonishment. "What made you think of that?" he asked.

I shrugged. "There weren't any other possibilities, not really."

"You realize, don't you," he said at last, "that this Chicago assassin will have a hundred witnesses—"

"Ready to swear he was in some restaurant near the Loop Saturday night and couldn't have been in Hollywood. Yes, I know."

"Still, better to know who committed the crime, even if he can't be touched," said Miss Pickford. "Maybe now the hysteria will die down."

"'Jessie Beckett, Girl Detective.' Sounds like a feature film, doesn't it, Mary? Too bad women can't be policemen. When this gets out, you'll be a heroine."

I squirmed. Here was the issue I couldn't get past.

"I can't tell the police. Everything starts with the packages of dope I saw at Bruno Heilmann's house on Sunday when I sneaked in to get Lottie's things."

"That's no problem. Just say you saw them Saturday night while you were at the party."

I shook my head. "Two detectives searched the house shortly after I saw those packets. But their report doesn't mention finding any dope, just liquor."

His eyebrows rose with comprehension. "Ahhh. They confiscated it."

"They took it to sell. There are lots of party guests who could say they saw the dope on Saturday night. The detectives who took it would deny it was there Sunday. They would say the killer took it after he shot Heilmann."

"Couldn't it have happened that way?"

"No, he wouldn't have had the time. Believe me, it was more than one person could carry, and Panetta couldn't have chased after the catering truck if he'd taken the time to search for something to carry it in or taken several trips to his car. Besides, why would anyone in Los Angeles tell him about the dope upstairs? He was hired to kill someone and get out of town, not take their dope."

I waited in silence as Douglas stroked his moustache. "If the detectives knew you were on to them, you'd be in as much danger from the police as from the gangsters."

"My thoughts exactly. Until I read this." I handed him today's newspaper, folded so that article on the hero detectives was facing up. With a puzzled frown, he took it. I waited until he had read the piece and passed it to his wife.

"Those were the detectives who stole the dope from Heilmann's. They were the ones who questioned me at the police station. They aren't heroes; they're crooks. They weren't trying to break up a smuggling ring in the desert. They were part of it. They stole the dope from Heilmann's on Sunday and were trying to sell it to one of the local gangs. Something went wrong—a double cross or an argument—and someone started shooting. Sounds to me like at least one man, one of the gangsters, got away with the car and the dope."

"And it's still drifting around somewhere."

"As far as I can tell."

"So the crooked detectives are dead. Now you can go to the police with your story, can't you?" asked Miss Pickford.

"No, she can't," Douglas answered for me. "We don't know how high up the corruption goes. The police captain could be in on it, maybe other detectives. This is what comes from bribing a police force to overlook illegal liquor . . . they start overlooking all sorts of other crime as well."

I knew one cop who wasn't corrupt, but I didn't want Carl Delaney to play hero and get himself killed for his pains.

We were silent awhile with our own thoughts. Finally Douglas spoke up. "Then the person who killed Lorna McCall and Paul Corrigan and almost killed Faye Gordon wasn't trying to get rid of party guests who saw something?"

"It doesn't seem like it. I don't know who killed the others, but it wasn't the hired gun from Chicago. We know when he left town and it was before those people were murdered. Besides, you know what Paramount is like, right? It's as tight as it is here. Everyone is logged in and out. No stranger is going to waltz in carrying a tommy gun and poison the coffee without someone noticing."

"To tell the truth, Jessie," said Douglas, "studio gates aren't really that effective. There are a dozen back entrances into any studio, including Paramount. The gate is really there to keep outsiders from wandering in—tourists who would get in the way, job seekers who would overrun the place, youngsters who might get hurt. It wouldn't have been at all impossible for someone who knew the business to get into Paramount."

"Well, no one broke into Lorna McCall's apartment like they

did Esther's. There were two cups and plates on the coffee table that her maid washed before the police could dust them for fingerprints. Lorna knew the person who killed her. She invited him in."

"Besides," said Miss Pickford, laying her hand on Douglas's arm. "This information will only fuel the publicity fires, now that dope rings and gangsters are added to the mix. Until Lorna's and Paul's murders are solved, the frenzy will continue. We can only hope no one else is killed, and that no one in Hollywood is damaged beyond repair."

Douglas nodded and squeezed her hand. Then they both looked at me.

30

That night Melva showed me how to toast a cheese sandwich with ham, adding another recipe to my short list of culinary accomplishments. Lillian had made a big pot of vegetable stew and we girls sat down at the little kitchen table to dine in style. Only Myrna was missing. She had not yet returned from Culver City. My ears strained for the sound of her footsteps on the walk. She should have been home by now. I was worrying like a parent.

"Perhaps she stayed over with her mother," Melva remarked when I voiced my concern.

As if on cue, Myrna breezed through the screen door. "Hi, girls!" she said with a flutter of her fingers. She didn't pause but continued through the kitchen and up the stairs to her room. I finished eating and cleaned up my dishes before following her.

"There's stew on the stove if you're hungry," I called through the door as I passed her room, leaving my door open to make it clear I was there if she needed to talk.

An hour passed before she crossed the hall and leaned against the doorjamb, looking as forlorn as a wilted flower.

"How was your day?" I asked carefully.

"Fine. Just fine. I changed my mind about the part. I'm doing it."

"That's your decision to make. You should do what you think best for your career." Her lower lip trembled and she dropped her face into her hands, unable to hold her emotions inside any longer. "And I see it's made you very happy," I deadpanned.

Myrna couldn't suppress the giggle that erupted beneath her tears. Wiping her eyes, she came into my room and sat on my bed, folding her dancer's legs Indian style.

"What am I gonna do?"

"What do you want to do?"

"I want to quit, of course. I tried! I told Johnnie Salazar I couldn't give the part the effort it deserved. And he got very, very angry. I'd never seen him like that . . . he's always, well, he's been so kind and understanding."

"Did he threaten you?"

"He said I couldn't quit now, or he'd lose a lot of money reshooting my scenes and a lot of time finding a replacement. He said I was a fool to leave, that this was my big break. And if I quit on him, he'd see to it that I never worked in the pictures again."

"So you worked all day?"

She nodded miserably. "More net scenes, most of them with Fred—he's Zeus—who was naked, too. I feel like a tart, Jessie. And I didn't like him touching me. I couldn't help thinking, What would my father say? I want to be a star like Mary Pickford or Greta Garbo or Gloria Swanson. They manage to keep their clothes on!"

"I wouldn't worry overmuch about Johnnie's threats. He isn't Mayer or Zukor or one of those big shots who really *can* ruin you if you cross them. Anyone who knew the circumstances would understand. If worse came to worst, you could change your name and poof! Start over."

"You think I should quit?"

"It isn't what I think that matters, Myrna. It's what you think."

"I think I should quit," she admitted, picking at a hangnail. "I'm just chicken. Johnnie was really . . . well, really mean when I told him . . . although, to be fair, I think it was because of his arm hurting."

"His arm?"

"His arm was in a sling. He broke it yesterday afternoon in a fall at his house. That's why he wasn't at the studio yesterday to talk to me. He was at the hospital."

"I see." Silence hung between us for a few minutes as we both pondered the best course of action. Finally Myrna cleared her throat.

"Would you—I hate to ask you but I don't know if I, well, if I can do it alone . . . would you come with me to Western Compass tomorrow morning when I tell Johnnie? Not to come inside with me, just to wait outside the studio so I know you're there, and I can say, 'I have to go now, my friend's waiting for me.'"

Tomorrow was Saturday, the last day of the week. I was supposed to be at work, but prying Myrna out of Johnnie Salazar's clutches took precedence over any paycheck.

"Sure," I said. "You realize he won't pay you for the days you worked, don't you?" She nodded glumly. "Cheer up! Everything will work out. Now, how about some of Lillian's stew?"

31

Like other slapdash studios in Los Angeles, Western Compass took a frugal approach to filmmaking. Although I couldn't see past the building's façade from where I was positioned, Myrna had told me the compound consisted of five or six small sets, a few offices, and some workrooms all squashed on a one-acre lot. Anticipating something squalid, I was reassured by the clean coat of pale yellow paint and the classy sign—the word "Western" in gold script superimposed on a gray compass—that gleamed in the morning sunshine. Maybe this wasn't such a disreputable operation after all.

I settled onto a bench at the bus stop opposite the entrance to wait for Myrna, whose confidence had returned. "Just knowing you're outside makes it easier," she had said. Then, lifting her chin, she crossed the street, every step revealing that regal posture so typical of classically trained dancers. I crossed my fingers.

Moments later a Cadillac pulled curbside and a man got out of the backseat, his left arm cradled in a muslin sling. Who else but Johnnie Salazar? I got a good look at him today: medium build, dark curly hair, a Roman nose, and dressed like a model for a clothier's advertisement. I was right, this was the same man I'd noticed with Jack Pickford at Heilmann's party last week. His high-pitched voice and fidgety motions gave him a nervous appearance today. I paid little attention to his conversation with the driver, but rather focused on his hand and his arm, which I could see quite clearly. At one point, he became animated and jerked his left hand, then winced with pain. Salazar had hurt his arm, yes, but it wasn't in a plaster cast. It was in a sling. It wasn't broken. Myrna must have misunderstood.

He disappeared into the building. The Cadillac waited. With nothing to do but think, I thought.

Johnnie Salazar was the Heilmann link to liquor. Probably supplied the French champagne I had so cheerfully downed at last Saturday's party. But that raised the question: the link to what? Who else dealt in bootleg liquor but the local gangsters? The same bunch who smuggled drugs from Mexico. Surely they were the ones who'd hired the assassin from Chicago to eliminate the Heilmann competition. David had said as much. And Johnnie Salazar was tied into all of this. Johnnie Salazar had gotten hurt Thursday afternoon. He'd missed his appointment with Myrna. Five other people had gotten hurt Thursday afternoon, so hurt they died. Was that where Johnnie Salazar had been? Had he been shot in the arm during the gunfight in the desert? At first, it seemed improbable, but the more I considered it, the likelier it became. I began to get nervous about Myrna.

Half an hour later, she burst through the door. Her eyes were bright and her lips pressed together in a bloodless line, but her head was high, and I knew she had done it.

"Well, I'm through with Western Compass. Johnnie was furious, but I stuck to my guns."

"Good girl."

"He threatened me again. Said he'd ruin me. Said the only way I'd ever get into the pictures is to buy a ticket."

I shook my head. "What else?"

"Now that I think about it, he wasn't as angry as he was yesterday. He said to get off his property, he never wanted to see me again, that he had more important things to worry about than a stupid little girl who was throwing away the only chance she'd ever get."

"Don't believe a word of it. You're going to be a star."

She gave me a big hug. "Thanks. I mean, for coming. I've made you late to work."

Together we rode the bus back to Hollywood, then went our separate ways. By the time I had arrived at the Pickford-Fairbanks gate, I'd formed my plan. I needed to know if my suspicions about Johnnie Salazar were more than imagination run amok, and I'd figured out how to do it.

Bypassing the *Son of Zorro* set, I went straight to the wardrobe mistress at *Little Annie Rooney* and told her what I needed. She eyed me suspiciously. "You want to borrow some children's clothing?"

"And a wig."

"This isn't a lending library, Miss Beckett," she said and sniffed.

"It's for a special assignment Mr. Fairbanks wants me to handle. I need to look as young as possible, right away."

I'd dropped the wrong name. "This is Miss Pickford's set," she reminded me coldly.

"I'll bring everything back in a couple hours. Look, you can call Miss Pickford; she'll vouch for my request."

She looked me up and down, twisting the black velvet pincushion on her wrist while she considered my suggestion, then went to the telephone on her desk. I sat in the nearest chair. While she made the call, I reached for the telephone directory and looked up the home address for John Salazar. Yes, he did live in Hollywood. It stood to reason that he'd have gone to the nearest hospital if he'd been badly hurt. Hollywood had two that were close by.

"Miss Pickford's office, please," I heard her say. After a minute, she said, "Thank you," and hung up. "Miss Pickford isn't in yet, but I'll give you whatever you want."

"Gee, thanks."

She gave me a thin smile. "I assumed you had approval when you didn't object to my call. Come look at what we have. What age did you want?"

Thirty minutes later, a pert fifteen-year-old girl left Wardrobe. She wore a blue and white sailor dress with white stockings, shiny patent-leather shoes, and a matching straw hat. Her golden curls bounced against her back when she walked. Her cheeks were sprinkled with freckles, courtesy of Miss Mildred Young, who didn't ask a single question when she heard my request. I was really beginning to warm to that woman. I scooted between buildings, taking a shortcut to the front gate, and when I came out in an open area that held *Thief of Bagdad* bazaar remnants, I was surprised to see David Carr crossing the middle of the plaza. I was hugging the adobe walls, and our paths were not going to intersect. There were several other people in sight: two men pulling a handcart loaded with boxes, a woman with a tray, and several *Annie Rooney* kids arguing in loud voices, and none of those gave my young self the briefest glance. Before I could call out to David and razz him about my disguise, a female voice turned my head.

"Oh, David! Just the man I wanted to see." A peek over my shoulder told me I didn't know the attractive young woman heading in his direction, but the warmth of his reply told me that he certainly did.

"Mornin', doll." He slowed. She slowed. He gave her cheek a kiss. Neither noticed the invisible girl who bent over to adjust her shoe buckle.

"Me and some of the girls are going sailing again this afternoon. A big strong man would sure be a welcome addition to the
crew," she teased. Her voice was sultry, her hair was dark, and my
mood followed. "The galley's stocked with lunch and liquor.
Wanna come along?"

"Gosh, thanks, Ruby. Sounds swell, and I'd love nothing
better. But I'm booked this afternoon."

Her lips pouted prettily. "What could be more important
than an afternoon on a sailboat? Your friend Stella will be there,
and I know all the girls would be thrilled for 'Stella's fella' to join
us again."

"Stella's fella" gave a hearty laugh and chucked Ruby under
her pointy little chin. "Sorry, hon. Another time for sure. I have
to meet a friend at the train station."

"Bring him along! You can't have too many sexy fellas on a
sailboat, that's my motto."

"My friend's train doesn't come in until two, and we've got
some business to take care of, but what about tonight—whoops,
no." He snapped his fingers. "Almost forgot. I've got another ob-
ligation tonight. How about a Sunday picnic?"

A shoemaker could have stitched an entire shoe by now, and
if I heard any more of this drivel, I'd rip off my wig and shout to
"Stella's fella" that he needn't bother with tonight's tedious obli-
gation. Neither of them paid the slightest attention to me as I
seethed my way around the corner, scheming about the blister-
ing set-down I'd deliver tonight when the two-timing bum came
calling.

I should have known. I damn well should have expected this.
What in heaven's name made me think David was any different
from the rest of them? I hoped the Oregon police caught up
with him, and he ended up doing forty years in the pen. I'd even
help put him there if I could. I was disgusted with my own gull-
ibility for believing his snake-oil-salesman lies. Never again was
my heart going to rule my head.

The girl in the sailor suit left the studio, stopped briefly at the Sunrise Bakery to buy a small cake, then hopped the east-bound Santa Monica Red Car, sitting demurely with ankles crossed and the box on her lap. She got off at North Vermont and walked the few remaining blocks to the new Clara Barton Memorial Hospital.

"What can I help you with, my dear?" The nurse at Reception looked up and smiled big beaver teeth as I approached.

"If you please, my mother sent me with this." I placed the cake box on the counter. "She said I should give it to the nurse who was so kind to my father when he hurt his arm Thursday. But we don't know her name."

"I can tell you that." She reached for a roster of some sort.

"My father's name is John Salazar. He was here in the afternoon, with a broken arm."

She ran her finger down a list of names and frowned. "What was the name again?"

"Salazar." I spelled it out.

"I'm sorry, dear. No one by that name was admitted Thursday or yesterday."

I had half expected that response. Nonetheless, I put my hand on my mouth in confusion. "Oh, no. Are you sure? I know Mama said to go to the Hollywood hospital and ask who was the nice nurse who helped Papa—"

"She must have meant Community Hospital, a little farther down Sunset, dear. Could you have mixed them up?"

"Oh, yes," I said with mock relief. "That's it! I'm at the wrong hospital."

"People have been making that mistake ever since we opened last year. We have flowers delivered here that are meant for someone over there, and visitors who come to the wrong place. Luckily, it's not far away. Do you know where to go? Just continue along Sunset to Vine . . ."

I told her I knew the way, and thanked her. It was a short ride to Vine where I repeated my performance for a similar audience. Hospitals are wary about saying too much about their patients, so my little act brought the desired result—I got more information than I would have had I made a direct inquiry. It was just as I thought: Johnnie Salazar had visited neither hospital on Thursday. Not for a broken arm and certainly not for a bullet wound. Of course it was possible that an injured man would drive past the two closest hospitals and go to another one in Los Angeles a long distance away, but I judged it unlikely.

No, Johnnie Salazar had not been treated at either Hollywood hospital yesterday. He had not fallen at home and broken his arm. He had been wounded in the gunfight with detectives Tuttle and Rios miles from the city. Hospitals had a way of asking annoying questions about gunshot wounds, especially right after a deadly gun battle with the police. Johnnie Salazar must have gone to a private doctor, then made up the broken-arm story for Myrna and everyone else.

32

I returned my costume to Wardrobe and myself to work. Not long afterward, a boy came by the *Zorro* set with a note for me.

"A band of horrid reporters has taken over the porch, demanding to see you," it read. "They are very, very rude. Call before coming home."

The nearest telephone was at the front office. I called Myrna back at once.

"They're still here," she wailed. I didn't need to ask what they were doing. I could hear fists pounding on the front door and muffled shouts. "They say they want to talk to you. We told them you weren't home, but they don't believe us. They've discovered you had something to do with the first two murders, and gosh, I'm afraid you're the latest suspect."

"Hell, I've been a police suspect; I guess I can handle a bunch of reporters. I'll come home now and get rid of them."

"I wouldn't do that if I were you, Jessie. I'd stay away. They'll get discouraged and leave in a while."

The legendary stubbornness of the press made me think otherwise. Those reporters would stay until I showed up, frightening the girls and bothering the entire neighborhood. I excused myself to patient Pauline Cox and got ready to return home. Bless her, she didn't bat an eye. "Just do what you need to do, Jessie. Nothing is more important to all of us than getting to the bottom of these murders."

Minutes later, I was standing at the curb with some of the neighbors taking stock of the commotion in my front yard. A dozen newspapermen in loud suits were milling about like a pack of hounds that treed a coon. Several pounded on the front door, others trampled the bushes, pressing noses against windowpanes. Shouts of "Jessie Beckett! Come out and talk!" rang loud. While I watched, one man threw handfuls of gravel at upstairs windows; some circled around back and began rattling the kitchen doorknob. They made me angry, but I wasn't afraid. I'd dealt with audiences rowdier than this at burlesque houses.

Drawing a deep breath, I approached a knot of men on the sidewalk. "Excuse me, gentlemen. You needn't tear down the house. I'll be happy to answer your questions."

"Yeah?" One of them looked down his nose at me and snapped his gum. "And who are you?"

"I'm Jessie Beckett."

"Yeah, and I'm the Easter Bunny. Beat it, kid." The men smirked and elbowed one another, then turned back to the house just as the gravel thrower pitched one rock too large and shattered the glass. "Jesus Q. Christ, Schaeffer, lookit what you've done now," someone said.

"Hey, stop that! Look here, I really am Jessie Beckett." I felt like the first act of a vaudeville lineup, doomed to be ignored by an audience waiting for the headliners to appear.

Finally one man said, a little more kindly, "Forget it, kid. Nice try, but she's inside. We've seen her. She's got dark hair." And he moved away.

I guessed they had caught sight of Lillian, who had probably taken to her bed by now with one of her towering headaches. I headed next door to ask old Mrs. Pritchard if I could telephone the police when, like magic, a police car pulled up to the curb. Two blue uniforms got out. The Widow Pritchard must have had enough.

The cops sauntered up the walk as a second car turned the corner. I hardly thought this altercation would require reinforcements. Then I recognized the newcomers: Carl Delaney and his partner, Officer Brickles. As the reporters caught sight of them, the catcalls diminished.

"Okay, boys. Break it up," said the first cop. "You're disturbing the peace. Time to go home."

"Hey, we aren't causing any trouble," protested the gum chewer. "We're just waiting for an interview. As soon as she comes out and talks to us, we'll leave."

The cop caught my eye, and I pointed silently to the broken window. "Who did that?" he growled. "Schaeffer," said someone, no doubt a reporter from a competing newspaper. By now Carl Delaney and Brickles had joined the party.

"Well, well, Officer Delaney," I said, trying for a little humor as they walked up. "What brings you out on this fine day?"

"Good afternoon, Miss Beckett. Brickles and I were at the station when one of your neighbors called in to complain about a ruckus next door, and I recognized the address. Not many ruckuses going on these days that don't find you somewhere nearby, so I thought we'd come see what you had to say about this one."

The reporter who had told me to beat it spun about when he heard Carl say my name, so startled that the gum fell out of his mouth. He stared at me as if I'd grown horns. "*You* are Jessie Beckett?"

"I told you I was."

"You look— Never mind. Jasper! Over here, boy, get a picture!" Thinking to get a jump on his rivals, he whipped out his pencil and paper. "Were you jealous of Bruno Heilmann's other girlfriends?"

"Too late, buster. I'm not talking to you now. Too bad you didn't believe me to start with—I was going to tell you just how I murdered all those people and who I'm going to kill next."

"That wasn't very smart," muttered Carl under his breath as he pulled me away from the reporters. He was right, but by then, I didn't care. I'd care tomorrow when I read myself quoted in the article.

For once, I appreciated Officer Brickles's finer qualities. "Clear out, boys," he said, his voice heavy with the boredom of a man who had seen it all a hundred times before. When no one reacted, he gave two of them a shove toward the street. "I'm counting to five and any of you bums left standing on this side of the street is gonna get arrested for trespassing and vandalism. One, two . . ."

"Let's get you out of the line of fire," said Carl Delaney, guiding me through the reporters who had, all at once, realized who I was and were jabbering questions at me about my affair with Bruno Heilmann and why I had murdered Lorna McCall. We gained the porch just as the door opened, revealing the pinched faces of Lillian and Myrna. They had been seriously frightened by the reporters' harassment and greeted the police with relief.

"They got meaner and louder until I thought they were going to break down the doors!" wailed Lillian.

"They did break a window," Myrna pointed out.

"You girls should have called sooner," Carl scolded, sounding like someone's father. "They won't bother you now. If they come back, you call the station and we'll lock some of 'em up. And we'll get Schaeffer's newspaper to pay for your window, don't worry."

Like dogs herding sheep, the police pushed the reporters onto the street where they gradually dispersed. After the last of them had muttered away, Myrna and I walked Carl back to his car. We stood for a moment in the warm afternoon sun, thanking the four men, and I marveled inwardly that I could ever have felt such appreciation—even affection—for the police.

All at once a third police car pulled alongside Carl's and the driver, wearing civilian clothing, rolled down the window. Ignoring us girls, he called to the four cops, "Get down to La Grande, pronto. We're surrounding the depot. A tip came in—the guys who murdered Tuttle and Rios will be there at two." And with a squeal of tires, he took off toward the station.

"What's that about?" I asked Carl, suddenly feeling very cold.

"I'll find out when I get there. Don't worry, we'll get 'em. Cops don't like crooks who kill cops." He set his lips and glanced at his wristwatch.

"What time is it?" I asked.

"One twenty-five."

It could not be coincidence that David was meeting a friend there at two.

33

Wait! Where are you going?" Myrna cried as I snatched my purse and banged out the door.

"The train station, fast."

"What for?"

"Tell you later."

"I'm coming with you."

"No. It might be dangerous."

I waited one second after the three cars had peeled around the corner in a dramatic display of police bravado before I took off running down our narrow lane toward Sunset Boulevard. I had reached the busy intersection when I heard the footsteps behind me.

"Myrna! What are you doing?"

"I'm coming with you."

"No, go back—"

"You stood by me when I needed you, and I'll do no less for you."

A taxi approached from the east. I thrust out my arm and flagged him down.

"A taxi?" Myrna gasped, astonished at my extravagance. If nothing else brought home my desperation, this single act did.

"Get in," I said grimly. Then, to the driver, "La Grande Depot, as fast as you can."

His foot slammed the pedal, knocking us back against the seat. Taking me at my word, he squealed a U-turn on Sunset, skimming past a farm truck loaded with crates of early asparagus, and motored east.

"What'sa matter, you gals gotta catch a train?"

"Yes. And I'll pay any ticket you might get."

That pledge brought on another spurt of speed, and we tore down the boulevard for many blocks until the driver snagged an unexpected right through a red light onto a side street. As we zigzagged through this sleepy residential neighborhood, he must have caught a glimpse of my startled expression in his rearview mirror. "It doesn't look like it, lady, but it's faster this way, honest."

I had my money ready, and as soon as we came within sight of La Grande, I tossed the cash on the front seat. "Pull up to the main door and we'll jump out."

The parking lot and all the entrances were eerily quiet. No uniforms, no police cars, no unusual activity. A few passengers walked out carrying suitcases; a few others headed in. Perversely, the calm only stoked my fears. Was I too late? Surely not. I must have arrived ahead of the police. Or else they were gathering somewhere out of sight, laying their trap.

I dashed into the station with Myrna at my heels, then stopped cold. The big clock said six minutes to two. "Wait here," I told Myrna. "I've got to find David."

Taking a deep breath, I scanned the station floor. It was not particularly crowded at this time of day, with a few dozen people milling about at the newsstand, queuing up at the ticket booths, resting on benches, and squinting anxiously at the arrival-and-departures board. Not a single blue uniform in sight.

I tried to think like a policeman planning an ambush. I would position the men in uniform, like Carl Delaney, outside where they could ring the building and make sure no one escaped. Those inside would be in civilian clothing, like the two who had come by my house. I was instantly suspicious of every man in the station who was not with a woman or child, anyone who stood alone or with a male companion. I spotted several whose eyes moved systematically from one person to the next, as if they were looking for someone. Cops? I couldn't be sure.

My eyes moved, too, from one end of the great hall to the other and back again, searching for David. I had to find him before the police did. What if they thought he had killed the two detectives in the desert? He hadn't. I was sure of it. The tip had to have been wrong. He couldn't have done such a thing. But they wouldn't arrest him and ask polite questions about his whereabouts. They would shoot him. Carl Delaney's words kept playing in my head: *Cops don't like crooks who kill cops.*

David was nowhere visible, but he had to be here somewhere. I had heard him with my own ears telling that actress that he was meeting a friend at two. The arrivals board confirmed that a train was due to arrive at two minutes past two and, no surprise, it was coming from the north. The passenger he was meeting would be coming from Portland. I had eight minutes to find David and warn him off. Eight minutes before the police sprung a trap that would end with David's death. His betrayal this morning played like a comic aside in a Shakespeare tragedy. I cared too much to lose him now.

Giving the ticket lines a wide berth, I traveled the perimeter of the vast hall, trotting toward the Harvey House with my silent shadow close behind. I didn't want Myrna anywhere near me, but she stuck like flypaper.

"Myrna, things might turn ugly here. It would help if you would wait out front." She neither replied nor changed her pace.

A quick survey of the restaurant told me David was not inside. Next I barged into the men's room, surprising two gentlemen in the act, neither of them David.

All at once I saw him, slouched in the shadows by the alcove where the luggage lockers were stacked three high. His arms were folded; his fists were clenched. Even at this distance, I could read his anger in the way he held himself. Evidently he'd been observing me with mounting displeasure for some time. I rushed over.

"David! Thank God I've found you."

David didn't look at me or Myrna. His eyes stared past us to the exit from the train platforms where someone would soon pass. If willpower alone could have eliminated me, I'd have vanished in a puff of smoke.

"Listen! It's a trap. Call it off. The police know something is up with some fellas at two o'clock, and they're surrounding the station. They think you killed Tuttle and Rios. Get out while you have the chance."

His eyes narrowed slightly and he worked the muscles in his jaw. Still, he ignored me.

"Look around! Some of those people are policemen wearing street clothes. If you walk into the Harvey House right now, you can get out. There's a back door in the kitchen."

He looked over my head and straightened, letting his arms fall slowly to his sides. I stole a glance at his face. Gone was the boyish quirk in his lips, the sparkle in his eyes. He seemed to have aged ten years.

I had come into the station afraid *for* David; suddenly I was afraid *of* him.

Before I could turn around, a rough voice from behind me said, "Well, well, what a coincidence finding you here."

Johnnie Salazar stood a few yards away. His left arm might have been useless, bound up in the sling, but the right one was fine and dandy, tucked inside his coat pocket holding something pointed and hard.

Myrna's hand flew to her mouth. "Johnnie! What are you doing here?"

"Shut up," Salazar snapped, his eyes never leaving David's face. "You dames keep still." Then, to David, "I believe you have something that belongs to me, and I want it back. Right now."

David held up two empty hands in a gesture that was meant to convey astonishment. I edged slightly closer to Myrna.

"Where are those suitcases?" hissed Salazar.

David gave a nonchalant shrug. "Sorry, Johnnie. I don't know what you're talking about."

"Well, you're gonna remember real quick." With his good arm, he grabbed a handful of Myrna's dress and yanked her against his chest. The gun was in plain view now as he held Myrna with his good arm, the gun in the same hand, pointed up at her throat.

I felt every eye in the train station must be on us, every breath drawn and held in horror as our deadly performance played out. In my mind we were center stage, caught under a dozen spot-lights, with an entire audience on the edge of their seats.

Incredibly, the spectators didn't seem to notice us. We were as good as invisible there in the locker alcove. Passengers surged out of arriving trains, off the platform and into the station, luggage in hand. They hugged family members or hurried for the nearest exit. Redcaps with baggage carts piled high wove through the throngs. Two smartly suited businessmen actually passed within a couple feet of our drama, circling around us without a glance, eager to reach the bank of lockers and retrieve their belongings. A woman holding her son's hand stopped almost at my side to study the departures board.

"Look, Mama," said the boy, pointing at Johnnie and the gun.

"Hush up." She tugged him along toward the trains, never turning her head.

"You think I didn't know who took my dope? You stupid mick. Never underestimate Johnnie Salazar, eh? Someone saw your car at the doc's house. I'm gonna see to it you don't sell what's mine."

"Don't be a sap, Salazar. Let the girl go. You shoot her in front of all these witnesses and you'll swing."

"I got nothing to lose. I'm a dead man anyway if I don't get the dope and the money back where it belongs." He cocked the gun. "Now where is it?"

For the first time that day, David's eyes met mine. They sent a loud cue. I didn't read it perfectly, but I knew enough to brace myself for what was to come.

"Have it your way, Johnnie. The suitcases are in locker 14." David opened his hand flat and held it out so Salazar could see. A small brass key lay on his palm. "Here, catch."

He lobbed the key gently toward Salazar's right side, toward the right hand that held the gun. Instinctively, as people do when something is thrown to them, Salazar grabbed for the key with his nearest hand, letting go of Myrna and lunging toward the right. At the same moment, I shoved her to the left, out of his reach.

"Run!" I commanded.

With only one hand, and that one still clutching his gun, Salazar was doomed to miss the key. He reached far enough that it struck his hand but it clanked against the metal gun and fell to the floor, bouncing away. At that moment, I locked my elbows, clasped my hands together and, with all the force I could muster, swung them like a club into his injured arm.

His scream of pain and outrage echoed through the depot, and he dropped the gun. It skidded on the smooth floor away from the key toward a cluster of potted palms. The key, meanwhile, slid into the path of several passengers who were arguing about the best place for dinner. One of them inadvertently kicked it farther away.

For one second, Salazar was paralyzed with indecision, looking from the gun to the key and back to the gun. That was all it took.

Although he had a greater distance to cover, David leaped toward the gun at the same moment that Salazar made his decision to do the same. They collided on the floor and struggled frantically for the weapon, knocking over one of the potted palms, scattering dirt and fronds everywhere, and *finally* drawing the attention of several nearby passengers who stopped to watch as if it were an intriguing publicity stunt.

Where the hell were the police when you needed them?

Salazar managed to get his finger on the trigger, but his one hand was no match for David's two. The struggle to point the barrel was brief. When the gun went off, it was pressed against Salazar's chest. The muffled bang left Johnnie Salazar dead.

34

The gunshot and the screams from onlookers turned the heads of the plainclothesmen positioned near the entrance to the tracks. Springing into action, they came running with guns drawn, shouting, "Don't move! Don't move! Drop your weapons!" to a huddle of unarmed people frozen in horror.

I rushed to David, who was kneeling on the floor breathing hard. "Are you all right?"

He nodded wearily, then looked over at Myrna. She was crouched against the lockers, her hands clasped so hard her fingers were white, but she was unhurt.

"Good job, kid," he said to me. "I knew I could count on you."

Under the circumstances, the safest place seemed to be the floor, so David and I sat and waited for the cops to assemble. David held the gun out flat on his palm to the first to reach us.

Only then did I notice Carl Delaney and Brickles. They had come inside along with the surge of blue uniforms. Carl hung back but his eyes moved from me to David, and I could hear his brain tapping like an adding machine calculating the odds of finding us together. On hands and knees, I made my way to the key to locker 14, nearly buried beneath the spilled dirt and broken palm branches.

One cop crouched over Salazar's body to satisfy himself that he was dead. "What happened?" he asked David.

David hadn't heard the question. He was staring intently at the entrance to Track 4. I followed his gaze and saw a man holding a large valise, taking in the mayhem in our corner. David shook his head. The man disappeared.

"Isn't it obvious?" I butted in before David had a chance to reply. "David Carr is a hero. He saved my friend Myrna's life as well as mine and shot this—this murderer here. That man"—and I motioned toward Salazar's body with my toe—"killed Detectives Tuttle and Rios out in the desert last Thursday. He was wounded during the gunfight, as you can see—his arm has a bullet wound—but he escaped, and he took the dope with him. Here's the key. He hid it in this locker until he could sell it."

I turned the key over to a redheaded cop who went straight to the bank of lockers to search for number 14. Finding it on the bottom, he opened the door and, as everyone watched, pulled out two large suitcases. They were top-drawer, made of dark leather with brass corners and catches. Even from where I stood I could see the bold initial *H*.

Just as I thought—Heilmann's suitcases. I knew Tuttle and Rios had taken the dope they found in the upstairs bedroom, but I was never sure how they got it out of his house. I asked myself what I would do in the same situation, and I answered myself that I would look for something large to carry the dope. Something found in every house. A suitcase. The detectives had made

a similar deduction, found Heilmann's luggage in a closet somewhere, and loaded up. They must have ruminated for a few days
before deciding that their likeliest customer was the local mob.
Big mistake.

If local crime bosses didn't like high-flying film directors
muscling in on their business, they liked cops even less. They
must have sent Johnnie Salazar and some of his gang to meet
Tuttle and Rios in the desert, ostensibly to buy the dope from
them. Someone started shooting, and Salazar walked away
with the goods. I still wasn't sure how David had gotten involved, although I suspected it had been my doing. I was the
one who had given him the information about the detectives
and the dope. I was the only one outside the mob who knew
the connection.

"Who was that man on Track 4?" I hissed.

"You don't miss much, do you, kid?" He shifted his weight and
I thought for a moment he wasn't going to answer. "A friend."

"From Portland?"

He nodded. I didn't have to ask anything else. David was
going to sell the contents of the Heilmann suitcases to someone
from Portland, probably someone from his old gang.

The chief of police arrived and took charge, dismissing
most of the officers and shooing away onlookers. A doctor who
chanced to be passing through the station pronounced Salazar
dead. "You ladies all right?" he asked. Myrna and I nodded.
"You're a couple of lucky girls. You should go home and have a
stiff drink . . . medicinal, of course," he added with a nervous
glance at the chief.

"As soon as you answer a few questions," said the chief, "I'll
have one of the men escort you home. Now, tell me what happened."

I repeated what I'd said to the cops who came first on the
scene. Enough time had elapsed since then that I had figured out
a plausible story and managed to convey in a few sentences how

my friend Myrna and I had come to the station with David to meet a friend.

"Salazar arrived at about the same time we did, to pick up his suitcases and leave town—at least, I presume he was planning to leave town. Unfortunately, he spotted the plainclothes cops hanging around. He panicked and grabbed Myrna, intending to use her as a hostage." The chief looked at Myrna, who nodded her agreement. She knew nothing different. "I distracted him and David knocked the gun out of his hand. They both dived for the gun and struggled for it, and it went off."

"And how did you come to know Salazar was the one who shot Tuttle and Rios in the desert?" the chief asked.

I pointed to Myrna. "Myrna overheard him talking. She was working at his studio and heard him boasting about it." I spoke louder, so Myrna could hear me. "He threatened you, didn't he, Myrna?"

Salazar had certainly threatened to ruin Myrna's career, which is what she thought I was referring to. Still shaken, she could only nod her agreement. I'd coach her a little more later, in case we were questioned further. It was a sure thing Salazar wasn't going to contradict anything we said.

David confirmed my account, as did several bystanders who had witnessed part of the fight. Names and addresses were jotted down in case the police needed to follow up, and two men arrived with a stretcher to carry off the late Mr. Salazar. The chief said we could leave.

I was congratulating myself on a masterful performance when I caught sight of someone standing just within listening range, someone I was beginning to know rather too well. Then our eyes met, and I knew there was one cop who wasn't convinced.

David drove us home. Questions burned inside me, questions I couldn't ask with Myrna beside us in the front seat. David was not similarly constrained.

"So how did you find out about the ambush?" he asked as we

pulled out of the depot parking lot. He displayed an extraordinary degree of sangfroid for someone who had just knocked off someone else.

"Some cops were in our yard shooing away a pack of reporters, and a police car came by with a couple of plainclothesmen to tell them to get to the depot right away. An informer had tipped them off that the man who killed the two detectives would be there at two o'clock. I remembered you were going to be at the depot to meet someone at two, and it was nearly two, so I grabbed a cab."

"You thought I had killed the detectives?"

The truth of it was, I hadn't been certain. That was part of what I was itching to ask. I had to know what David's role was in this affair. But with Myrna next to me, I chose my words carefully. "Noooo, but it looked like you were going to get caught up in it anyway."

I translated his grunt to mean that he understood I couldn't talk freely. We drove west in silence for a couple minutes before he spoke again. "I don't remember telling you I was going to the depot at two."

I gave a resigned sigh. No one was going to slip anything past David. "Yeah, well, you did. I heard you talking to someone named Ruby at the studio about a boating party. You begged off because you had to meet a friend at two."

"How—? You weren't—"

"I was the girl in the blue and white sailor suit."

He looked at me with disbelief. "Hey, watch the road, buster," I reminded him. "I've met my danger quota for today."

He pulled up to the curb in front of our house on Fernwood, and Myrna and I got out. "Dinner?" he asked. I remembered our engagement and my intention to break it off in some dramatic fashion. It seemed so petty now. I wanted—I needed—to talk to him alone, but there was no way I could handle being out in public tonight. I could not fathom how he could think of food at a time like this. What I needed was a hot bath and a glass of relaxant.

"Not in the mood," I replied.

He nodded. "Tomorrow, then?"

"Tomorrow." I'd have to wait to hear his story. I wondered whether it would be fact or fiction.

35

Turned out Johnnie Salazar was the Hollywood Killer. News-papers across the nation blared headlines like SMALL-TIME HOODLUM CRASHED HEILMANN ORGY, RETURNED FOR REVENGE AFTER BEING TOSSED OUT, and WAITRESS WITNESSED MURDER, HUNTED DOWN. Stories explained that Salazar feared other late party guests had witnessed his actions and so had had to murder Lorna McCall in her home. Then he had gained ac-cess to Paramount by pretending to be a director and poisoned Paul Corrigan and Faye Gordon. Meanwhile, two detectives were preparing to bust up Salazar's dope ring, one of California's most notorious, and they surprised him as he was taking deliv-ery of a shipment from Mexico. The ensuing gunfight left two of Los Angeles's finest detectives dead, not to mention three worthless gangsters. Much was made of the heroism of Tuttle and Rios, and their funerals received extensive coverage.

The police were pleased to have wrapped it all up. Their detectives had been avenged. Case closed.

The big studio bosses—the Warners, Zukor, Mayer—were giddy with relief. They knew the puzzle parts didn't fit together that well but preferred not to challenge an explanation that so neatly deflected criticism from the film industry without linking Heilmann or any other movie people to dope, sex, or liquor. They took every opportunity to point out piously that Hollywood was as much a victim of gangland mayhem as any other city in America.

It was really very tidy. Too bad none of it was true.

I didn't remember the money until the following day. I broached the topic over dinner with David in my usual subtle way.

"What the hell happened to the money?"

"What money?"

We had just been seated in a dark corner at one of Musso & Frank's red leather and mahogany booths.

"Don't go innocent on me. The money that wasn't with Heilmann's suitcases. The money Johnnie Salazar was going to pay Tuttle and Rios for the dope."

"Oh, that money. When the dust settles, I'll find some worthy charity . . ."

"Right, you and Andrew Carnegie."

"I won't be building libraries, but the public will certainly benefit. I plan to invest the proceeds in sound films and color process."

A waiter came to take drink orders. I asked for a highball; David ordered whiskey.

"I'm sorry, sir, we don't serve alcohol."

I swallowed my surprise and ordered ginger ale.

"Make it two," said David.

"A law-abiding proprietor," I said. "Who could have imagined?"

"Most likely they have it for regulars. They don't know us here. And anyway, we're inside the city limits."

"What's that got to do with it?"

"Los Angeles cops don't have jurisdiction beyond the city limits. Why did you think that far end of Sunset Strip had so many cabarets and nightclubs?"

Trust a bootlegger to know the ins and outs. "This is the first time since I arrived in Hollywood that I haven't been served. I thought liquor was available everywhere. Mexico is so close, I hear people drive across the border and come home with cases of the stuff in the trunk."

"Yeah, this is a pretty easygoing town. But it isn't all Mexican, you know. Plenty of bathtub gin is brewed right here. A friend told me most of it starts downtown at L.A. General Hospital. They're allowed to buy alcohol for cleaning surgical instruments— a legal exception, like the Catholic Church's sacramental wine. The funny thing is, though, before Prohibition, the hospital bought denatured alcohol by the gallon. Now they buy it by the boxcar. Someone gets hold of the extra, 'renatures' it, dilutes it with water, adds a little juniper juice, and presto! Gin." He shook his head with admiration as we sipped our sodas. "Pure genius. Ideas like that keep me humble. In all my years in the business, I never thought of the hospital angle."

I waited until we had ordered our steaks and the waiter was out of range before I steered him back to my original topic.

"All right, I want to know the whole story. How did you get the suitcases from Johnnie Salazar? And don't lie to me."

A smile softened the angles of his face. "I don't dare. Besides, I have you to thank. You told me about the detectives stealing the dope from Heilmann's. I was following them to see where they'd stashed it, thinking I might be able to relieve them of it without much trouble and sell it out of town. Do you know where it was all along? In the trunk of their damn police car! I had binoculars. I saw them out in the desert trying to sell the stuff to Salazar's boys. A very stupid plan. Anyone over the age of eight could have told them that."

He shook his head, baffled at such naïveté. "When the dustup was over, I followed Salazar back to town. I could tell by the way he was driving he'd been hit pretty bad, and I saw my chance. I figured he'd go to a hospital, and I could grab the suitcases then. But he was no fool. He stopped at a doctor's house, some fella who knew better than to talk about bullet wounds. While he was getting patched up, I moved all three suitcases to my car, the dope and the cash. I didn't think anyone saw me."

"Someone did. Someone must've told Salazar. Maybe described your car."

"Probably got a license plate number. Anyway, I went straight to the train station to put the luggage where it would attract the least attention and contacted an old chum to buy the contents. Heilmann suitcases in one locker, money suitcase in another. Never mix dope and money, that's my motto. The man I was meeting had a satchel full of Grover Clevelands that he was going to put into a locker, then we were going to swap keys and go our separate ways."

"Nothing like selling the dope twice."

"Double the money. That was the idea. Still, I came out ahead. Thanks to your warning." He lifted his glass in a toast.

"I wasn't trying to help you get rich. I was trying to pay you back for saving my life in Oregon last year. The cops thought you'd killed Tuttle and Rios, and you were not going to live to see a trial."

"I am forever in your debt."

"No, the score's even now."

"Let's see if we can't both stay out of trouble."

"I'm still wondering who could have tipped off the police. Who else knew you were going to the depot at two o'clock?"

"Salazar must've followed me there. As for the police . . . I have my own ideas."

"Such as?"

"The only people who knew about the two-o'clock swap were

me and the Portland boys. I hear there's a struggle going on between some of the old gang now that I'm not there to keep a lid
on things, and I'm pretty sure one of them sent word to the L.A.
cops in order to be rid of Danny. That's the guy I was meeting.
Maybe also to make sure I wasn't planning a comeback."

"And are you?" I asked.

"I told you. I'm done with all that. Gone straight."

Our steaks arrived. "You promised your whole true-life story."

"In exchange for yours."

A nod sealed the deal. He waited for the waiter to finish
serving, then surveyed the room again. Musso & Frank's was
popular with film people, but I saw no familiar faces, and no one
was close enough to eavesdrop.

"When I was about fourteen," he began, "I fell in with some
lads who were bringing whiskey in from Canada. Oregon went
dry before the rest of the country, you know, and there was good
money to be made for doing nothing more than driving through
Washington, across the Canadian border, and back again. Over
the years I worked harder and smarter than anyone else, and it
got noticed. I moved up in the ranks, supervised local purchases,
organized overland and sea runs, and branched into speakeasies.
Pretty soon I was running the show."

He paused to cut into his steak.

"What sort of show, besides the hooch?"

"Some gambling around town."

"Dope?"

"The Chinese handled most of that through their opium
dens. And you don't want to cross the Chinese when it comes to
opium."

"Brothels?"

"A couple high-class houses attached to the speakeasies, to
keep customers and cops happy."

"Did you kill people?"

He put a large piece of steak in his mouth and chewed it

slowly. "Only in self-defense. Like yesterday." Something in the way he replied told me further questions on that topic would not be welcomed. Besides, I wanted to believe him. "When the cops came after me last fall, I skipped to Vancouver, changed my name, and lay low for a while. After things quieted down, I came back to the States, but no one knew where you'd gone. Finally I tracked down some of your vaudeville friends who told me you were living in Hollywood, so I came south, figuring Hollywood would be just the right starting-over business for David Carr. I have plenty of money, and that makes me very popular in the film industry. And now that you know more about me than anyone on this earth, you'll have to marry me."

I looked up, startled, and my face flushed hot. David had a way of getting under my skin with a single word. I raised my eyebrows and looked my question at him, hoping the dim light was hiding my discomfort.

"Wives can't testify in court against their husbands," he continued.

"Ahhh, I see." He was toying with me, the way men do, trying to rattle me. Our conversation paused as another couple was seated in the booth behind ours.

"And what about your activities now?" I asked, careful to use innocent-sounding words and a quiet voice.

"You mean here in Hollywood? Like I said, I've gone arrow-straight."

"Except for Salazar's cash."

"That doesn't count. It fell into my lap. I didn't go looking for trouble. I could not in good conscience let all that money get into the hands of some undeserving crook, could I?" The deserving crook grinned. It was all a game to him.

Over apple pie and ice cream, it was my turn. I gave David a brief synopsis of my life in vaudeville, describing the hungry times as well as the successes. I told him a little about the mother who raised me and the grandmother I had only recently discovered.

He wanted to know more about my acts, the best ones and the worst.

"That's a hard question; there were so many." I thought a while, then told him the best act was probably the Little Darlings, a lighthearted song-and-dance team where I played one of the older children. "And the worst? Let's see. Well, I guess I'm not too proud of my stint with the fakir when I impersonated a grieving widow to help swindle other grieving widows. And the time I worked as a magician's assistant was pretty sleazy. As I was telling Myrna last week, I was practically nude on the stage."

"I'd like to have seen that!" I tried to keep a stern face but the mischievous look on his face drove off all my resolve. "Any chance of an encore later tonight?"

"Nope."

"Mmmm. And you started over when you came to Hollywood, just like me."

"Hollywood's a new start for a lot of people."

"You sure you're not operating a swindle now?"

"No!"

"Don't give me any outrage. Are you going to tell me you've never run afoul of the law?"

I sighed. "It was a long time ago. I . . . well, I got off light—if anyone had known my real age, the story would be a lot worse."

"So here we are, two reformed delinquents. Two upstanding citizens. No reason we can't let this fine friendship grow into something stronger, is there?"

36

In *Son of Zorro*, Douglas Fairbanks plays two roles, reprising the original Zorro from the first film, now a graying aristocrat but still a formidable swordsman, as well as Zorro's son, Don Q. Thanks to the wizardry of the studio's film crew and cameramen, he could play them both in the same scene. This delicate procedure, perfected a few years earlier for Mary Pickford's astonishing dual role in *Little Lord Fauntleroy*, calls for the cameraman to matte part of the frame, then rewind the film for a second pass. One of these double-exposure scenes was on the schedule for Monday.

Douglas Fairbanks emerged from a lengthy session in Makeup looking so much older that Frank Richardson called him Gramps. Douglas scowled, and Frank didn't repeat the joke.

We worked hard until noon. Frank called a lunch break, and Douglas motioned me to his side. "What happened this morning? Did you get to talk to Faye Gordon?"

"Nothing happened. I went to Faye's home at about nine with some flowers. A snooty maid let me in and took my name, then returned to tell me Miss Gordon wasn't feeling well enough for visitors."

"You really think she can tell you anything you don't already know?"

"It was worth the try."

He tapped a cigarette out of its box and struck a match. "I'm glad you haven't given up on the case. It spooks me knowing the person who killed Lorna McCall and Paul Corrigan—and very nearly killed Faye—is still walking around. What if you went to see Faye again this afternoon?"

"I don't think I'd have any better—"

"What if my Mary went with you?"

I considered it. "That might work. Although as I recall, Faye wouldn't see Miss Pickford when she was in the hospital."

"But she might now."

"She might."

That's how, a few hours later, I found myself in the backseat of a Rolls-Royce with Mary Pickford heading to Faye Gordon's apartment on the west side of Hollywood. I took the opportunity to ask her something that had been pestering me. "What was Faye's relationship with Paul Corrigan?"

Miss Pickford thought for a moment. "I suppose you'd call it the love/hate sort. They were lovers once, and she threw him over. He took it hard. Lately they had been friendly. I suspected they were back together again, which is why I invited them both to dinner last week." She sighed and shook her head sadly.

"Paul said some pretty harsh things about her at dinner."

"Paul . . . well, one hates to speak ill of the dead, but Paul had a way of saying cruel things quite unconsciously. I never held it against him."

Not sharing Miss Pickford's generous nature, I believed Paul Corrigan's remarks were quite deliberate, but I didn't voice my thoughts. We had reached Faye Gordon's apartment building.

This time, I stood back and let Miss Pickford handle the maid. The maid oozed deference, returned promptly, simpered, and showed us into a fussy, red and white living room with large windows overlooking the gentle western hills.

"Miss Gordon will be with you in a moment," she said, and I pictured the actress hurriedly applying more makeup and changing her dress. "May I get you ladies some tea?"

It was some time before Faye glided into the room, clad in a Chinese silk dressing gown that puddled on the floor when she paused. "Darling." She greeted her friend with a kiss on both cheeks. I got a limp hand. She sat facing us with her back against the afternoon sun, taking care to position herself in the flattering backlight.

I allowed the pleasantries to flow over me for a few minutes. Faye was delighted to see Mary, Mary was charmed to see Faye, the flowers were lovely, the weather was grand, and Douglas sent his regrets but wished her well. I had agreed with Miss Pickford on the drive over that she would steer the conversation to Faye's health, at which point I would take over.

"Well, I must say, my dear, you look divine after such a monstrous experience," said Miss Pickford. "Douglas and I were very worried about you, and everyone is most grateful that you have had a complete recovery."

That was my cue. "I wonder, Miss Gordon, do you expect to return to the *Cobra* set soon?"

She gave me a slightly startled glance as if she had just noticed I was sitting on her sofa. "Joe Henabery was kind enough to adjust the filming schedule to work around my . . . my illness," she said delicately, facing Mary Pickford as she replied, as if Mary had asked the question and not her upstart little companion. "He won't resume filming my scenes until next week, so I have plenty of time to recuperate."

I am not that easily deterred. "I—we were wondering if you might tell us about what happened last Tuesday morning."

She straightened her back and peered down her nose at me like an affronted duchess. "And what earthly business is that of yours?" she asked haughtily.

"Now, Faye, you mustn't take offense," said Miss Pickford, trying to smooth the ruffled fur. "Jessie is helping Douglas with his own investigation of these tragic deaths, and she only wanted to ask you a few questions on his behalf. I told her you wouldn't mind. It's the least we can do, in Paul's memory."

"Well, I don't know . . . I mean, naturally, Mary dear, I'd do anything for you and Douglas, but, well, heavens . . ."

I interpreted that as a green light. "Were you expecting Mr. Corrigan that morning?"

"Of course not. He just dropped by the studio unannounced."

"I was wondering what his purpose was."

"His purpose? Why, to see me. What a ridiculous question."

"But didn't it seem odd that he would come by the set when he had just seen you at Pickfair the night before?"

"Really, you sound like those nasty policemen. What is the reason for all this? The murderer has been identified and the police have killed him."

"Oh, I know what the newspapers are saying," said Miss Pickford, "but you and I know better than most how they make things up. That awful director Salazar was part of the shootout that left the two detectives dead, but we believe someone else—another gangster from Chicago—killed Bruno Heilmann and the waitress after his party."

Faye looked at me now. Really looked at me. Her eyes flashed angrily, and at that moment, she appeared quite capable of killing someone herself. "And what evidence do you have for this extraordinary conclusion?"

"A good deal of evidence," I said, "showing the movements of the gangster who killed them. The gangster left Hollywood a few hours after the killings on an early Sunday morning train."

"There is a serious lapse in your theory, my dear," she said in a patronizing manner. "Lorna McCall wasn't killed until Sunday afternoon. And your gangster was still around on Tuesday morning to poison Paramount's coffee."

"I'm afraid not," I said. "Someone else killed Lorna McCall and Paul . . . and would have killed you if you had swallowed more coffee. And the means used in those murders were entirely different. The man who murdered the first two was strong, violent, and good with a gun. The other murderer was more devious in his methods."

"Jessie and Douglas believe that Lorna's and Paul's murderer wanted us to think that the same person killed them all," said Miss Pickford in her quiet way. "But it isn't true. I know you'll want to help us catch him before he strikes again."

"Oh, my. But surely that's all over. No one has been killed in a week."

"It may be over, and it may not," I said.

"You mean to say I might still be in danger?" Finally we had Faye's attention.

"You might," I said. "So might others."

Faye gave a long sigh and picked up a sandalwood fan lying on the table beside her. "Well, to tell you the truth . . . and I hope it won't go any further," she said, fanning herself gracefully, "Paul and I had a little spat at your dinner last week, and he had come by the studio to apologize."

"I see. What time did he arrive?"

"Sylvie came by at about ten with a message that Mr. Corrigan had come to see me. I said show him into my dressing room, and we talked for about fifteen minutes. He was very sweet. Then we went down the hall for some coffee. The studio had set up coffee in an empty dressing room so we wouldn't have to walk all the way to the commissary."

"Was anyone else in the room when you entered?"

She looked scornful. "Naturally not, or there would have been another death. No, the room was empty. We sat and poured our coffee. Paul takes his—I mean, he took his with lots of cream and sugar; I drink mine black. While we talked, he drank two cups rather quickly. Mine was so hot without the cream to cool it, I drank just a little. I noticed a funny taste, but thought nothing of it." She shivered at the memory, and for the first time, I felt sorry for her. It must have been a horrible experience.

"Bad coffee is the bane of every studio," said Miss Pickford. As if I hadn't noticed. "All that cream and sugar probably covered up the taste and prevented Paul from noticing it as unusual."

"Then what happened?" I asked. "Did Mr. Corrigan collapse right away?"

"He complained that his stomach hurt. We kept talking. Then it got worse, and he doubled up, then started writhing about on the floor. I thought it might be appendicitis, coming on so sudden like that, and I was going for help when I felt a stomach cramp myself, sharp as a knife, and I couldn't move. I don't know how much time passed, maybe seconds, maybe half an hour. I was in terrible pain. If Sylvie hadn't come by, I'm sure I'd have died, too. She found us both on the floor. Paul wasn't dead, and he tried to talk, but she couldn't make out anything he said."

"Not a single word?"

"That's what she told me."

"Could you?"

"No."

"Then what happened?"

"Sylvie called for help and the Paramount doctor came right over, but Paul was unconscious by then. I managed to warn them that I thought it might be the coffee. I could hardly breathe, but

I forced myself to speak so that no one else would drink from that deadly pot."

"How very brave of you." Miss Pickford sighed.

Faye tilted her head modestly. "I couldn't live with myself if I had failed to prevent an innocent person's death."

"And then what happened?" I prompted again.

"They rushed us both to the hospital and pumped my stomach just in the nick of time. I very nearly died. They told me Paul passed away several hours later, never regaining consciousness." She reached for a lace handkerchief and dabbed her eyes, then took another tiny sip of tea.

I reached for my cup and found I'd drained it. Miss Pickford's cup was empty, too. Faye's was almost full. As I watched, she lifted her cup and once again barely wet her lips with the tea. She looked at our empty cups and then directly at me. Her eyes glittered like ice.

Panic seized me by the throat. The scene was being replayed. The tea was poisoned. Faye was hardly drinking any. Miss Pickford and I had drained our cups. My stomach ached. We were about to fall on the floor. She wouldn't call the ambulance until it was too late. We were going to die.

I squeezed my hands together to give my common sense time to rein in my galloping imagination and tell me how silly I was to even think such a thing. I took a deep, calming breath. We weren't being poisoned. My stomach didn't hurt. The maid, not Faye, had made our tea, and Faye was drinking it, too. A nasty look did not equate with murder. Faye may have thought me pushy and rude, but that was no reason for her to poison me and her longtime friend. All this intrigue was making me fanciful.

To prove to my head that the rest of me was convinced, I poured myself a second cup, used the antique sugar tongs to pinch a lump of sugar, added a dollop of warm milk, and stirred the concoction with a silver teaspoon. Defiantly, I took a sip. There! See? No stomachache, no poison.

What had set my imagination running like that? Did I really believe Faye capable of poisoning anyone? Just because I didn't like her didn't mean she had poisoned Paul Corrigan.

But she could have, whispered a voice in my head.

Don't be ridiculous, I answered it. Why would Faye want to kill poor Paul Corrigan, her friend, who had come to apologize for some rift? She hadn't even known he was going to come by the studio that morning. Did I seriously think she carried a vial of poison in her pocket in case someone she didn't like dropped by?

She didn't like Lorna McCall, either. Remember that fierce argument at the party when Faye slapped Lorna?

So what? Things like that happened all the time in Hollywood.

Faye could have been the one at Lorna's that Sunday. She could have gone to see her and . . . and . . . somehow . . .

And what? Did she barge in, demand coffee and cake, force Lorna to go into the bathroom and throw up, then push her head in the toilet bowl? Come now . . . It sounded more plausible the other way around. Lorna McCall had more reason to be angry with Faye than vice versa. Besides, the person who killed Lorna had probably intended it to look like another Heilmann witness murder, like Esther's. If so, that meant the killer had to have known that both Heilmann and Esther Frankel were dead. The newspapers didn't carry that information until Tuesday.

But Faye was at Pickfair Monday night. Everyone there knew the details.

The person who killed Lorna had to have known about Heilmann's and Esther's murders before Monday's dinner, in fact, before Sunday afternoon. The only people who knew about both at that point were me, Douglas Fairbanks, Mary and Lottie Pickford, Adolph Zukor, and the police.

*Doesn't that mean one of those people killed Lorna? Or could
one of them have told someone I didn't know about?*

Miss Pickford's voice intruded into my mental debate. "No,
thank you, my dear," she was saying, "you know I can't allow myself to indulge in sweets. But I will have more tea, please." Faye
left off urging the teacake on her friend and poured her another
cup of tea.

"Do you remember when you first learned of Bruno Heilmann's death?" I asked Faye.

"Let me think . . . I believe it was from the newspaper. I can't
remember what day that was."

Miss Pickford corrected her gently. "No, Faye, the newspaper
story came out on Tuesday, and you were at our house Monday
night when we were all talking about it."

"That's so. I forgot about that."

"No one told you before you arrived at Pickfair?" I asked.

"No."

37

Jessie!" Melva called up the stairs to my room. "Jessie, there's a policeman here to see you."

Geez Louise, now what? Hadn't I answered all their questions at the train station? Was I headed for another prickly round of interrogation? It was almost seven and I'd just slipped into a dressing gown after the long day.

"I'm not dressed," I yelled. "I'll be right down."

Step out of the dressing gown. Pull on an everyday skirt. Tuck in a simple blue blouse. Freshen the rouge and lipstick. Add a touch of kohl. Now I looked the part—an honest, sober citizen, ready for whatever the police threw at me.

The effect was wasted on Officer Delaney, who was waiting for me on the front porch.

"Why, Carl," I said sweetly. "This is a surprise. What brings you here tonight?"

Before I knew what he was doing, he'd taken hold of my wrists and snapped them together with a pair of clunky handcuffs.

"What the hell—"

"I'm sorry to have to place you under arrest, Miss Beckett."

"Arrest! For what?"

"Withholding information, lying to the police. If you'll just come with me, please . . ."

Melva's jaw dropped and she dithered helplessly, but Carl whisked me out of the house and into his police car before she could marshal her thoughts into any semblance of coherent speech. "I'll . . . Should I . . . I'll tell Myrna as soon as she gets home . . . What do you . . . Is there anything else I should—" But the car door slammed and I couldn't hear the rest.

I fumed. I seethed. I stared straight ahead and vowed not to utter another word, even if they tore out my fingernails. It was humiliating being trussed up like some common criminal for all the world to see. They'd be sorry they treated me like this! They wouldn't get a peep out of me. I had already told them everything I was going to tell. I would stick to my story like glue. Come what may, I was going to protect David.

I kept my head turned away from Carl, glaring out the window until I emerged from my self-absorbed sulk long enough to notice a couple of deer on the edge of the road, turned to stone by the headlights. We were beyond the edge of town.

"Wait a minute," I blurted. "You've turned the wrong way. The police station is—" Then it occurred to me that Officer Carl Delaney knew very well where the police station was located, and a watery chill trickled down the back of my neck. "Where are you taking me?"

"To a nice quiet spot where we can talk."

"I'm not under arrest?"

"Not really."

"What the hell are these for?" I shook my manacles.

"Just making sure you don't hurt yourself. Or me. I saw you

light into that Salazar fella at the depot the other day. You're a tough customer."

I hate men who patronize me. Then I realized Carl was missing his shadow. "Where's Brickles?"

"It's his day off. Mine, too, for that matter."

"This is kidnapping!"

He gave a patient sigh, as one would to humor an unruly child. "Simmer down, Jessie. You're not in any danger, and you know it. You and I are going to have a nice, uninterrupted chat, that's all. Then I'll take you home." He gave me his choirboy smile.

"You bastard! You'll take me home right now—I'm not *chatting* with you!"

The car continued north until Carl turned onto a narrow paved road that snaked into the hills of Hollywoodland. "You ever been to see that big sign on Mount Lee close up? It's quite a sight, all lit up like that."

It was a lonely sight, that's for sure. We passed no other cars, and while there were a few skeleton houses in various stages of construction scattered about the development, no one was working on them at night and no light shone from any windows. If I hadn't been in such a fury, I would have enjoyed the panoramic valley view.

It wasn't long before we pulled off the road onto a dirt turnaround that ended near the giant *H*. Carl cut the motor. "This is as close as we can get with the car. We could walk up farther, but there's a nice spot over there to sit and look over the city lights."

"I'm staying right here."

"Suit yourself. It can get pretty cold here without any covering," he said, indicating that the gray blanket folded over his arm was going with him. "It's warmer over there with the heat from the sign."

The sun was slipping below the horizon in a gorgeous display of orange and red that would normally have thrilled me. The western sky glowed as the shadows vanished, taking with them

every drop of warmth that had heated the air. I sat in the motorcar until I nearly shivered off the front seat before I surrendered
to reality and walked to the sheltered spot where Carl was sitting, puffing on a cigarette. The smoke drifted straight up in the
still air. He stubbed it out on a rock as I approached.

"Why are you doing this?"

"Got tired of listening to lies."

"I don't know what you're talking about."

"Brickles, now he says you're the problem here. I said no, she's
the answer."

"I have nothing to say to you."

"Then we'll be here a long time."

I sat near him on a warm, flat rock and felt on my back the
heat that radiated from the Hollywoodland sign. Carl draped the
blanket over my shoulders. Behind us loomed the fifty-foot *H*, lit
up like a giant theater marquee spilling light as bright as day. I
could wait the bastard out. I looked down on Hollywood spread
out below like a toy village under a Christmas tree. Behind me
the enormous white letters with their thousands of lightbulbs
made sure this portion of Mount Lee never saw darkness, and I
tried to decide whether they were a point of interest or an eyesore. It didn't matter; either way, they'd be gone in a year or two.
I sat so still a lizard crawled over my shoe. A half hour passed,
maybe an hour; I didn't have a wristwatch. I did have an idea.

"I have to go to the bathroom."

"There's a bush over there in the dark. I'll keep my head
turned."

I stood up and held out my wrists. He raised his eyebrows in
an unspoken question. "I can't do it with these on," I said impa-
tiently.

"You'll manage."

I sat down again. "I'll wait."

"Suit yourself."

I heard the motorcar coming up the road before I saw its

headlights. I willed it to come our way, although I wasn't sure how, exactly, it was going to help my situation. It finally came to the end of the road where Carl had left his police car. The motor stilled. A man got out. Here was my opportunity.

I was about to call out when I heard a dog bark. "Hey there, Carl," the man shouted. He was in the dark and I was facing the lightbulbs, but I could sense movement behind the lighted sign.

My heart sank. "A friend of yours?"

"Caretaker," he said, pointing up the hill. "You can't see it from here with the lights in your eyes, but he lives in a cottage behind the *H*."

"Somebody lives behind the sign?"

"Not all the time. His job is climbing up the letters to replace burned-out bulbs. Keeps vandals away, too."

"How does he know it's you?"

"I come up here sometimes. It's a good place to sit and think. Calms me down."

The idea of Carl needing calming flummoxed me. Here was a man whose highest level of agitation was manifested by a raised eyebrow, talking about nerves? I thought about that awhile, until he stood and walked back to the police car. The next thing I knew, he was settling a basket on the rock beside me. "I brought something to eat. How 'bout a sandwich? I made two kinds, not knowing your preference. A roast beef and a cheese. Take your pick. It makes no nevermind to me."

I was starving. I hadn't had much to eat at lunch and it was way past dinnertime. "I'm not hungry," I snapped back as rudely as I could.

Carl bit into the roast beef. My eyes ignored him but my stomach, recognizing food just inches away, protested loudly at this injustice. Carl heard. Without a word—without even looking in my direction—he handed me the cheese. As I tore into it, he fished out a couple of apples and a Mason jar of cool water.

When we'd finished, he creased the waxed paper and put it back into the basket.

"Enough is enough, Carl. You can't keep me here forever."

His nod acknowledged the truth in that. "But I can keep you here a good long while."

"You don't mean to stay here all night!"

"In France, I slept outside every night for months, until it seemed strange sleeping under a roof. I've got a warm coat. I'll do fine. Kind of you to worry about me, though."

"I wasn't worried about you," I snapped.

Every minute seemed like an hour. The rock had long since cooled and even with the blanket, I shivered in my thin blouse. My temper was decomposing rapidly.

"You are without a doubt the stubbornest man I ever knew."

"You're no piker yourself. What say we call a truce and start with something easy, like why you don't like cops."

"Not all cops. Just you. *Hey, what the hell are you doing?*"

He had started unfastening the brass buttons of his blue uniform. Calmly, he took off the coat, folded it over his arm, and walked to the car where he took a thick coat out of the trunk. Buttoning it up, he returned to my side and sat down. It was army issue, well worn and sturdy, something that had, quite literally, been through the war. "Thought you'd be more comfortable this way."

"Uniform or not, you're still a cop."

"You got that right, lady. Over in France, I told myself if I got home in one piece, I wasn't going to follow my father and take on the farm, I was going to be a cop."

My curiosity got the better of me. "Why?"

"I saw what happens to decent people when law and order disappears, when the strongest man with the biggest gun gets away with doing whatever he wants to because there's no police, no jails, no consequences."

The damn rock was turning my fanny numb. I crossed my legs

under me Indian style—an unladylike pose my mother would have deplored—and hunkered down with the blanket.

"I figure you being in vaudeville all your life and moving around the country all the time, you had some run-ins with the police that soured you on the whole lot. I can understand that. There are some pretty rotten apples in the police barrel."

"You can say that again!"

"The way I see it, you got yourself mixed up in this mess and now you're stuck. You can't come clean about what you know or your own part will come out. That about sum it up?"

All too well. I twitched uncomfortably.

"And maybe you could tell me your real name?"

"There's nothing suspicious about my name."

"Didn't say there was. Just wanted to know it."

I turned the question every which way in my head but could find no harm in it. "My mother named me Leah. She was using the name Chloë Randall at that time, so I guess my last name was Randall, although I never saw a birth certificate. Don't think I have one. No one ever called me Leah. Mother called me Baby. My name changed with my acts until last year when I learned who my father was, and took his name, Beckett. I had a cousin named Jessie. She's dead but we were close once and she wanted me to have her name. What is a real name, anyway? It's whatever fits. Jessie Beckett fits me. I'd hate to lose it."

"Why would you lose it?"

"If I had to disappear."

He considered what I'd said for a few minutes, then he came closer and tucked the blanket firmly around my knees. "You know how in court they make witnesses swear to tell the whole truth and nothing but the truth? Well, you don't need to do that. You can just tell me the parts you can tell me. We could start with that funny business at the train station Saturday."

I began to thaw. "What do you mean?"

"Those suitcases came from Heilmann's house, didn't they? I

saw the H. And the dope, too, of course. It didn't come from Mexico. At least, not that day. Others saw the H, too, but they don't have such a suspicious mind as me. Not that it matters; there aren't any detectives investigating anymore. The case is closed. The detectives are dead."

He was already so close, it couldn't be that risky for me to nudge him the rest of the way. In spite of his antics, I did trust Carl. He was the first honest cop I'd ever known. Maybe the only one in Los Angeles. "The detectives were crooks," I said.

"Tell me something I don't know."

"You knew?"

"Everyone knew Hank Rios and Sam Tuttle took favors on the side. What more do you have?"

"They were the ones who stole the dope from Heilmann's to begin with. They found it in the bedroom when they searched the house and put it in his suitcases and put them in the trunk of their car. A few days later, they set up a meeting to sell it to Johnnie Salazar."

Carl whistled softly. "So Salazar double-crossed Tuttle and Rios, kept the money, and took the dope out of their trunk." He didn't ask how I knew, and I was relieved not to have to mention David's temporary ownership of the suitcases or my own sneaking into Heilmann's house. "Well, I see why you didn't want to blab that around town. Who knows if those two were acting alone? There could be others involved, and you might have met with an accident." He ruminated a while on what I'd said, then shifted gears to the first murder. "So Salazar didn't kill Heilmann. And Lottie Pickford didn't, either. Who did?"

What the heck. I had nothing to lose by sharing this part. I took a deep breath. "Sal Panetta, a hired gun from Chicago." And scene by scene, I laid out the plot for him, from the moment Panetta stole the motorcar from La Grande until he stepped off the Chicagoan at Dearborn Station three days later. Carl bit his lip rather than demand to know how I came by my information, and naturally I didn't volunteer David's shady connections. It wasn't ideal but it was working.

"You can check out everything I've told you," I said. "Then it will be your information, and you can do what you like with it. Just leave my name out of the credits. And be careful you don't get killed yourself."

"So who murdered Lorna McCall and Paul Corrigan?"

"I have no idea." That wasn't strictly true, but I was not ready to share my thoughts on that subject with anyone.

"I have one. It was someone Lorna knew. Remember the broken lock on Esther's door? Lorna McCall's door was in fine shape. She let the killer in. Gave him coffee."

"That doesn't limit the suspects much. Lorna had a lot of Hollywood friends, men and women. What about the poisoning? Did the police find anyone suspicious in the drugstore poison books?"

"Nary a one. Only a few dozen purchases of mercury bichloride in Los Angeles in the past month, and all of them accounted for."

"Did the police learn anything from Faye Gordon?"

"Not much. I wasn't the one who talked to her, but according to the report, she arrived at the studio at nine. The makeup person did her face, the wardrobe mistress delivered her costume, someone told her Corrigan had come to see her, and she invited him into her dressing room. They talked maybe fifteen minutes and went for coffee. The studio had a coffeepot and some chairs in an empty dressing room so the cast and crew wouldn't have to walk to the commissary every time they wanted some. Corrigan put cream and sugar in his. Miss Gordon drinks hers black. She noticed a funny taste but thought nothing of it. Corrigan drank fast and had a second cup. She drank less than half of hers. That was the difference between life and death."

So far what he said tallied with my information from Faye earlier today. I didn't tell him I'd just talked with her myself.

"Miss Gordon warned that it could have been something in

the coffee, so they took the coffee away to test it. She was right. What I wonder is, did someone want to kill Paul Corrigan, or Faye Gordon, or both of them, or did he want to kill someone else and accidentally get the wrong people? If so, is he still after Faye Gordon or someone else?"

I started to throw my hands up in a "who knows" gesture, but it only served to remind me I was still handcuffed. I glared at Carl until he reached into his pants pocket and found the key.

"You aren't going to wallop me if I take them off, are you?"

"I ought to."

"You got a left-hand swing Ty Cobb would trade for. You ever play baseball?"

"Just take these off."

"Yes, ma'am."

38

T hat's it, boys and girls," called Frank Richardson through his megaphone. "Mother Nature says class dismissed. We'll hope this blows through by tomorrow."

Nothing shuts down Hollywood quicker than a cloud bank. Filming couldn't continue without the famous southern California sun lighting up sets all over town, so whenever the day turned gray, filming went indoors or ceased entirely. After all, it had been the lure of year-round sunshine that coaxed production companies away from the East Coast in the first place. That plus favorable temperatures allowed cameras to roll 325 days a year. Few in the audience realized that most of the moving pictures they watched in their local theaters were filmed outside—even the indoor scenes were often done on sets that opened to the sky. It was hard to get good shots indoors, even using the three-

or four-point lighting techniques Mary Pickford had helped develop.

Before the grips started packing up the scenery and the actors disappeared into their dressing rooms, Pauline Cox and I scribbled notes about the placement of all the props and the condition of the costumes and makeup, so we could pick up tomorrow where we left off without a break in continuity.

We had been filming Lottie's scene, the one where, as Don Q's servant Lola, she tells her master that the corrupt Don Fabrique is blackmailing Sebastian. Lottie was in rare good form today, making the weather delay doubly regrettable since no one knew how she'd feel tomorrow. Douglas was there in his dashing Don Q getup, toying with his whip. He motioned me over to where he and Lottie were standing.

"I'm glad Mary got you in to talk with Faye yesterday. Mary tells me her story was quite chilling. I hadn't realized how close to death Faye was herself."

I nodded, although privately I thought Faye guilty of some overacting in that regard. Hadn't her doctor said she had swallowed too little bichloride of mercury to threaten her health? But it seemed a petty thing to say, and I had something else on my mind.

"I'm glad we got in to see her," I said.

"Did you learn anything new?"

"Maybe. Enough to make me wonder about something. Exactly who knew about both Bruno Heilmann's and Esther's murders on Sunday? Not one of them, but both."

He squinted into the distance and stroked his thin moustache as he contemplated my question. I peeked at Lottie's face to see her reaction, but she had none. She didn't seem to be listening.

"Let's see," Douglas began. "Zukor told me about Heilmann, but he didn't know about Esther. You told me about Esther. I knew about both. You knew about both. I told Mary. Mary told you, right, Lottie?"

"What?"

"I said, Mary told you about Heilmann's death and Esther's. The waitress."

"Oh, yes, she did, I think."

"That's when Lottie became concerned about her belongings left at Heilmann's," he said to me.

"Douglas! Don't tell people about that!"

"Jessie already knows. She was responsible for getting your things out of Heilmann's house, Lottie."

"Oh, I didn't know that. Well," she continued, turning to me, "you missed the cigarette case so it really didn't help."

You're welcome. "Lottie," I said, "did you tell anyone on Sunday about the murders?"

"Who, me? No! Douglas said not to."

"Not even later?"

"Oh, well, later, sure. The next day, sure. But Sunday afternoon, no. Not a soul. Except for Paul Corrigan."

"What?" Douglas and I exclaimed in unison.

"Well, don't make a fuss. I couldn't help it. We were going to meet friends later that night and I wasn't feeling up to it, what with the shock and all, so I telephoned to let him know, and of course he asked why I wasn't coming, so I had to explain. Anyway, what difference does it make now? He's dead."

I forced myself to sound calm. I didn't need Lottie to get defensive and start lying to me. "Oh, it's nothing, really. I just wondered . . . can you remember, by any chance, about what time it was when you talked with Paul?"

"Oh, I don't know. A little after lunch maybe."

"And do you remember the conversation?"

"Gee whillikers, let me think . . . I was upset. I told him Bruno had been shot dead. Paul had been at the party, too, you know, though he wasn't a great friend of Bruno's, but he was horrified. Very much. So we talked about that for a while. Who could have done it, and so forth and so on. Paul had lots of ideas—he was good at thinking."

"Did you happen to mention the waitress who was killed? Esther."

"Sure, I told him like Douglas told me, that the waitress must have seen the murderer at the party, and so he had to kill her or she'd have identified him to the police. We talked about that some, about wondering if we had seen the killer, too, and not even known it, and wondering if anyone else would get killed. And boy, did they ever!" She gave her shoulders a shake. "It's enough to give a person the creeps. Oh geez, there's Lily and I'm still in rags." She waved to a smart young woman across the set and called, "I'll be there in a jiffy, darling!" Then to us, "We're going shopping in Lily's new Packard Roadster, and I'm driving. It's the top-of-the-line custom Packard, and if I like it, I might buy one myself. In a different color, of course. Ta-ta!"

With the usual frown he wore when his sister-in-law was around, Douglas watched her flit away. "I want to apologize for Lottie—"

I held up one hand. "Thank you, but it's not necessary. That's just the way Lottie is. I understand."

"You understand a lot."

"I've known plenty of vaudeville performers like Lottie. It's part of show business."

"Sit down a minute." He indicated the canvas chair with LOT-TIE PICKFORD stenciled on the back. "Where do we go from here?"

"That's what I'm wondering. Just when the list of potential murderers was shrinking, it opens up wide. Paul Corrigan could have told anyone in Hollywood. In fact, he could have told several people and they could have spread the word further."

"Someone was quick to grasp the possibilities. Someone knew that the waitress had been killed and why, and that person figured a subsequent murder would be construed the same way. If and when someone was apprehended for the murders of Heilmann and the waitress, he'd deny killing Lorna McCall and Paul Corrigan, but who would believe him?"

"Maybe we're going about this backward. We'll never know now who Paul Corrigan might have told, but if we knew the killer's motive, we might figure out a likely suspect. Why would anyone want to kill Lorna?"

Douglas played with his moustache as he considered the possibilities. "Envy over her success. A romance gone sour. Something in her past we know nothing about."

All reasonable possibilities, but no bells rang. "What about Paul Corrigan and Faye? Who'd want to poison them?"

"We don't really know that anyone was trying to kill them both. The murderer may have intended to kill one of them, and the other was unavoidable."

"What do they have in common? Besides the fact that they were both at Heilmann's party."

"This isn't very nice to say, but they've both passed their prime."

"I gathered that."

"Paul wasn't working much and the parts he got were minor. And Faye lost several parts to younger actresses—Lorna for one. That's what brought on their quarrel at Heilmann's party, when Faye slapped Lorna. Mary says Faye and Paul were lovers once, some years ago. She thought they had reunited."

Ever since yesterday, thoughts of Faye Gordon had pestered me from the blurry edge of consciousness. Her fight with Lorna, her inability to get help when the poison struck Paul, her own mild reaction to the poison. It wasn't much, but the thoughts wouldn't leave me alone.

"Do you think Faye could have been angry enough at Lorna to kill her?"

Douglas didn't bat an eyelid. "I've been wondering the same thing. That brawl at the party must have left some pretty hard feelings."

"And if," I said, "Faye and Paul had reunited, she could have been there with him when he received the telephone call from Lottie. Or he could have telephoned her to share the news. If Faye knew about Heilmann's and Esther's murders, she could have decided it was an opportune moment to kill Lorna and make it look like another witness being eliminated."

Douglas picked up my train of thought. "And as for Paul Corrigan, maybe he suspected what she'd done and threatened to go to the police. If she knew he was coming to see her at Paramount, she could have planned to poison him to keep him quiet, and . . . Oh, for heaven's sake, it really is rather far-fetched, isn't it? Where would she get the bichloride of mercury? The police checked all the sales in Los Angeles for the past month and found nothing suspicious."

"Unless . . . what if she didn't buy it in Los Angeles?"

"You can't check every pharmacy in the state."

"But I might be able to check the ones in Bakersfield. At your house, Faye was talking about having missed a yachting party the previous weekend because she had to visit her sick mother in Bakersfield, and Paul made a snide remark to our end of the table about how that was just an excuse to distract from the fact that she hadn't been invited."

"I remember. But that puts her in Bakersfield long before the first murders."

"True. Maybe she was planning something before the murders, and when they occurred, she altered her plans to fit the circumstances."

"It's possible."

"I could go to Bakersfield and check the drugstores there. It's a long shot, but we haven't any other leads to follow."

"I don't know that it is such a long shot, now that I think about it. I'm sure Bakersfield is Faye's hometown. I've heard her mention it before. Let's not say anything about this to Mary, though, at least not until we know more. I'll let them know at the studio that you won't be in tomorrow. And don't worry about the cost. I'll pay any expenses." He took out his wallet and handed me twenty-five dollars, brushing aside my protest that it was far too much. "You take this and I don't want to see any change."

"I'll need a recent photograph of Faye."

"I'll telephone Paramount and ask for a publicity shot from *Cobra*."

39

The next morning I stopped by the Paramount office for the photo on my way to the station. There I hopped a northbound train. Several hours later I stepped off in Bakersfield, a small city known to most of us in vaudeville as a friendly place. Sizing up the taxi drivers waiting out front, I hired the bald one with the big belly because he had a sincere smile. His name was Charlie.

"First stop, the public library, please," I said, introducing myself.

"You'd be wanting the Beale Library. That's not far, just over to Seventeenth."

"I plan to visit all the drugstores in Bakersfield today, and I think the city directory would be the place to start, don't you?"

"Yes siree, Miss Beckett. I know where some of 'em are, but with a list, we'd miss nary a one."

I was prepared to explain my quest in brief terms but Charlie showed no curiosity, only a helpful enthusiasm, so I left the subject alone. The library wasn't far. Nothing in Bakersfield was far. I left him waiting at the curb while I went inside to ask for the current directory.

I'd have ripped out the page I needed and been done with it had it not been for the steely-eyed librarian who could read minds. She fixed her stare on me when I sat down and never once blinked. Outfoxed, I took out a pencil and copied all eleven drugstore names and addresses to a piece of paper.

"Here." I handed the list to Charlie. "We won't have to go to all of them, just until I find the one I'm looking for. With luck, it will be our first stop. Where do we start?"

Charlie drove around the block to a corner building on Nineteenth and Chester where a large sign proclaimed KIMBALL & STONE: DRUGS, LUNCHEONETTE, PRESCRIPTIONS, and pulled up to the entrance.

"If you don't mind, I'd rather you stopped a block away, so I can walk up to the door." I didn't want the taxi to raise any suspicions about why a girl would come from a distance to buy poison.

Charlie grunted his assent and moved forward.

"I won't be long."

It took only a few minutes to find what I wanted: a box of Rough on Rats. Living in cheap hotels and boardinghouses had acquainted me with the virtues of this fine product early on in my career, and my eye picked out the familiar package with its comforting image of a dead rat on his back, his little paws in the air. I went to the counter and waited my turn. Sixteen cents. The druggist rang up, then pushed a ledger toward me to sign.

I took my time. I opened it to the wrong page and turned slowly, looking not in the names column but at the dates until I found Saturday, April 4, the day Faye Gordon had last been in

Bakersfield. Then I checked to see what poisons were sold that day. I was looking for a drugstore that had sold a woman some bichloride of mercury on April 4. The name wasn't important—she almost certainly would have used a false one—it was the poison and the date that mattered.

There were no entries at all on April 4. I signed the ledger, thanked the proprietor, and left the store.

I saw a good bit of Bakersfield that day, more than I had seen when I played here in years past. It seemed like a good place to call home. The town had long been a regular stop on the Big Time vaudeville circuits—Keith-Albee and Orpheum—and I had been there a few times, once with my mother and later when I was with Kid Kabaret and Kids in Candyland. We passed one theater that looked particularly familiar.

"Oh, there's the Opera House!" I said to my driver. "My mother played there years ago."

"In vaudeville, was she?"

"Chloë Randall. She was a singer. We were on the circuit for years."

He was kind enough to pretend he had seen her. "I think I remember a Chloë Randall singer from years ago. Yeah, a pretty woman, beautiful voice. That old Opera House just got a new name. Now it's the Nile Theater, see?" I couldn't miss the large vertical letters. "Fancy you remembering that place."

"Performers remember enthusiastic audiences."

"Coming up, Globe Drug Store, ahead on your right."

Globe Drugs was the old-fashioned sort with two parallel counters stretching from front to back and virtually all the stock on wall shelves behind them. It was a popular place and there were several customers ahead of me. When it came my turn, I asked the clerk for rat poison. He pulled down two red and white tins, one large, one small, both with prominent skull and crossbones, and set them on the wood counter. "This will do," I said, picking up the smaller one. "What do I owe you?"

"Fifteen cents," he said. "And wait a minute, you need to sign the book." He crossed the room and pulled out a heavy red-bound volume that he set before me. I handed him the money and took my time finding the place to sign. Someone had purchased a poison on Saturday, April 4, but it wasn't bichloride of mercury and the signature looked very masculine. I thanked the man and left.

"Two," I announced as I got back in the taxi. "Next?"

Charlie and I hit three drugstores before my stomach demanded a break. "I'm hungry. What's next and do they have a luncheonette?"

We ate chicken potpie and cherry phosphates at Kahler's soda counter and, since lunch was on Douglas Fairbanks, ice cream sundaes for dessert. Charlie waited as I bought another box of Rough on Rats, scanned the poison book for April 4 entries—there were two but not for bichloride of mercury—and signed my name. If he was curious about what I was doing, he didn't show it.

"Back to the salt mines," I said as we left Kahler's. "What's next on the list?"

Fortune was frowning that day. Doggedly, Charlie and I tracked down Baer Brothers, Eastern Drugs, Riker's, and Proctor's, paused for a soda at Elgin's, and resumed the routine. In an odd way, it reminded me of the vaudeville circuit: repeat performances at each stop with a jump in between. At the ninth shop I found someone had purchased bichloride of mercury on April 3, but it was a man's name and a man's bold signature, not to mention the wrong date. Meanwhile, arsenic was piling up on the floor of Charlie's taxi and the afternoon shadows were growing longer. If I missed the last train back to Los Angeles, it was no catastrophe—I had enough money to spend the night in a decent hotel and finish tomorrow—but I much preferred my own bed. I was tired and discouraged. My hunch wasn't playing out.

The sign on the tenth drugstore read PIPKIN DRUGS AND SO-
DAS. I heaved a sigh and got out of the taxi, walked the block to
Pipkin's, and went inside.

The soda fountain was crowded with lively young people,
making me suspect there was a school nearby. In the back of the
store, however, the pharmacy counter was deserted. The familiar package of Rough on Rats called to me, and I picked up the
smallest size and took it to the druggist.

"Fifteen cents," said a grandfatherly pharmacist as he peered
at me over the top of his spectacles. Taking the poison book out
of a cabinet, he set it on the counter for me to sign. I handed
him a dollar . . . I had the correct coins but making change took
attention away from me and gave me a couple extra seconds to
peruse a page of entries.

And there it was. April 4 in the date column. Bichloride of
mercury beside it. A carelessly scrawled name in a feminine
hand next to that. That's what I'd come to Bakersfield for. That's
what I'd been searching for all day. I was so startled, I almost
forgot what to do next.

I had spent a lot of effort trying to come up with a plausible
explanation for why a young woman was investigating poison
sales, with absolutely no success. Everyone knew there was no
such thing as a female detective or a female policeman or a female Pinkerton, and the reporter act just didn't play well here. I
was left with no other recourse than the flimsiest justification of
all—the truth.

"Here you are, miss," said the man, handing me my change.
He must have seen the surprise on my face, for he said, "Are you
feeling all right?"

"Yes. Yes, I am, I just, I mean . . . I wonder, were you here on
Saturday, April 4, when a woman purchased some bichloride of
mercury?"

Now it was his turn to look startled. "I'm here every Saturday," he said cautiously.

I pulled the publicity photograph of Faye Gordon out of its envelope. "Would you happen to remember the woman who came in that day and bought it? Was it this woman?"

He looked at the photograph without showing a flicker of recognition. Then he looked sternly down at me. "Why do you want to know about such things, young lady? You're not the police."

"I'm Jessie Beckett and I work for Douglas Fairbanks. We are investigating the murders that took place last week in Hollywood. The police believe that one person murdered all four people, and since that person is now dead, they have closed the case. Mr. Fairbanks and I think there's a strong possibility that the woman who bought this bichloride of mercury from you"—and I tapped the page—"killed two of them."

I'm afraid I lie better than I tell the truth. My story sounded feeble even to my own ears. The man's expression didn't change one whit. I tried again.

"The police checked all the drugstores in Los Angeles for sales of bichloride of mercury in the past month, and they didn't find anything suspicious. They didn't think to check here in Bakersfield, which is where this woman was on April 4. And here is a purchase on that very day. I can't read the signature, can you?"

Without looking down he said, "No."

I wilted. He wasn't going to help me. I couldn't blame him. Why should a medical man discuss such things with a young woman from out of town who had no official status? I gave it one last try. Holding up the photograph once more, I said, "I figure she made it illegible on purpose. And I'll bet it's a phony name anyway."

The pharmacist seemed to look through me for a long moment, then his eyes shifted to the photograph. "It was the same woman. Her hair was dark, but it could have been a wig or hair dye."

My pulse leaped. "You remember her well enough to be sure?"

"I tend to pay attention to strangers who come in and buy poison. And I remember looking at the book after she had left and noting that I couldn't make out her name. That made me uneasy, and I don't mind saying so. It was my own carelessness that she got out the door before I noticed and could call her back. Is this about the murder of that director and the people who came to his party that was in all the papers?"

"Yes, sir."

"And what makes you think this woman had anything to do with it? There are honest reasons why people buy bichloride of mercury and those people don't deserve to be bothered by nosy reporters."

"I'm not a reporter," I said, relieved that I hadn't attempted that impersonation. I couldn't explain what had really made me suspect Faye Gordon—the inexpressible fear that came over me as Mary Pickford and I drank tea at her house and the malevolent look in her eyes that made me think she could read my thoughts. I couldn't explain that, but I could tell him the facts, and I did so as succinctly as possible.

"And people who buy bichloride of mercury for honest reasons don't disguise their signatures and come into out-of-town drugstores in wigs. I think there were two different killers in these deaths, one a Chicago gangster and the other this woman," and I tapped the page again, "who planned to kill a rival, a young actress, and she bought your bichloride of mercury to do it. And then she used it to kill someone else, another actor."

"That young actress was the girl named Lorna McCall, wasn't it?"

"Right. She thought that if she killed Lorna immediately after the other deaths, it would be blamed on someone else. The police would see it as the death of another witness. And she was right. That's exactly what the police think. I believe Faye went to Lorna's apartment, sweet-talked her way inside with the intention of pouring some poison into Lorna's coffee. She may have done so, or she may not have had the chance, but something made Lorna start to feel sick, and she went to the bathroom to throw up. Faye followed and pushed her head in the toilet, drowning her quickly."

"I read about that, too. A gruesome way to die."

"I don't think Faye planned that in advance; she couldn't have known that opportunity would present itself. But it worked out well for her. Since Lorna died from drowning, no one ever considered that she might have been poisoned first. Some even thought it was an accident or suicide. Which it may have been, but I doubt it."

The pharmacist shook his head. "I wish I were more shocked, but I've seen a lot in my lifetime. Sad to say, I'd believe just about anything."

"I think Faye was the one who put bichloride of mercury in the coffee at Paramount. To make it look good, she drank some of the coffee herself, not much, but enough to make sure the doctors found traces in her stomach."

"A little of the stuff won't kill you," he said. "In small doses it's good for treating anemia or tonsillitis. It's only dangerous in larger amounts."

"And the victim, Paul Corrigan, drank at least two cups of coffee."

"What are you going to do with this information?"

"I'm going to go back to Hollywood and tell an honest cop I know. He can come up here and have a look at your book, and if he agrees with me that it's suspicious, he can arrest Faye."

He closed the book with a bang. "I'll keep this safe right here until then, little lady."

"Thank you, sir. I appreciate your help." Euphoric, I turned and nearly floated toward the door. I had done it! I had found the proof we needed to implicate Faye Gordon in both murders. I couldn't wait to tell Douglas.

"Miss Beckett!" I turned. "If you're right and this woman killed two people, she isn't going to take kindly to you making the information public. You take care."

"Don't worry about me. I'm going back to Los Angeles right now and straight to the police."

40

The return trip to Los Angeles took longer than the one to Bakersfield, and it was dark when the train pulled into La Grande. Most of the seats in my car were occupied, but the entire ride was eerily silent, as if no one knew anyone else in the car. We were slowing into the station when out of the blue, the young woman beside me, who hadn't uttered a word since she sat down, suddenly remarked that if her husband wasn't able to meet her, she was supposed to take a taxi. Did I know where they waited?

"They line up out front."

She settled back into silence, and I looked out the window. There wasn't much to see.

I was famished. There was no dining car on the train. The "Blue Plate Special" was calling me from the Harvey House, and it wouldn't have taken fifteen minutes to gobble it up. But no, I told my stomach sternly, I needed to get to the police station as quickly as possible.

I followed the flow of passengers that surged from the platform through the station where it parted into streams, some to the restaurant, some to the main exit, some to the luggage lockers. The potted palms had been righted and the dirt and blood cleaned up, making what had happened last Saturday seem like a bad dream. The smell of fresh bread and roast beef wafting out of the Harvey House nearly mugged me, but I trailed toward the exit where taxis congregate.

Wouldn't Carl's mouth drop when he heard what I'd learned in Bakersfield? I hoped he would handle the case now. I didn't know how these things were done, perhaps he would go to Pipkin Drugs to see the poison book himself, perhaps they would send a detective. Or maybe it was more tactful to inform Bakersfield's police and let them take over. I hoped to high heaven the drugstore evidence was enough to arrest Faye Gordon tonight. The idea of that lunatic strolling around Hollywood with a bottle of mercury bichloride in her handbag made me queasy. The evidence seemed sufficient to arrest her, if not for the murder of Lorna McCall then at least for the murder of Paul Corrigan. Maybe nabbing her for one would make her confess to the other.

It wasn't until I stepped outside that I remembered I had driven the studio's Ford flivver to the depot. How had I forgotten that? It was parked in the lot behind the station. I didn't need to take a taxi. I made my way around the station to the rear lot. At least half the cars parked there were flivvers, all of them black and boxy, but I had planned for that this morning by putting mine in the far corner where I would not mistake it for another.

The merest fingernail of a moon hung in the sky. The air was chilly. My footsteps echoed on the pavement as if I were alone in the parking lot, and yet I wasn't. A man started up his car one row over. Another turned on his headlamps and pulled out onto the main street. A Mexican couple with a baby passed me on their way toward the station. A dark-haired woman behind me headed down my row. Two men were struggling to fit all their luggage in the trunk.

I paid none of them any attention. That was my mistake.

The flivver was waiting for me where I had left it. I scrounged in my purse for the key. The dark-haired woman passed me and went to the car on my right. As I settled into the front seat, she wrenched open the door on the passenger's side and climbed in beside me. Startled, I turned toward her thinking hazily that she wanted to ask directions.

I was facing Faye Gordon.

A dark wig covered her bleached hair, and a hat brim obscured part of her face, but I couldn't miss those angry eyes burning with hate. I could also make out the small pistol in her right hand.

"You little bitch. Drive or I'll shoot you, and don't think I won't."

I didn't think it for a second.

"What's wrong, Faye?" I asked, reacting automatically with an exaggerated calm as we always did onstage when a mishap occurred and we needed to keep the show moving forward at all costs.

"You damn well know what's wrong. Drive!"

I shifted into reverse and eased out of the parking space, searching frantically for some explanation that would put her off, all the while knowing it was too late.

"Maybe if you were to tell me—"

"Shut up!"

I had come to the main street. "Which way do you want me to turn?"

"Back to Hollywood."

I pulled into traffic and headed west with a gun eighteen inches from my chest. I had to assume she knew I'd been to Bakersfield and why I'd gone, although for the life of me, I couldn't figure out how she had found out. Only Douglas knew, and he certainly wouldn't have warned her. The only other person was the pharmacist at Pipkin Drugs and, unless he was Faye's uncle in disguise, I couldn't imagine him telephoning her. But I hadn't time to ponder where I'd stumbled. I needed to figure a way out of this mess.

"Douglas Fairbanks knows where I am, Faye, and he knows the whole story. He's expecting me right now at his house. He'll have the police out looking for me if I don't show up at Pickfair in a few minutes."

"Shut up."

If she noticed I was taking a longer route, she didn't object. I spent some time wondering if I could slow down, get my door open, and jump out before she could shoot me, and decided I couldn't. Her eyes never left my face. Her little gun never wavered. I remembered David telling me how inaccurate those short-barrel handguns were, but it was cold comfort. At this distance, a monkey couldn't miss.

"Killing me will only make things worse, Faye. Everyone will know you did it."

"You stupid little bitch. Shut. The hell. Up!"

So maybe she didn't plan to shoot me. She needed me dead; that was certain. How would she accomplish it? I keenly regretted not having telephoned ahead once I had the information. I should have told Carl Delaney to meet me at the station. I should have taken a taxi. I should have passed along the information to Douglas immediately. It dawned on me then that Faye would also need to kill Douglas. He'd be a lot harder to do in than me—he was never alone—and he'd be forewarned by my own disappearance. I thought longingly of Carl and his gruff partner. Any policeman would be a welcome sight about now.

"Turn right up ahead," she snapped. I turned on Cahuenga and headed north toward the Hollywood Hills. Toward the reservoir? Was she going to push me in and make it seem like a drowning accident? How did she know I couldn't swim? Maybe I could make a break for it as we got out of the car. Or maybe the reservoir would provide a chance to get away. Faye would have to drag me in and hold my head under until my lungs filled with water, and to do that, she'd need two arms, which would necessitate laying aside the gun. Or maybe we were headed to a sheer drop somewhere in the desert where my death would look like an accidental fall. She'd find me hard to push over the side and here, too, she would need both arms free to do it. Faye had a good eight inches on me and a couple dozen pounds, but I throw a solid punch. And I don't fight fair.

"This will never work, Faye. If I disappear, Douglas will know it was you. If I drown or fall off a cliff, he and the police will know it wasn't an accident."

"Shut up."

"Play it smart. You can still get away. All you have to do is dump me here and keep on driving. I won't tell a soul, I promise. Go east to some city where no one knows you. Change your name. No one will ever find you."

Her eyes blazed with the fury of a maniac insulted beyond all reason. "They know me *everywhere* in the whole country," she hissed, spewing flecks of spittle on my arm. "In the whole *world.* I am famous. I am a star."

I kept driving.

Until Faye ordered, "Turn here," I was confident we were heading to the reservoir for an accidental drowning. This optimistic scenario vanished when she demanded I turn right, away from the reservoir, on an all-too-familiar road that led up into the hills. Last time I had traveled this road, I'd been handcuffed.

The pavement meandered as if it had all the time in the world. I had very little so I drove slowly, following the turns by the light of my headlamps, trying to stretch the seconds and keep my wits about me as I figured out what this madwoman intended to do to me and, more urgently, how I was going to prevent it.

The engine coughed once. Twice. It sputtered to a stop in the middle of the narrow road and choked again. "It's out of gas," I said.

I knew what had happened. I hoped Faye didn't.

She did.

"No it isn't, you fool. Turn around."

I gestured helplessly, asking without words how I was supposed to accomplish such a feat without gasoline, hoping her disgust with my ineptitude would cause her to set down the gun and take the wheel herself. No such luck.

"You don't need gas. Roll backward and turn."

I released the brake and did as I was told, letting gravity pull the car downhill as I turned the wheel hard left and reversed direction.

"Now start the car," she ordered. "Drive backward."

The car started right up, as I knew it would once the fuel could slosh forward to reach the carburetor. Ford flivvers were notorious for having to be driven backward uphill when fuel was low.

"You'll run out of fuel before you can get away," I told her as I twisted around to see the road behind me. Now her gun was pointing straight at my heart.

She sent me a smug smile. "Never you worry about me, dear."

We stuck to the main road until Faye said stop. It was almost exactly the same place Carl had left his police car Monday night, below the Hollywoodland letters but far enough away to be outside the light cast by all those bulbs.

I thought of the caretaker, the one Carl said had a cottage behind the H. I had not seen it that night, nor could I tonight— all performers know that light in your face erases the audience, so anything that might have existed behind the letters was obscured from view. Carl had said that the caretaker wasn't on duty all the time. I fervently hoped he was home tonight. He was my one chance.

"Get out."

I slammed the door hard and began talking very loudly. "What are you planning to do, Faye? You can't get away with killing me, you know. Everyone will know Faye Gordon did it."

"Shout to heaven, fool. There's no one around to hear." She motioned toward the sign with her gun, a tiny pearl-handled pistol that looked familiar. A lady's gun. I'd seen it before. Of course. It was the one David had pried from Lottie's fingers that night at Pickfair and handed to Douglas, the one Douglas had set on the mantel. Faye must have picked it up later when no one was looking. And now Crazy Faye was going to shoot me with Lottie's gun and pin my murder on Lottie Pickford.

41

I t will never work, Faye. You may have Lottie's gun, but no one is going to believe Lottie shot me. For one thing, your finger-prints will be on the gun, and if you wipe them off, you'll wipe off Lottie's, too, and leave nothing to connect the crime to her. You still have time to get away. Leave now and you'll have a huge head start."

"Shut up. You don't know anything."

I picked my way over the rocky terrain toward the edge of the light. Faye stayed close behind me. By then, I'd decided on an escape plan, sadly predictable but the only one that came to mind. I would make a run for it, gambling on Faye's poor marks-manship, the inaccuracy of Lottie's stubby Belgian pistol, and my own agility. If I could dash out of this lighted area, I could disappear into the darkness behind the sign.

Maybe she could read minds, or maybe it was the obvious

move of a desperate person, but just as I tensed, preparing to spring to one side, a hard shove against my back sent me sprawling to the ground. Prickly scrub scraped my hands and elbows and thistles tore the sleeves of my blouse.

"This is far enough."

Bleeding, I started to get to my feet but she kicked one leg out from under me. I fell forward, my skirt tangled in my legs. "Stay right there. You're not going anywhere." She reached into her large handbag and pulled out a thermos. Tossing it to me, she stepped back out of reach and sneered. "No more wasting time. Pour yourself a cocktail."

Faye's beverage of choice. Bichloride of mercury. I was going to suffer the same fate as Paul Corrigan.

Slowly I unscrewed the thermos. The lid made a cup with a thin handle. Slowly I poured a little liquid into the cup. I considered dumping it out, but then she'd use the gun, her ace up the sleeve. "Don't stint yourself," she taunted. "Fill it up."

I realized our position had not been chosen randomly. At the edge of the light, Faye could see what I was doing quite clearly. There was no cover of darkness to hide me, no spilling the poisonous brew without her noticing. And once I swallowed it, it wouldn't matter if the caretaker were home or not. He could have telephoned for the whole U.S. Cavalry to come riding over the hills, and it would be too late.

Long experience with magic acts had taught me that the secret of most tricks was misdirection. There on that cold, scrubby hill in Hollywood, it came to me that misdirection was the only chance I had to see tomorrow. Carefully holding the full cup by its handle in my right hand, I set the thermos on the ground beside me and palmed a rock with my left. I rearranged my legs a bit so that the loose fabric of my skirt folded into my lap between my thighs. Positioning my cup hand inches above my lap, I held it rigid. When I was ready, I locked onto Faye's glittering eyes for a long moment, then I looked pointedly over her shoulder and gave a stage gasp.

"What's that?" I cried and at the same instant, let fly the rock in that direction. It clattered harmlessly to the ground.

Most people will instinctively follow motion and noise with their eyes, and Faye proved no exception to the rule. It was all I needed, one fleeting second when her attention flickered away from me; one blink of the eye when her head turned slightly. Then she was facing me again with a look of incredulity mixed with fury. The gun wavered in her hand. Clearly she wanted to shoot me, and holding back took a lot of effort.

"Oh, that was clever!" she said in a voice heavy with sarcasm. "What an ass you are. Now drink up, and be quick about it."

During that moment of brief distraction, while her eyes left me for the time it took to blink, I had twisted my wrist a quarter turn, dumping the poison into my lap and righting the cup in the exact same position. The tiny movement went unnoticed. The cup was empty.

I put it to my lips and pretended to drink, making my throat bobble as best I could by swallowing saliva. I took my time.

"Let me see," she demanded as I took the cup from my lips. I held it out so she could see it was empty. She gave a satisfied smile. "Now the rest."

A trick like that was not going to work twice. I clumsily tipped over the thermos, spilling the remaining poison in the dirt.

She merely shrugged. "So what? You've already drunk twice as much as Paul. But just in case, I'll wait right here till the stuff works like it's supposed to." She lowered herself onto a flat rock, her elbow resting on her knees and the gun pointed square at my face. "I'd hate to have to shoot you after all this trouble. I'd planned this to be another sad case of suicide."

"Suicide? Like Lorna McCall's supposed suicide?"

"No, not at all like hers. That was an impulse. I gave her the poison, too, you know, the same mercury stuff you just drank. There's no harm in telling you now. You're already dead. Poor Lorna. So very, very dumb. She actually believed me when I came to her door, begging her pardon for my behavior at the party. I said we should be like sisters from now on. It was a stellar performance on my part, if I do say so myself. She was still suffering from a hangover, but the nitwit invited me in and served coffee and cake. I poured the poison in the coffeepot, and the little slut gulped it down. So there we were, getting along famously, when she was taken with a sudden stomach cramp. I followed her into the bathroom where she got violently sick, and as she sat there retching, her head hanging over the toilet, I got the idea to hold it down. It was a kindness really—a faster death, putting her out of her misery. And it meant that no one looked in her stomach for poison. They just figured the same person killed Lorna as killed Bruno and that waitress."

"Just like you planned." Once Faye thought I'd swallowed the poison, her whole demeanor changed. Eager to demonstrate her own cleverness, she became downright chatty, confiding in me as if I were an old friend. An occasional prompt from me was all it took to keep her going.

"Not like I'd planned at all. I'd been thinking about how to get rid of her for months, and I'd already bought the poison when Bruno conveniently got himself murdered. And when that waitress who had seen his murderer got herself killed, it gave me a better idea, to make it look like Lorna was another witness being bumped off."

"Lorna took parts away from you?"

"That little piece of trash went around telling people I was responsible for her Big Break . . . that my lousy screen test got her hired. It was humiliating. And she told everyone I was thirty-five, when I'm only twenty-nine."

"Why kill Paul?"

Her lips curled. "That has-been?" She switched the gun from

hand to hand as she thought about something. "You know, I really didn't want to kill Paul. We were lovers once. He forced my hand. I was afraid he would figure out what I'd done to Lorna, and he did. He was threatening to go to the police. I couldn't let that happen."

I recalled Paul's odd behavior at the Fairbanks' dinner table. "He figured it out at Pickfair that night, didn't he?"

She nodded. "He telephoned me after we got home and accused me of killing Lorna. I denied it, of course. But he remembered that I was with him when Lottie called to tell him about Bruno and the waitress being killed. Lottie was all atwitter about the unmentionables she had left at Bruno's house, worried her husband and the press would find out and cause a ruckus. Paul and I talked about Lottie afterward, and that's when I got my idea. I went straight to Lorna's house with the poison I'd bought the week before. Well, Paul said he was taking his suspicions to the police in the morning. I told him I was innocent and that I could show him proof if he'd stop by Paramount first. He walked right into my trap, the poor old fool." She smiled and shook her head.

"You poisoned the coffee."

"Luckily no one came by while he was writhing on the floor. He almost got out of the room to get help, so I bashed him over the head with the chair."

"No one noticed his head?"

"I told the police it was from when he fell. Once he was down, he lay still, gasping and blinking at me something fierce and turning purple and so ugly I had to look at the ceiling. By the time Sophie came in for Rudy's coffee, he couldn't speak. Do you know, he wasn't dead for hours. People thought he was dead when they carried him out on the stretcher, but it takes longer than that. I know. I was at the hospital with him. He died hours later in the hospital. It took hours and hours to finally kill him." Reminded of the time, she looked at her watch, probably gauging how much longer before the poison began working on me. I thought it prudent to clutch my stomach and make a face. No doubt poor Lorna had done the same.

"It won't take so long for you. You drank lots more than Paul did."

I grimaced and bent double.

Faye heaved an impatient sigh. "I hope you won't be much longer. I've got a long walk ahead of me back to town."

"You're walking back?"

"Well, it wouldn't make a very convincing suicide if I were to take your car, would it?"

"No one will believe I committed suicide."

"They will when they read your confession." She took a folded piece of paper from inside her blouse and wafted it like a fan. "Typed, of course." She played as if to show it to me, taunting me and waving it closer before pulling it out of my reach, then finally putting it back inside her blouse.

"That won't work, Faye. Douglas knows everything I know. He'll go to the police when I don't show up at his house tonight."

"Douglas Fairbanks is dead."

She paused on a dramatic note, as if waiting for applause. My stomach really did hurt now. "What?"

"You killed him. You'll be in all the newspapers. 'The girl who murdered Douglas Fairbanks, then took her own life in remorse.' It's all in here." She gave a smug smile and patted the letter, wordlessly inviting me to coax it out of her. She wanted me to beg. I wanted to deny her the satisfaction, but I had to know what she had done to Douglas.

"Tell me, Faye. Please tell me, before I die."

"Well . . . all right. Why not? Who are you going to tell out here? The snakes?" She laughed gaily. "It goes like this: you and Douglas have been having a love affair for weeks now—everyone knows you're in and out of his dressing room—but he decided he couldn't continue to deceive his dear Mary, so he broke it off.

You couldn't bear it. You sent a lovely box of chocolate-covered cherries to his house as a parting gift. But you put a dose of cocaine in each one, enough to kill him if he eats more than one, and everyone knows he can't stop at one."

She looked at a dainty wristwatch and frowned. "They probably aren't finished with dinner yet, but they will be soon. You know how their dinner parties go. After the meal comes the film and the cigars and chocolates."

I tried to convince myself that Douglas would be suspicious of a box of candy unexpectedly delivered to his home, but the man was so trusting he seldom saw any deviousness in others. My name on the card could indeed blind him to the danger. The plan was so transparent, it just might work.

"How could you do this to Mary? She's been your friend for years."

"Oh, pooh. Mary will be fine. She never eats sweets. Too bad about anyone else who dips into Douglas's chocolate box."

"You'll never get away with this, Faye," I said with as much conviction as I could, considering she was well on her way to doing just that. If only I could get free, find the caretaker's cottage, and telephone Pickfair to warn Douglas!

It was time for me to die.

42

Fortunately, dying came easy. I had played Cleopatra so many times, on stages from Alberta to Alabama, that once I'd launched her death scene, the motions followed of their own accord. Instinctively I clutched my hand to my breast, as if holding the asp that killed the Queen of the Nile, gasped, and doubled up like a jackknife. Deleting the dialogue, I concentrated on choking piteously, groaning a little—I was saving the louder groans for later—and doubling up until my head had dropped almost between my legs.

If I stood up, the curtain would fall. Even the dullest of murderers would see the large wet stain on my skirt and realize I had spilled the poison in my lap. But it required only minor adaptations to perform the scene from the ground, and I went on, stretching out what had been a two-minute death scene as long as I could in order to mimic the slow agony Faye had witnessed during Paul's death.

Just before the part where Cleopatra bids farewell to her maid Charmian and collapses dead to the floor, I began again at the beginning, as if I were rehearsing for a hard-to-please director who was demanding multiple takes and greater melodrama. With louder groans, more writhing, and longer pauses between contortions, I ran through the scene at a slower pace. Much as I ached to hurry so I could get to Douglas, rushing the scene would only arouse Faye's suspicions. I rubbed a little dirt in my eyes to make them water. Then it was time for a third run, my final take. This time, my imaginary director required a toned-down version, so I made the gestures feebler and drew out the still segments.

Faye came closer. I labored over my breathing. With my face in the dirt, I stared at her shoes and gave the most heart-rending cough I could muster. I hoped it was good enough. When all was said and done, Faye was a consummate actress who would spot a fake in a second. I lay stock-still on my stomach, my eyes closed, panting unevenly and hoping I was giving an accurate imitation of Paul's death throes before he lapsed into a rigid silence.

She prodded my shoulder with her shoe to see if I would react. When I did not, she stepped very hard on my outstretched hand, grinding it into the rocky ground so hard I felt small bones crack. It took ten years' worth of willpower to keep from crying out.

Satisfied that I was genuinely incapacitated, she fumbled for my skirt pocket and stuck something inside. The suicide letter. She set the thermos and cup closer to my hand, and gave me a hard kick in the ribs for the fun of it. I heard her footsteps crunch on the uneven ground and the car door open. I guessed she was wiping away any fingerprints. The door slammed. I didn't hear anything for a while, and it made me suspicious. Was she watching me from a distance, waiting to see if I moved? Or had she taken off on her walk back to town?

I was frantic to move. What time was it? What was going on at the Fairbanks house? I knew the sequence, and it played out in my head like a film. They had finished dinner. They all rose from their chairs and ambled into the living room, oblivious to the peril that awaited them. Were the Chaplins there tonight? Probably . . . certainly, if there were foreign dignitaries or other important guests in attendance. Were they making themselves comfortable in the sofas while the projectionist set up the film? What if the butler was opening the box of chocolate-covered cherries right at that moment? Had the Chaplins excused themselves early, or would young Lita eat the chocolates and kill her baby as well as herself? *What time is it?* What if I missed warning them by minutes? I almost groaned with frustration. But if Faye was watching me and if I so much as twitched, she'd come back and wait longer.

Out of nowhere, I heard footsteps. Heavy feet, then men shouting from a short distance away.

"There she is!"

"Hold on, there, lady!"

I heard Faye's voice, gentle and calm, coming from the direction of the car. "She's over there, Officer. Thank God you're here. I tried and tried to talk her out of drinking the poison, but she wouldn't listen. Douglas Fairbanks broke off their affair—she's been out of her mind ever since. I was just going for help when you arrived."

I pushed up with one arm as they hurried to my side. Blue uniforms. Half a dozen of them. I opened my eyes to see a terrified expression on Carl's face.

Throwing himself on his knees beside me, he lifted me with one arm behind my back. "Jessie! Jesus Christ, what happened?"

"She wasn't making any sense at all," said Faye, dabbing her eyes with a handkerchief. "Babbling about killing Douglas Fairbanks. Killing herself. She's too far gone now—"

"Don't believe her. I'm fine." I grabbed his coat with my good hand and watched the horror in his eyes fade to confusion. "There's no time to waste. Get to the caretaker's cottage and call the Fairbanks home. Warn them not to eat any chocolates! Quick!"

"What the hell . . . ?" said Carl.

"She poisoned his chocolates. Hurry, it's life or death."

"The poor child, she's delirious," said Faye in a voice so convincing I almost believed her myself. "She's swallowed almost a pint of undiluted mercury bichloride, and it's affecting her mind."

Carl didn't have to ponder over which of us to believe. He turned to Brickles standing behind him. "You get all that?"

Brickles nodded and took off toward the cottage, at his heels a thin man in street clothes I took to be the caretaker. He must have heard us; he must have called the police. I heaved a great sigh and prayed the message would not come to Pickfair too late.

"My God, your hand . . ."

"She brought me here to kill me. She made me drink poison. I didn't really drink it. She's the one who killed Lorna McCall and Paul Corrigan. She knew I had figured it out—oh, my God, I forgot. She's got a gun."

I twisted my neck just in time to see Faye backing away from the officers who had clustered close around me. As soon as she realized I wasn't dying, she knew the jig was up. She darted uphill, wrapping herself in the darkness behind the huge sign just as I had planned to do earlier.

"There she goes!" I cried.

Four cops with flashlights scrambled up the hill after her, but Faye had several seconds' and several yards' start, and she moved surprisingly fast. Soon they had all disappeared into the night and I heard shouts from the cops as they stumbled over the rough terrain.

"There now, don't you worry, they'll get her," said Carl, sounding like he was soothing an injured child. "You look pretty bad. Bet that hand hurts. Let's get you to the hospital and then you can tell us all about it."

The minute he said that about my hand, it started to hurt like the dickens. I began shaking with cold. Or shock. Someone handed Carl a blanket and he wrapped it tight around me.

"She's crazy," I said. "She told me how she killed them. Oh, God, I hope Douglas and Mary haven't—" A shout came from the hills, and I strained to make out the words. "Oh, no, it sounds like they've lost her."

"They'll get her," Carl reassured me, but I wasn't reassured. Everyone underestimated Faye, myself included. We were all in mortal danger while she was still free.

"If she gets away . . ."

"We're not leaving here until we have her, so don't worry."

Moments later Officer Brickles came hustling down the hill toward us, watching his feet so he wouldn't stumble. My mouth opened but fear had robbed me of my voice. My heart pounded in my throat. Carl called out for me, "What did they say?"

He lumbered over. "They didn't know about any chocolates. Turns out someone delivered them to the butler this afternoon, and he set them aside and forgot to tell Mr. Fairbanks. They're holding them for the police."

Faye had failed. This time, at least. The news took the starch out of me and my knees refused to hold me up any longer. Chilled to the bone and exhausted, I sagged against Carl like a marionette with its strings cut.

"Come on," he said, scooping me up against his chest. It felt so good, I made no protest. "No need for you to hang around here. We'll get you to the hospital and have someone take a look at that hand."

A shout stopped him in his tracks. It was the caretaker's reedy voice coming from behind the sign. "Hey, lady! Don't go up there! It's dangerous!"

"She's climbing up the *H*!" yelled one of the cops.

Most of the men were still chasing shadows in the hills. Faye had eluded them and circled back toward us, for what purpose, I don't know, but she still had Lottie's gun so I doubted it was anything benevolent. I looked in the direction of the great Hollywoodland sign and thought I could make out some movement on the *H* about twelve feet off the ground. It dawned on me that the giant letters must have some sort of ladder built into them—there had to be a way for the caretaker to reach the lightbulbs when they needed replacing. With the light in my face, I couldn't see Faye, but I could hear the commotion on the ground as all the men started trying to talk her down.

"Come on down, lady. You'll get hurt up there."

"Come back, we just want to ask some questions."

"What's her name?" asked one.

"It's Faye Gordon, the actress," said another.

"Never heard of her. Miss Gordon! Come back down, honey. No one's gonna hurt you."

"Fool woman, thinking she could hide up there and we'd never notice."

Faye continued to climb. A brief debate on the wisdom of going up after her followed, with the caretaker settling the issue. "I'm the only one who knows how to climb the letters without getting electrocuted," he said. "It's hard enough during the day. Just wait here. I'll go help her down."

It was then that I knew how the story was going to end. I knew how Faye's mind worked. She wasn't trying to escape. She wasn't trying to hide. She had no intention of coming down from the *H*. She was crazy, but she wasn't stupid. She knew exactly what awaited her—months in a prison cell and a sensational murder trial splashed across the world's newspapers, followed by a hangman's noose or an insane asylum. Faye Gordon could spit in Death's eye, but not if she were wearing a gray prison smock and no makeup, with her hair pulled back in a knot. She was a star.

"She's going to jump," I said to Carl.

He tightened his protective hold on me. "No, she wouldn't do that, I'm sure. She—"

Jumped.

Without a farewell speech, without a long scream, without a dramatic gesture, Faye Gordon stood atop the highest row of lightbulbs where the ladder ended and dove out of the darkness into the bright light of a thousand bulbs. With her clothes flapping like a bird's broken plumage, she plunged in silence fifty feet to the rocky ground, landing on her head, breaking her neck instantly. Like the bird against the window glass.

43

You might say I went to bed with Carl and woke up with David.

The last thing I remember, after the doctor had finished setting my broken bones, packing my hand in ice, painting my scrapes with Mercurochrome, and dosing me with some sort of medicine, was Carl's solemn face watching me from the wooden chair beside my hospital bed. When I opened my eyes the next day and my gaze fell on the same expression, it took my fuzzy head a moment or two to register the substitution. Someone had waved a magic wand and changed Carl into David.

"I came as soon as I heard," said David.

"Heard what?" I was still feeling woolly from the medicine.

"I saw Mary at the studio this morning. She told me what happened last night. Or as much as she and Doug knew. I came straight here. You look great, kid."

Everything came back in a rush, playing through my head like a film running triple-time. Remembering, I winced, but the movement only reminded me of the cuts on my forehead. With red-orange splotches of Mercurochrome decorating my skin and bobby pins sticking out of my hair, I could imagine how great I looked.

"Flatterer. What time is it?"

"Eleven."

The door to my room opened and a nurse walked in. She was short, with curly gray hair peeking out from under her starched white cap and a moustache to match, and she bustled about in a motherly way. "There you are, dearie. And top of the morning to you. And to you, too, sir. How's our little patient this morning?"

"A little woozy but otherwise pretty good."

She set about changing the ice packs on my hand. "That's the Luminal the doctor gave you last night to help you sleep. It'll wear off. Does your hand hurt?"

"Some." In truth, it hurt a lot, but I hated to sound like a baby.

"I'll bring more aspirin. Are you hungry?"

I thought back to my last meal and realized I had missed dinner last night. The hole in my stomach woke up angry. "Starving. I haven't eaten in almost twenty-four hours."

"Well, I'll call down to the kitchen and get a tray sent up right away, dearie. Meanwhile, drink some of this."

"What is it?" I think to the end of my days I'll be suspicious whenever anyone says, "Drink this."

"Water. Do you want ice in it?" I shook my head and drank deeply. "Where's that nice policeman that was here last night?"

I shrugged that I didn't know and emptied the cup. David stood and held out his hand in a wordless offer to refill it.

"Such a polite young man he was. Here, hold this under your tongue." Silencing me with the thermometer, she picked up my good wrist to take my pulse. "Reminded me of my brother killed in the war. He was still here when I left at midnight. Said he wanted to make sure you were sleeping soundly. Above and beyond the call of duty, that's what I say." She nodded knowingly. David set the full cup on the bedside table and scowled.

"I feel well enough to leave," I said when she removed the thermometer, squinted at it, then shook it down.

"Sure you do, dearie. As soon as we get a hot meal inside you and the doctor has a look at you, we'll see if that's in the cards. He'll be doing his rounds this afternoon. Until then, you just rest quiet." With that pronouncement, she gathered up her ice packs and charts and bustled away.

"What am I going to do with you?" David asked softly. "The minute my back is turned, you get into another scrape."

I gave an apologetic grin. "It's not like I go looking for trouble, you know. I'm not even sure how trouble found me. All I did was travel to Bakersfield, ask some questions, and come home, and there was Faye, lying in wait like a cat at a mouse hole, trying to kill me and Douglas both. I don't know how she found out what I was doing. For that matter, I don't know how the police got there. I suppose the caretaker telephoned them, but I sure didn't hear anyone coming. No cars, no headlights, not an echo of a footstep. They just appeared out of thin air, like ghosts."

"Lookahere, dearie." The nurse breezed in again, bursting with importance. "Look who I brought." Close behind her came Mary Pickford and Douglas Fairbanks, each carrying an armful of flowers. "My, my. Who'd've thought I'd be showing Mr. Fairbanks and Miss Pickford themselves in to visit one of my patients! What a day! What a day!" Douglas made her a courtly bow in acknowledgment, bringing a bright red patch to each round cheek.

"Well, well, if it isn't our own Girl Detective," said Douglas. "Looking swell, I'm glad to see. Now, Nurse, might you have something to put these in?"

"Oh, my, yes, Mr. Fairbanks. Right away. I'll run find a vase. Or two . . . or maybe three . . ."

"My first thought was for roses. Pink, I said to myself. Jessie's a pink sort of girl. But Mary here, Mary said asters suited Jessie better. Matched her pretty eyes. So rather than fight it out, we compromised and brought both."

I smiled. How typical. The king and queen would both get what they wanted. As always.

"Oh, Douglas, you do go on," Miss Pickford protested. "Jessie, dear, how are you?"

"I'm fine. Truly I am. I wanted to go home last night after the doctor set my hand, but he wouldn't hear of it. He insisted I spend the night. 'Just to make sure,' he said. And the police were there to back him up, so I had to give in."

"I'll send our driver to bring you home as soon as you're released," said Douglas.

David answered for me. "That's good of you, but I can drive Jessie home. I'm staying until the doctor comes."

Douglas laid a morning paper beside me. "There's nothing in here about last night's adventure, but I thought this might help you pass the time. The afternoon papers will have the story, or at least a version of it. Zukor and I talked last night and squared it with the police chief, so what went out to the press this morning is pretty tame."

"What's the story?"

"You don't figure in it much," he said. "Neither do I, thank God. Faye was insane—that's indisputable. They're saying she became despondent over some casting disappointments and Corrigan's murder and drove up to the Hollywoodland sign to kill herself. The police were unable to prevent her death."

"But she murdered Paul Corrigan and Lorna McCall!"

"The public already believes they were done in by Johnnie Salazar. He's dead. Now Faye's dead. There can't be any trials, so what's the point? Both of them were murderers—does it really matter who killed whom? No one's getting off scot-free to kill again. Zukor convinced the chief that it was a tidy solution, one that's fair yet does no harm to the film industry."

"But all those policemen know I was up there at the sign with her."

"If that comes out, you were a friend trying to talk her out of suicide."

There were no other holes I could see in the story. It harmed no one and kept scandal away from the Pickfords. It wasn't very satisfying, but I had to agree it was the best solution for all concerned, under the circumstances.

"There's still one thing I don't understand . . . how did Faye catch on to my trip to Bakersfield yesterday?"

"Oh, my dear, that was all my fault," said Miss Pickford, her smooth brow wrinkling with distress. "I'm so ashamed; I'll never forgive myself."

Douglas patted her hand. "Nonsense, the blame is all mine. When Faye reported to Paramount yesterday morning, one of the secretaries asked her whether she was being considered for a part in a Fairbanks picture. Of course, Faye didn't know what the woman was talking about. The secretary told her I had just sent my red-haired assistant—you—over to pick up one of her publicity photos, so naturally she concluded that Faye was in the running for something. Faye knew better. She knew you and I were pursuing our own little investigation into these murders, and she must have felt us coming too close to the truth. She telephoned the studio and asked for you. No one knew where you were."

"So Faye called me next," said Miss Pickford. "She said it was important that she get in touch with you, something about the murders that you needed to know right away. And Douglas had mentioned to me that you were out of town on an errand for him in Bakersfield and wouldn't be back until evening. When she heard that, she put two and two together and knew exactly what you were doing. Douglas hadn't told me what your errand was, so I didn't know not to tell Faye."

"My mistake, darling. I didn't want to upset you about Faye until we were certain."

"You mustn't be so protective of me, Duber," she chided. He gave her a look more tender than any I'd seen on the silver screen.

"Faye was waiting for me in the depot when I got home. She couldn't have known which train I would take, so she must have met every one from Bakersfield that afternoon. After she made her chocolate-covered cherries."

Miss Pickford shivered. "That was despicable. She truly was insane."

"I'm so glad the warning came in time."

"To be honest," said Douglas, "we didn't even know the chocolates were in the house. When Officer Jackson called, I hadn't the faintest idea what he was talking about."

"Thank goodness no one ate any," I said. "When I asked the doctor last night if eating cocaine could kill you, he told me it could cause a heart attack and death, but he didn't know how much it would take."

"Well, I'm very glad we won't be finding out."

The nurse interrupted with some aspirin and another visitor.

"Hi, Jessie—oh, gosh, Mist—I mean, hello Mr. Fairbanks. Miss Pickford. Good morning. And Mr. Carr. Geez Louise, you don't need any more visitors, I'll just—"

"You're Jessie's friend, aren't you?" asked Miss Pickford. "I remember you from the Heilmann party. What was your name, my dear?"

"Myrna Wi—Myrna Loy. That is, it's really Williams, but I've changed it . . . just recently."

"Very melodic. A wise choice, my dear. And now, Douglas, we should be going before we overtire Jessie." And after insisting I not come back to work until thoroughly rested, they took their leave.

"Gosh, Mary Pickford liked my name! It really must be a very good choice, huh? Oh, by the way, Melva and Lillian sent you their love and said they're coming by after work with Helen to see you."

"With any luck, I'll see them at home before that. The doctor is bound to release me shortly."

"What happened?"

I shot David a look. No time like the present to try on the official story. In short order, I told Myrna that I had followed Faye into the hills to talk her out of suicide and failed. I explained my injuries as a fall. She would read something like that in the newspapers this afternoon and tomorrow morning.

"I'm so glad you aren't badly hurt. And guess what? I have divine news!"

"You got a break?"

"They called me back for a part in *What Price Beauty?*" she said, jiggling with excitement. It was as if Saturday's events at the train depot had been nothing more alarming than a stage play. "Natacha Rambova remembered me from the test I did with her husband—the one where Valentino said I was too young, remember? And she thought of me for this picture."

"Congratulations!" said David warmly. "You're on your way."

"It isn't a big part, mind you. Just one scene, actually. A dream sequence. Natacha says I'll be an intellectual type of vamp without race or creed or country. Sounds thrilling, doesn't it?"

David and I professed ourselves thrilled just as the nurse came in with a tray of chicken and mashed potatoes. As I forked through my food, Mildred Young arrived on the scene carrying a potted begonia. "Gracious, it looks like a florist shop in here," she exclaimed. "And voilà, the gifts of the magi," she said as Pauline Cox and two grips from the *Son of Zorro* production team came down the hall bearing large boxes of candy.

Just as long as there were no chocolate-covered cherries.

44

From the *Los Angeles Times*, April 24, 1925

HOLLYWOOD KILLER
STRIKES FROM THE GRAVE!

Actress Faye Gordon leaps to her death

Couldn't live without love

Miss Faye Gordon, an actress well known to Hollywood, took her own life on the night of April 22 in a dramatic leap off the highest point of the Hollywood-

land sign on Mount Lee. Falling 50 feet to instant
death, Miss Gordon was pronounced dead of a broken
neck at the scene. Police were summoned to the site
by a longtime friend of the actress, Miss Jessie Beckett,
an employee of Pickford-Fairbanks Studios, who had
tried unsuccessfully to dissuade her from senseless
self-destruction.

Friends of the late actress attributed her acute de-
spondency to last week's death of her fiancé, Paul Corrigan, one of the victims of the Hollywood Killer, Johnnie
Salazar. The ruthless gangster and drug smuggler poisoned both Corrigan and Miss Gordon while they were
in the Paramount Studios, although the latter consumed
too small an amount of the poison to harm her at that
time.

Mr. Adolph Zukor of Paramount Studios expressed
profound sadness at learning of Miss Gordon's suicide
and immediately announced a donation to the Im-
maculate Heart School in her name. "We all grieve
for Faye. She was a fine actress and friend to many and
will be sorely missed. In the final analysis, she could
not face life without her beloved Paul, so in that sense,
she was a posthumous victim of the Hollywood Killer."
Miss Beckett could not be reached for further comment.

Blond, vivacious, and intelligent, Miss Gordon had
played a variety of roles, including most recently: *Right
to Love, Enchantment, The Last Payment, Bluebeard's
Eighth Wife, Java Head, A Sainted Devil*, and *Dorothy
Vernon of Haddon Hall*. At the time of her demise, she
was acting in Paramount's *Cobra*, staring Rudolph
Valentino and Nita Naldi, directed by Joseph Henabery.

Miss Gordon will be interred at the Hollywood Cemetery on Wednesday. She is survived by her mother, Mrs. Josephine Schlect of Bakersfield; her brother, Arnold Schlect, of Chicago; and two nephews. Miss Gordon was 36.

ACKNOWLEDGMENTS

My special thanks to Dr. Mark Pugh, a pharmacist who helps me figure out historically appropriate ways to poison people; Donna Sheppard who, more than any teacher, taught me to write; Mike Shupe, the world's best librarian and book sleuth, who can lay his hands on any obscure tome I request; Mark Young, an L.A. producer who reviewed the manuscript and improved my local references; John Hollis, for gun terminology and advice; Brooks Wachtel, a prolific Hollywood writer, producer, and director, for his advice on period filming techniques; and everyone in my very excellent writing critique groups: Vivian Lawry, Marilyn Mattys, Linda Thornburg, Susan Campbell, Kathy Mix, Sandie Warwick, Heather Weidner, Susan Edwards, Josh Cane, Tom Fuhrman, and Libby Hall.

I hope you enjoyed reading *Silent Murders* as much as I enjoyed writing it. If you'd like to see what Jessie's world of silent movies and Hollywood looks like, visit her Pinterest page at www.pinterest.com/mmtheobald/jessies-world-silent-murders/.

If you have any questions or comments on *Silent Murders* or any thoughts for future books, you can contact me through my Web site www.marymileytheobald.com, my Facebook page, or my Roaring Twenties blog www.marymiley.wordpress.com. I'll be glad to let you know when the next in the series comes out.

HISTORICAL NOTE

Although this is clearly a work of fiction, I find that I, like most historians, am incapable of riding roughshod over historical fact. Fortunately, the detective work involved in research is as much fun as writing the story, so I don't begrudge the amount of time I spend making sure the details and descriptions are as accurate as possible. To readers who wonder about such things, several of the main characters are real: Mary Pickford, Douglas Fairbanks, and Charlie Chaplin were the foremost stars of their era. There are many excellent biographies written about them, as well as Mary Pickford's autobiography, *Sunshine and Shadow*. Myrna Loy broke into pictures during this time, and all the details about her early life, including the story about the bird against the window and her posing for the statue in front of her high school, come from her autobiography, *Being and Becoming*. Her brief stint as Io in the mythology film is the only part of her story that is fictional, but pressuring young, inexperienced actresses into appearing in such films was standard fare for Hollywood. Mary Pickford's brother, Jack, and his second wife, Marilyn Miller, were genuine stars, as was Lottie Pickford. While not as talented as their megastar sister, Jack, Lottie, and Marilyn were film personalities who partied hard and died young, probably from an excess of alcohol and drugs, and in Jack's case, syphilis. Chaplin's sixteen-year-old wife, Lita, also a budding actress, gave birth to sons in 1925 and 1926; the couple divorced the next year.

As often as I could, I used real characters, including Adolph Zukor, Ernst Lubitsch and his wife, Helene, Frank Richardson, Joseph Henabery, Zeppo Marx, Johnny Torrio, Al Capone, Rudolph Valentino, and the actual casts of the two silent movies being filmed in the spring of 1925: *Don Q, Son of Zorro* and *Little Annie Rooney*. Both are highly entertaining and available on DVD. All theaters, train stations, drugstores, restaurants (except Lucky's), and hotels (except the Riordin) mentioned are real, and a few are still in existence today.

The early 1920s saw four sensational scandals erupt from Hollywood onto the front pages of the nation's newspapers, three of which I mention in my story: the poisoning of Olive Thomas, Jack Pickford's first wife, in Paris; Fatty Arbuckle's trial and eventual acquittal for the rape and murder of a would-be actress; and leading man Wallace Reid's death from drug addiction. These scandals ruined actors and studios alike and convinced an idealistic American public of Hollywood's immorality. The threat of government censorship brought the motion picture industry to adopt self-censorship through the Hays Code, which prohibited a variety of topics, certain language, and anything sexual, until it was replaced in 1968 by a ratings system similar to the one we have today.

The fourth scandal is the one that inspired my own fictional account of the murder of the fictional director Bruno Heilmann.

It was the mysterious shooting in 1922 of famous director William Desmond Taylor. The police investigation was completely botched, and every single one of the dozen or so suspects was hiding secrets. Newspaper reporters shamelessly sensationalized all aspects of the story, exaggerating or fabricating outright lurid tales of sex, homosexuality, drug dealing, gangsters, hit men, bribery, theft, forgery, insanity, and prostitution. William Desmond Taylor's murder was never solved. If you like wading through true-life tangles of lies, cover-ups, and mystery, you can read more about this intriguing case online or in *A Cast of Killers*.

Eight years after my story takes place, on September 16, 1932, a depressed, twenty-four-year-old actress named Peggy Entwistle hiked to the base of the HOLLYWOODLAND sign, took off her jacket, folded it neatly beside her purse, which contained a short suicide note, climbed a ladder to the top of the *H*, and jumped. Her body was found two days later. The huge sign, meant as a temporary advertisement for a housing development of the same name, fell into disrepair. When it was restored in 1949, the last four letters were removed and it looked as it does today.